DIG TOO DEEP

AMY ALLGEYER

DIG
TOO
DEEP

AMY ALLGEYER

ALBERT WHITMAN & COMPANY
CHICAGO, ILLINOIS

Library of Congress Cataloging-in-Publication
data is on file with the publisher.

Text copyright © 2016 Amy Allgeyer
Published in 2016 by Albert Whitman & Company
ISBN 978-0-8075-1580-8

Printed in the United States of America
10 9 8 7 6 5 4 3 2 1 BP 24 23 22 21 20 19 18 17 16

Cover illustration and design by Jordan Kost

For more information about Albert Whitman & Company,
visit our web site at www.albertwhitman.com.

To Hazel, Julie, Kristen, and Sarah,
who kept believing in me…
even those times when I stopped

ONE

Union Station is crisscrossed with spotlights, lit white against the dark DC sky. I step out of the car and wait for Iris's mom to pop the trunk. "You don't have to stay," I say to Iris. "I'm okay by myself."

We each grab one of my suitcases. Iris slams the trunk, and we set the luggage on the sidewalk in front of the art deco bus station.

"No way." She untangles her sapphire bracelet from my luggage tag. "I won't get to see you for *how* long, and you think I'm going to give up my last few minutes of Liberty time?" She pulls me into a hug as her mom drives off to park the car. "I'm going to miss you, girl."

My eyes sting a little, but I don't cry. I never cry. "I'm going to miss you too. Hugely much."

"Seriously. When are you coming back?"

I open my backpack and riffle through the papers, looking for the ticket I printed online. I really hate that question. "It depends." On whether the woman who gave birth to me is guilty or innocent. On whether her lawyers are crappy or decent. On whether she ends up getting life in prison or not. But I don't have to say those things. Iris already knows.

"Best-case scenario?" she prompts.

"It's fourteen months till the trial. After that…" Shrugging, I unfold the paper ticket and smooth out the wrinkles. *Ebbottsville, KY* is printed across the center. Below that, it says *One-Way*. All six letters are little knives to my soul.

"So if everything goes well, you'll be back just in time for graduation." Iris gives me her famous grin, all wide eyes and pretty teeth. "Perfect timing, yeah?"

I know she's trying to cheer me up, but it's not working. How could it?

We head for the bus terminal, dragging my luggage behind. The station's pretty quiet this late at night, the loudest sound being the clicking of our sharp heels on the marble floor.

"At least you'll get to see your granny," Iris says after a while.

"True." I am looking forward to that. When I was little, Mom and I lived in Ebbottsville and I stayed with Granny all the time. She and I would milk the goats and collect the eggs, and by the end of the day, she'd have me laughing so hard my stomach ached. But after we moved to DC in mom's never-ending quest for *A Better Life*, there wasn't time for the six-hour drive to go see her. It's been five years since we last visited. So yeah—Granny's the one bright spot in this whole debacle.

"Do you remember anybody there?" Iris asks. "Any of the kids?"

Thinking back, I try to recall. "Not really. We moved here when I was seven, so it's not like I'd formed any deep and lasting emotional ties."

"Well, I'm sure you'll charm them all to pieces."

I snort. "I think you have me confused with you."

"You'll be fine," Iris says. "It might even be nice to have a break from the norm. Think of it like a trip abroad."

Easy for her to say. While she's finishing our junior year at Westfield Academy, I'll be at Plurd County High, where I'm just sure they'll have Comparative Religion, Anthropology, and German III. I'll be lucky to have a math class that doesn't involve flash cards. "People don't go abroad to rural Appalachia," I say. "There's no immunization against poverty and unemployment."

"It can't be that bad," Iris says. "I mean, your mom grew up there and—"

"I rest my case."

My phone buzzes in my hand. I glance at the caller ID: Pender Federal Corrections Institute. I silence the phone and keep walking.

Iris glances at the screen. "You'll have to talk to her eventually," she says.

I glare sideways at her, but I know she's right. There are things I need sorted out—money stuff, school stuff—and Mom's the only one who can explain them. Sighing, I let my suitcase bump to a stop against my leg and answer the phone.

An automated voice tells me I have a message from Jamie Briscoe at the Pender Women's Corrections Institute. I have about a second to think "institute" sounds so much better than "prison" before Mom's voice fills my ear.

"Hi, Lib. I know you're probably on your way to Mommy's now. I just wanted to tell you that I love you. I know things look pretty bad right now, but you have to trust me. They'll get better soon. We just have to pull together and be a team. We'll get through this. I promise. I love you, sweetie. Hang in there!"

Then there's silence—except for the blood pounding in my head. Did she really, *really and freaking truly* invoke the speech? *We just need to pull together and be a team.* How many times have I heard those words? During her double jobs and night school and the stupid rallies she had to attend, all while I was cooking dinner, paying bills, and going to bed in an empty house. The birthday cakes I baked myself. The volleyball games and teacher conferences and school plays she missed, that was us pulling together, I guess. We were a team when I was alone.

"Lib?"

I realize I'm frozen in the middle of the concourse, still holding the phone to my ear. "She wants us to be a team."

"Say what?"

"Be a team," I say.

There's a disgusted look on Iris's face. She's too polite to say it, but I know she doesn't think much of my mom. Never has. Chalk that up to years of watching Mom let me down. Too many examples of that Briscoe teamwork.

My fingers are bloodless, wrapped tightly around the phone. She's in prison, for God's sake, and she acts like she got a parking ticket. Meanwhile, my whole freaking life is upside down.

"You know what? Fuck the team. I'm done." I slam the phone into the side pocket of my backpack. "No more picking up her slack. No more disappointments. From here on out, I no longer have a mom."

I'm surprised how easy that is to say. Like throwing away a sweater that never really fit, I write the woman who gave me life right out of it.

Iris is quiet for a second or two then squeezes my hand. "We better go. Your bus should be here by now."

The number above my gate blinks as we approach. A handful of people line up to give their luggage to the cargo guy. There's an older couple and three backpacking students, chatting in what I think is Korean. Suddenly, I feel very alone.

Iris links my arm through hers and pulls me close. "You can visit me on the weekends. Whenever you want."

Leaning into her, I say, "Thanks, 'Ris. That'd be great." But I know it won't happen. She'll be busy with the newspaper, school, and theater. Weekends will be packed with group projects and extra rehearsals, parties that I'm not invited to. There'll be no time for catching up. No time for me. People who leave get forgotten pretty fast.

There's a reason my ticket says *One-Way*.

* * *

Fourteen hours later, I'm standing alone on a cracked sidewalk wearing the same clothes. I thought Granny'd be at the station to pick me up, but when I call her, she says I should take a taxi. After dialing the only cab company in the phone book, I wait thirty minutes until an ancient Monte Carlo pulls up in front of the bus station. There's no sign on it though, so when the guy rolls down the window and leans over, I back away.

"Yew call fer a taxi?"

God, I'd forgotten about the accent down here. "Yeah. Are you it?"

He nods and I pull my suitcases toward the car. It doesn't look like he's going to open the trunk or, you know, get out to help me. So I shove my bags across the backseat, climb in after them, and slam the door. "Thanks so much for all your help," I say.

He glares at me in the rearview mirror. "Where you going?"

"The Briscoe farm."

"Figures," he mutters.

I grin. The women in my family aren't exactly shrinking violets. This guy must have tangled with Granny at some point in the past. "Do you know how to get there?"

He doesn't spare me a glance, so I assume he does and settle in for the winding trip up the mountain. Eastern Kentucky isn't at its best in February. The trees are bare, the snow is melting, and the sky's full of clouds. Granny calls this mud season, and that's mostly what I see in the bare fields we pass. Red mud, little white farmhouses puffing out woodsmoke, and the curving gray sky holding it all down.

I feel the shift in the engine as the road tilts upward. We pass the ancient billboard proclaiming, *Coal Keeps the Lights On*. Then trees close in on either side, disappearing only when walls of craggy rock take their place. I'm not one of those people who wax all poetic about nature, but I like the way this place makes me feel. Like my bones are made of the same rocky stuff. I've missed it.

It takes about fifteen minutes to get to Granny's. Her driveway's long and really muddy and the taxi guy refuses to go up it. He's worried he'll get stuck. I pay him seven dollars, call him chickenshit under my breath, and haul my backpack and suitcases a quarter mile up the hill.

There are so many things I'd forgotten about: the haunted bird-houses we made one Halloween; the split-rail fence my granddad built; two little terriers nipping at my ankles; and Goldie, the old retriever, licking my face and covering my coat with muddy paw prints. I push them away, and they race back to the old brick ranch at the end of the drive, barking nonstop. It's nice to know things haven't changed that much in five years. I'm picking my way across the drier parts of the dirt yard when the front door flies open.

"Liberty, s'at you? God almighty, yer all growed up."

The woman on the porch is a far cry from the wiry, spitfire of a redhead I remember. She's tiny. Thin and stooped. Her cotton-candy hair is a shade I'd call Strawberry Jolly Rancher. If I hadn't just heard my granny's voice come out of that body, I'd swear I'd never seen the woman. Is this really what sixty-one years does to a person?

"It's me." I climb the steps and drop my suitcases. She hugs me and I try to find something to put my arms around. It's like hugging a bird skeleton. "Granny, you're so…" Skinny. Feeble. Old.

She launches into a cough that makes my throat burn. Before it's done, she's bent over, hanging on to the porch rail.

I put a hand on her bony back. "Let's go inside, and I'll get you some water," I say.

I sit her on the same ugly plaid couch we used to play Clue on and head to the kitchen. Everything looks exactly the same—green-striped wallpaper, bright yellow curtains, coffee pot on the stove, glasses in the cabinet. I'm reaching for the faucet when Granny calls out.

"Don't use the faucet, Libby. There's bottle water in the fridge."

I grab a bottle and take it in to Granny, watching as she downs half of it.

"Thanks, sugar pie." She rubs her chest.

I sit down next to her and put my arm behind her. "You sound terrible. What's wrong?"

"Just a cold, but the cough's sticking with me." She smiles, a picket-fence grin with missing slats. "Now, tell me what all you been up to at that fancy school o' yours."

I tell her about my best friend, Iris, about drama club, volleyball, and newspaper staff. About Georgetown, my dream college. I'm hoping to get early action this year. I have a good chance. But there's this complicated equation of Mother + Prison = Legal Bills = *I can't freaking believe she spent my college fund!* = Must earn scholarship.

Luckily, Plurd County High School should be a cakewalk compared to Westfield. Straight As...here I come.

My eyes wander over Granny as I talk. Her T-shirt's faded to a dingy brown, the Natural Bridge decal peeling off. Sweatpants swim around her, like adult clothes on a kid, and she's wearing tube socks with flip-flops. I realize if I saw her in DC, I'd think she was homeless.

"You sure turned out beautiful!" she says. "Just like your mama. I bet you got a dozen boyfriends up there too, don'tcha?"

"I didn't have time for boyfriends, Granny." I don't go into the fact that, after my homework was done, I had the cleaning and the bills and the grocery shopping to take care of because My Former Mother was running around the capitol with some hand-lettered sign yelling badly rhymed slogans about the dangers of genetically modified peaches or whatever cause she was supporting that week.

"I reckon not," Granny says. "Your mama says you're a bookworm."

"Granny, I don't want to talk about that woman, okay? Just pretend I don't have a mother. It's always been easy for me."

"Liberty!"

"I'm serious." I feel my jaw jut out in what Iris calls my "don't eff with me" face.

Granny mashes her lips together and shakes her head, which I recognize as her "you're full of shit but I ain't gonna say nothin'" face. She squeezes my hand. "Well, I'm'a let you get settled in. If you need anythin', I'll be righ'chere."

I get my suitcases from the front porch. When I roll them through the living room, she's already stretched out under a fleece throw. I walk toward the little room at the back where I always slept, stopping to look at the pictures lining the hallway. My Former Mother (MFM) as a toddler, playing in the creek with Uncle Mark. MFM at Tanner's Peak in her cap and gown, the black robe hiding the fact that she was four months pregnant. Granny holding me at the blackberry patch, my face and hands stained purple. Granddad in his army uniform, back when he had two hands. Just a couple weeks after that, he lost the left one on Hamburger Hill. Granny says he left it there on purpose, so he could keep giving the finger to the Vietcong.

The photos leave me feeling lonely. I feel even lonelier as I stand in my old room, imagining the look on Iris's face if she could see it. Ruffled muslin curtains. A worn, patchwork quilt under a framed, faded magazine story about starfish. Just like the rest of the house, they're shabby and cheap. I'm embarrassed by it all and disgusted with myself for feeling that way.

I drop my backpack on the cedar trunk. Granny must not have cleaned in here for a while. There's yellow dust on everything—like when the pine pollen drops in the spring. Only it's February, and the pines aren't dropping yet. I unpack my clothes and lay my makeup and stuff on the dresser. It doesn't take long. Most everything from our apartment in DC went into storage. It's hard to believe how much my life's changed in two weeks.

I check my phone, thinking I'll call Iris. She'll be in the school newsroom, finishing up the layout for the next issue of the *Westfield Word*. But there's no signal. I should have guessed that. Granny's house is tucked up in a hollow (or, as people here call it, a "holler"). The steep hills on either side mean I'll have to hike up to the ridge just to get my messages.

Which I do, because there's nothing else *to* do. Granny is snoozing on the couch as I walk by. The dogs follow me across the yard, all wagging tails and happy panting. Granny must not walk them much anymore. I pass the apple tree and turn up a tiny path that disappears into a rhododendron thicket. I'm pretty impressed with myself for even finding it. Five minutes later, I'm panting harder than the dogs, climbing steadily through the trees toward the gray sky above.

One foot in front of the other, I tell myself. Volleyball hasn't exactly conditioned me for climbing, and the trail is steep. By the time I hit the ridge, I'm totally out of breath. I stand with my hands on my knees as Silkie and Beethoven streak down the other side after some rabbit or vole.

I squint after them, wondering if they'll come back or if I should chase them down. And that's when I see it. Or rather, don't see it. Tanner's Peak. The whole top of the freaking mountain…it's just gone.

TWO

Instead of a rocky point poking through the trees, there's just raw dirt, hundreds of feet lower than it should be. It's covered with roads and equipment of every kind—big diggers, little diggers, bulldozers, an army of dump trucks, and a behemoth crane. It looks like they're getting ready to build a mall or something, except for the huge square pond halfway down the slope. It's filled with water—not natural water, but sludgy swirls of brown and electric green.

I'm wondering what they did with the rest of the mountain when I realize the valley floor is only half as deep as it used to be, and filled with raw dirt, rocks, and tree roots. They must have carved off the top third and dumped it into the valley between Tanner's Peak and the next hill over.

I'm staring, openmouthed, thinking about all the things that are gone: the lookout where you could see all the way to Bakersville, the blackberry patch, the little cave Granny and I hid in once when a thunderstorm blew up, the best hole for crawdads in the whole county.

The dogs come panting back, trailing a guy about my age who looks vaguely familiar and almost too cute to be real—blond hair, brown eyes, a few freckles across his nose. His dark eyes widen when he sees me. "Sorry. I thought...aren't these Kat Briscoe's dogs?"

"They are." I stare, trying to figure out who he is.

He stares back and suddenly grins. "Oh my God. Liberty?"

I nod, finally recognizing the ten-year-old I used to know. "You're Cole, right?"

"Yeah." He looks me up and down, but not in a creepy way. "You've changed a lot since the last time I saw you."

"I'll take that as a compliment, since the last time we saw each other, we were covered in mud war paint, playing Indian Attack."

Cole laughs and reaches down to scratch Goldie's head. "Yeah, I hardly ever do that anymore." He winks at me and my insides do some weird, squirmy thing. "Just the second Tuesday of each month."

He's funny. I like that. "I'll put it on my calendar."

We smile at each other, not sure what else to say. Finally, I point to the mountain. "What's going on there?"

Cole's eyes flick to the mountain. "Peabody Mining's new big thing—mountaintop removal."

"A coal company did that? On purpose?"

"It's an easier way of getting the coal out."

"Yeah, along with the trees and the dirt and everything else. Is it legal?"

"Of course it is." Cole's still staring across the valley. "Federal government issued the permit for it."

"And nobody's complained?"

"Complained? Why would they? Mining jobs are good jobs. My daddy's lucky to have one."

"Yeah, but—"

"That right there is progress," Cole says. "All those jobs are going to bring Ebbottsville back to life."

I think about the boarded-up shops and empty streets downtown. "That's great, I guess. It's just…" The sky looks empty without the craggy peak. "My granddaddy walked me all over that mountain."

Cole smiles. "Mine too. There was a honey hole for brook trout on the back side, up by…" He glances at me then shakes his head.

"Up by what?"

His nose crinkles under his freckles. "I can't tell you. Granddaddy swore me to secrecy."

I raise one eyebrow, like Iris taught me. "But it's gone."

"A secret's a secret."

That's exactly the kind of weird reasoning I remember from my own grandpa. Mountain people are an odd breed. "You realize that makes no sense."

He smiles and shrugs. "What are you doing here anyway? I thought you and your mama moved to DC."

"We did." I wonder how much to tell him. Having a mom in prison is probably as gossip worthy in Ebbotsville as it is in DC. "I live here now," I say and hope he leaves it at that.

"No shit. Really?"

"Really."

"That's great," he says, and I get the feeling he means it. "Will you go to Plurd?"

"Is there any other high school here?" I'd give my favorite sweater for him say yes. A private school, a Catholic school, heck even a charter school would be better than Plurd County High, with its 60 percent graduation rate and test scores in the thirtieth percentile.

"Nope. Plurd's it." I try to smile, but I must look like I'm in pain, because Cole says, "You probably went to a fancy school in DC, huh?"

"Kind of fancy." I turn and start down the rhododendron trail.

He follows me. "I can tell by the way you talk. Really proper."

"Sorry." Sorry? Did I just apologize for speaking correct English?

"No, I like it," he says.

"It's not like we were rich or anything," I say. "I was only there on scholarship." I frown, remembering the paperwork for that scholarship. A scholarship that *I* heard about. And *I* applied for. And I got—no thanks to MFM, who was so busy saving spotted seals that she wouldn't have noticed if I'd decided to homeschool myself.

"Well, that's good," Cole says. "I mean…it *was* good. I guess."

The trail is narrow, and he's walking behind me. I'm wondering if he's staring at my butt. I try to walk normal, which suddenly seems very hard.

"I was thinking maybe…" He puts his hand on my arm and I stop. "There's a party tomorrow night. You should come, meet some people from school."

His ears are turning a little red, and I can feel my face doing the same thing. He's not technically asking me out, but I think he kind of is. "Okay," I say. "Sure. Where is it?"

"West of town on Highway 52. I can pick you up, if you want."

"That'd be great." The thought of walking into a party alone is terrifying. People here aren't too quick to warm up to strangers.

"Eight o'clock?"

"Sure."

He walks backward up the trail. "A'ight, then. See you tomorrow."

I wave and start down the trail, smiling since I know he can't see me. I'm not looking forward to being the new girl at school. Knowing Cole will be there gives me some relief and, if I'm honest with myself, something to look forward to. He is pretty cute…but then I always have been a sucker for dimples and a crooked grin.

THREE

Back at the house, I tiptoe in so as not to wake Granny, but she's sitting up, watching *Wheel of Fortune*.

"Hey," I say.

"Hey back atcha. You find somethin' to do?"

"Just went for a walk." I watch the television as Vanna turns over two *A*'s in what is clearly *Amsterdam* and I realize I never did check my messages. "I saw that mess up on Tanner's Peak."

"Goddern Peabody!" Granny grumbles. "He'll have the whole county ground up and left for dead if he keeps on." She starts coughing again, and I watch her bony shoulders clench together as she hacks away.

"Your water's on the end table," I remind her. "Take a drink."

Between coughs, she manages to get a couple swallows down.

"How long have you had this cold?" I ask.

"Just a little bitty while," she says, which I know could mean anything from a couple minutes to a year and a half.

"And aside from the cough, how are you feeling?"

"Fair to middling." That could mean anything from perfectly fine to nearly dead.

I sit on the arm of the couch and put my feet on the cushion. "I ran into Cole Briggs. Up on the ridge."

"Did ya? I see him at church now and again." Granny cuts her eyes at me sideways. "Turned out cute, didn't he?"

One corner of my mouth turns up. "Fair to middling."

Vanna flips over the *D.* "Amsterdam," Granny yells.

I remember sitting on this same couch, watching *Wheel of Fortune* ten years ago. Honestly, I think it's how I learned to read. "How about I make us some dinner?"

"That'd be a paradise," Granny says.

I hop off the couch and head into the kitchen to check the cabinets. The options are slim—half a loaf of white bread, a block of moldy cheese, and a couple cans of soup. The bottom shelf of the fridge holds a stash of Mountain Dew.

I cut the mold off and lay thick slices of cheese on the bread. After checking the date on the mayo, I toss it in the trash. Then I melt some butter in the cast-iron skillet and mash the sandwiches into it, waiting until cheddar globs out the sides.

"Do you want to eat in there?" I call. "Or at the table?"

"In here, if you don't mind."

I slide a spatula under each sandwich and put them on plates. After grabbing a bottle of water from the fridge and a Mountain Dew for Granny, I take one last hopeless look around for veggies or fruit. There's nothing. A trip to the store tomorrow is at the top of my list.

I hand Granny her plate and sit down next to her.

"Muchie grasseras, darlin'."

"*De nada,*" I reply.

My sandwich is hovering deliciously close to my mouth when Granny says, "Hold yer horsies! Ain't you forgettin' something?"

"Oh right." I can't remember the last time I said grace. Something about eating alone doesn't lend itself to giving thanks. "Sorry." Putting down my sandwich, I take Granny's hand and stumble through the words I haven't said in four years.

"God is great. God is good. Let us thank him for our food. By his hands, we are fed. Give us Lord, our daily bread. Amen."

"Amen and how," Granny adds, squeezing my hand before she lets go.

Wheel of Fortune is over. She turns off the television just as *Jeopardy!* comes on. "I don't care for that man," she says. "Alex Trebek."

"Why not?"

"He's a gol dang know-it-all," she says through a mouthful of grilled cheese.

I've always felt the same way. Like, he acts like he knows the answers to all the questions, but I bet he really doesn't.

"Sure is nice to have you here." Granny puts her hand on my leg. I guess I'm not used to people touching me, because I jump a little. "I know you'd rather be up home. Hell, this is probably the last place you want to be." Her blue eyes bore into me like a welding torch. She never was afraid of saying hard things right to people's faces. "But I'm happy to have you, even if it is selfish."

"Thanks, Granny." I glance out the front window, where the yard is already dark in the shadow of the hill. On the ridge opposite, sunshine lights the tops of the bare trees, making them glow like skeletons against the pink sky. It's gorgeous and I'm not really lying at all when I say, "It's nice to be back here."

We eat in easy silence, watching the clouds roll through. Slowly, they go from pink to purple to indigo. I swear I can feel my blood thickening, slowing down, matching the pace of the mountain. It's a stride that feels natural, even after so many years away.

"How's your dinner?" I ask Granny.

She's finished about half the sandwich. "Dee-licious. But I'm 'bout full as a tick. I believe I'll wrap this up and save it for tomorrow lunch."

She struggles off the couch and shuffles into the kitchen. I shove the last bite into my mouth and follow. "I'll get the dishes."

I turn on the faucet to rinse the plates and almost drop them in the sink. The water's orange. Like neon. "Whoa. Is this water safe for washing?"

"County claims it is."

"What's going on with your well?"

"It's the mine," she says. "Ever since they started pulling down that mountain, ever'body's well water been orange."

"Everybody's?"

"Them that ain't dried up all together. Reckon they busted up a rust layer or something, and it's all running downhill."

"Hm." I've seen rusty well water. Granny's used to get like that if we had a long dry spell. But this isn't rusty. It's neon. "Can't the county do anything about it?"

"They had the waters tested." Granny shrugs. "They say it's safe to drink."

I blink twice. "It's. *Orange.*"

Granny chuckles and opens the dishwasher. "I get ya. I don't drink it. Tastes funny to me. But there ain't much I can do about washing in it. Hard to fill a washing machine with bottle water."

I wonder what it's going to do to my clothes as I look at the stained inside of the dishwasher. I nudge Granny toward the living room. "I said I'd do the dishes. You go sit down."

"I don't need you waiting on me hand and foot," she snaps.

"Good thing. Because I didn't come here to be your maid," I say, matching her tone. We glare at each other for a few seconds. "God, I'm just being nice."

"Well, I reckon there's a first time for ever'thing," she grumbles. But I see her smile as she turns away.

Loading the dishwasher takes all of thirty seconds, then I'm back on the couch, watching a *Matlock* rerun. "Oh, I forgot to tell you. Cole invited me to a party tomorrow night."

"Whose party?" She sounds wary.

"Some friend of his."

"What friend?"

"I'm not sure." I try to recall the conversation. "I don't think he said a name."

The wary look remains. "That friend's parents going to be there?"

I can't remember the last time Mom asked where I was going or with whom. It's nice having someone actually care about me. Nice, but also a little annoying. "I don't know."

"Find out," she says. "Then we'll see."

I'm not used to having to ask permission to do things. And I'm definitely not used to people telling me no. "Granny, I'm seventeen years old. And it's just a party."

"I am not letting you go off to who knows where, to do who knows what."

She's actually shaking her finger at me. I'd laugh if it wasn't so irritating.

"I'm responsible for you, darlin'. What would your mama say if anything happened to you?"

"First of all"—the mention of that woman puts an edge on my voice—"nothing is going to happen. You know Cole, right? You know his family. They're good people."

"Well, yeah. They go to church regular like."

"Second of all, it would be nice to meet some kids from school before I start on Monday." I let that sink in for a second. "Being at a new school sucks, you know?"

"I reckon it does."

I'm making progress. "And last, it's just a party."

"Well," she says. "I don't know. What d'you reckon your mama'd say?"

I feel the blood rush to my face. "I do not *have* a mother."

I know I've gone too far when her cheeks turn red and that wagging finger pops back up. "That's enough of that! Your mama loves you. I know she's made some mistakes, but ain't nobody perfect. Lord, if I had a dime for every mistake I ever made, I'd be richer than God hisself."

"You don't understand," I say.

"I understand she's disappointed you."

"That's the understatement of the year."

"And I bet having a mama in prison probably don't go over too well at that fancy school of yours." She rubs her chest as she goes on. "But that woman is still your mama. She deserves your respect, even if you can't love her right now."

"*Respect*? Are you freaking kidding me?" The struggle to keep my voice calm isn't working. "You don't know what it was like. She was never home. Never. I made my own dinners. I did the laundry and kept the house clean. I paid the bills because she always forgot. Most every night, I came home to an empty house because she had 'work' to do. I went weeks—I'm not kidding, *weeks*—without seeing her." I'm pretty much yelling now. "She deserves a lot of things, but respect isn't one of them. I'm glad she went to prison. I hope they find her guilty and she stays there for the rest of her miserable life."

"Liberty!"

I storm past her, heading for my room, when she starts coughing again. I get about halfway down the hall before I realize she can't stop. Turning back, I head to the fridge to get her some more water.

"Hey, stop that," I say as I hand her the open bottle.

She's bent nearly double, clutching her chest. When she manages to take a drink, her cough quiets.

I sit next to her and rub her back. "Monday, I'm taking you to the doctor."

"Psh, he can't do nothing," she says.

"Have you been to see him?"

She shakes her head and takes another sip of water.

Figures. "You're going on Monday, then."

"You're right bossy," she says. "You know that?"

I smile and squeeze her shoulder. "Yeah. I get that from my grandmother."

FOUR

Most grocery stores I've been in look the same—fluorescent lights, bad music, moms with full carts, and screaming kids. You can be totally anonymous in a grocery store anywhere in the world. Except here. People in the mountains have a sixth sense about strangers. They know you don't belong, didn't grow up here, didn't morph out of the dirt and rocks like their ancestors did a billion years ago, so they stare. The employees, the moms, the old men standing in front of the store, even the kids—they all stare. It's rude. And unnerving.

I hurry through the shopping, trying to ignore the stares and wishing I'd taken Granny up on her offer to come along. At least I'd have somebody to talk to. Before I left, she gave me twenty dollars and a SNAP card. SNAP stands for Supplemental Nutrition Assistance Program, which is a fancy way of saying food stamps. I'm embarrassed that I didn't know Granny was on food stamps. Almost as embarrassed as I am to be using them myself.

When I'm done, the cart seems awfully empty, considering this food has to last us a week. The two cases of bottled water and the twelve pack of Mountain Dew take up most of the cash. I put back the green pepper and fresh broccoli and toss in a bag of rice and a big carton of oatmeal instead. More food, less money. I count up the change from the bottom of my purse and have just enough to buy a package of cough drops for Granny. It feels weird to be scrounging for money. MFM's job might have taken her away from home, but she got a halfway decent paycheck every month. Enough, at least, that I usually had more than sixty-seven cents.

As I'm standing in the checkout line, hiding the SNAP card in my sleeve till the last minute, I overhear a woman in the next lane talking about her daughter.

"Doctor says she might have some trouble with the birth, her being so young," the woman says. "But so far she's doing good."

"What d'you reckon will happen after the baby comes?" asks the woman behind her.

"She says she's gonna keep it." The first woman shakes her head. Her hair is streaked with gray and her eyes are so tired they look like they're sinking down into her cheeks. I feel sorry for her and guilty for eavesdropping, but it's like a train wreck. I can't stop.

"She don't have any idea what it's gonna be like. Thinks she can get a after-school job to pay for day care and still finish school."

"Pff. That ain't gonna happen."

"Don't I know it? She don't listen though."

"They never do."

I wonder if Granny stood in line here seventeen years ago and had the same conversation with one of her friends about MFM.

The lady sighs. "I reckon we'll end up raising the baby, at least till she graduates."

"Where's the daddy?"

"You tell me. Worthless piece o' work ran his sorry ass out of town the same night Jess told him the news."

That sounded familiar too. Granny always said the only thing my father could be depended on for was not being depended on.

It's totally stupid and makes absolutely no sense, but I think I'm kinda jealous of Jess. Not because she's going to have a baby. God no. But because she screwed up, like in a major way, and here her mom is, trying to help her through it. It's hard to imagine MFM doing that for me. Impossible, actually. I'd probably be eight months along before she even noticed.

"Hey! You checking out or what?"

I look up and realize the guy ahead of me is long gone and the checker is waiting. I start unloading the cart, reminding myself for the millionth time...

I don't have a mom.

* * *

I put the groceries into Granny's rusted out 1987 El Camino and leave the cart in the middle of the parking lot like everybody else. Driving back up the mountain, I pull off at the overlook and check my messages. Thank God I prepaid my cell bill for the year before closing out MFM's accounts. Everything that was left went to her lawyers. Now I wish I'd prepaid a credit card or two for living expenses, but I had no idea money would be so tight here.

There are two voicemails from MFM that I delete without listening to and forty-three text messages from Iris. I read the latest few.

Dress rehearsal was a disaster.

Newsflash...Chet and Ally broke up!

Miss your face. : (

I reply, telling her about the party tonight. Granny hasn't technically said I could go, but she did call Cole's dad this morning and leave a message. All she wants is to know the who and the where, and I have to admit that makes sense.

In a 1950s sort of way.

Climbing back into the car, I'm thinking about Iris. She'd be all over this party, knowing exactly how to walk in and own the room. Me, I'm hoping I can sneak in the back door. The last thing I want is a repeat of the grocery store staring. I wonder if people here will ever accept me. I really need them to.

I've decided no matter what happens with MFM, I won't go back to DC. Not to live with her. We're just too different to ever get along. Sometimes, I'm certain I got switched at birth, and my real mom is out there somewhere dropping the wrong kid off at volleyball, cooking four-course dinners for the wrong kid, and helping the wrong kid with her lines.

* * *

The driveway is still muddy, and I spin out a couple times before making it to the house. Luckily, I'm used to driving in DC slush, so at least I don't get stuck. Granny is waiting for me on the porch, wrapped in an afghan and smoking a cigarette. She doesn't smoke much—just a couple a day—but it can't be helping her cough.

"Hey," I say, climbing out of the car.

"Hey back atcha." She flicks the butt out into the yard, joining a hundred others dotting the mud like little white flowers. "D'you get my cookies?"

"Nope." I walk around to the passenger side to get the bags. "They're like two dollars a bag. Plus, they have no nutritional value at all."

"I don't care. I need them cookies," she snaps. "Ever'body's gotta have a vice."

With my arms full of groceries, I'm too busy navigating the puddles to mention smoking counts as a vice. "Did Cole's dad call?"

"Not yet." She pushes the door open for me and I head for the kitchen.

"Can you call him again?"

"No I can't, Miss Impatient. I called him once and that's enough."

Granny has a strict idea of what constitutes good manners. "Fine." I wave the carton of oatmeal. "Where's this go?"

She snorts. "Outside with the pigs."

"Don't be stubborn. Oatmeal's good for you."

"That don't mean I have to like it."

"I'm sure you won't," I say. "Just for spite."

I finish putting the groceries away while she wipes at the furniture with a damp rag. By the time she works her way through the living room, it's yellow from the dust that covers everything.

"Whew." She drops onto the couch. "I'm tuckered out."

"You want me to dust the rest of the house?"

"That'd be a blessing."

I rinse the rag out in the sink, which turns it orange instead of yellow. I'm thinking, no matter what the county said, there's no way orange water can be healthy. Granny starts coughing again, so I drop the rag and take a cough drop out of the bag. By the time I get into the living room, I'm afraid she's going to pass out she's coughing so hard. I rub her back, waiting.

"You need to stop smoking," I say over her hacking.

She shoots me a nasty look, sideways through her watering eyes.

"I'm just saying."

When the cough finally passes, she drops her hand from her mouth and wipes it on her sweatpants. It leaves a red streak.

"Whoa. What's that?" I ask, pointing.

"Just a little phlegm."

"Phlegm my ass," I say. "That's blood!"

"Naw."

"Granny, you're coughing up blood. God..." I'm trying to remember from health class what that might mean. Tuberculosis? Pneumonia? "How long has that been going on?"

"Just a little bitty while."

"How *long*?"

She lies back on the cushions and wipes her eyes. "Lord, Libby, I don't know. It don't happen so often. Just now and then."

"Blood is blood," I say. "And when it comes out of your body, it's never a good thing. I'm taking you to the doctor. Right now."

Granny snorts. "On Saturday? Where you think you are, Worshington, DC?"

I stop on my way to grabbing the car keys. She's right. The nearest doc-in-a-box is probably an hour and a half away. And the car has maybe a quarter tank of gas. "Fine. Monday then."

"You told me that last night, Bossy."

"Yeah, well…just don't forget."

"How can I," she says, "with you reminding me ever' day?"

She grins, but I'm too worried to smile. I can't stand the thought that there might be something really wrong with her. She's the only family I have now.

The phone rings, jarring me out of my worried thoughts.

"That'll be Darryl," Granny says. Cole's dad. Then she starts coughing again, so I answer it myself.

"Hello?"

"Liberty?"

"Yeah?"

"Hey. It's Cole."

"Oh, hi."

"Kat left a message for my dad," he says.

"Yeah. About the party."

"Right."

"So?" I say. "Where is it? When's it over? Will there be any adults? And all those other questions adults have a deep and burning desire to torture us with."

Cole laughs. "It's at my buddy Dobber's house, and it probably won't be over till Sunday morning."

"Okay, well, I'll need to be home before that," I say.

I can almost hear him smile. "I'll get you home by midnight."

"And the adults?"

"His daddy'll be there." Cole kinda snorts.

"Great. I'll tell Granny." She's still coughing on the couch.

"What? Naw, you can't tell her any of that."

"Why not?"

"Well, Dobber's daddy...I mean, he's not..." The silence on the other end stretches on a little too long.

"He's not what?"

"Look, just tell her the party's at Jillian Coffey's."

"But you said—"

"I know, but your granny's not gonna let you go if she knows it's at Dobber's."

"Why not?"

"Liberty?" Granny calls from the living room. "Is 'at Darryl?"

"I gotta go," Cole says. "Don't say anything about the Dobbers. I'll pick you up at eight!" The line clicks dead.

"I want to talk to him." She's just walking into the kitchen when I set the phone back in the stand.

"He had to go," I say.

"What'd he say?"

I wonder what to tell her. On one hand, I really want to go to that party. Showing up at school on Monday would be a lot easier if I knew a few people. But I'm a little worried about the Dobbers. I mean, what's so bad about them that I can't even mention their name to Granny? Are they murderers? Moonshiners? Does it matter? I can take care of myself. And I'm looking forward to seeing Cole again.

I think all that in the span of one eyeblink. Then I look at Granny and say, "The party's at Jillian Coffey's house."

FIVE

I don't have the slightest clue what to wear. Will we be outside? Inside? Is it super casual or do people dress up? What I really want is an invisibility cloak, some way to walk in and not be stared at. But since I know that's impossible, I try to hit something in the middle, wearing jeans tucked into suede boots and a red cashmere sweater. I twist my hair into a bun, slap on my regular makeup plus extra eyeliner, and walk out to the living room to wait with Granny.

"Hoo wee. Ain't you gorgeous!"

"Hardly," I say, flopping down on the couch.

"Didn't nobody ever teach you how to take a compliment?"

"No." *Nobody* taught me almost nothing at all.

"Ya just say, 'Thank you.'"

"Fine. Thank you."

She hmphs and crosses her arms. "Well, I guess that's some better. You might try a smile next time."

"I didn't ask you for the compliment," I say. "Why am I supposed to be grateful for something I didn't ask for?"

She shakes her head at me. "Libby, a whole lotta people in your life are gonna give you stuff you don't want—in my case, it was mostly bad advice. Your best course of action is to say 'thank you' and throw it away when they ain't lookin'."

I hear an engine growling up the driveway and jump off the couch to grab my coat. "I'll remember that."

"When you coming home?" she asks as headlights cut through

the darkness outside.

"Midnight, I guess." I lean down to kiss her cheek. She smells like cough drops.

"Midnight? Well, don't expect me to be waiting up."

"You better not be," I say, pulling my scarf out of the collar of my coat. "I want you to get plenty of rest until that cold's gone." In the back of my mind, a little voice says, *Colds don't make you cough blood.*

"Okay, Bossy. You get on to that party before all the fun gets gone."

"I'm going." I pull the door closed behind me just as Cole steps onto the porch. He's wearing faded jeans, cowboy boots, and a PCHS hoodie. His cheeks are pink and his breath clouds up in the cold night air. "Hi."

"Hey there." He smiles and stares a little too long at the three-inch heels on my boots. "You look great."

"Too dressy?" I ask, as he starts down the steps. "I can change."

He turns back to me and his eyes crinkle at the edges. "I said you look great, Lib. Can't you take a compliment?"

I follow him into the dark yard. "Apparently not."

It's a cold ride down the mountain. Cole's car is older than my mom. It's kinda cool looking but only about half of it works. Heat is part of the nonworking half, as is the thingy that rolls up the window on my side. It's only open a crack, but Cole drives fast and the air streaming through is icy.

"Is it much farther?"

"Just a couple miles." He glances over at me. "Shit, you're probably freezing." He reaches into the backseat and hauls over a blanket crusted with dead leaves. "Put that over you."

Even without the leaves, the blanket has an ick factor I'm not really comfortable with, but I'm freezing my butt off. Hopefully, whatever germs the blanket has will be too cold to infect me.

Cole seems impervious to the temperature and keeps up a running stream of information on who I'm about to meet and who I should avoid. Oddly, Dobber, who appears to be his best friend, is at the top of the avoid list. So of course, I'm looking forward to meeting him.

Ten minutes later, we turn onto a gravel road. An orange glow shines through the trees, casting long shadows that fade into the night.

"Is that a fire?"

"Bonfire," Cole says. "You ever been to a bonfire party?"

"No." I'm thinking about bonfires and how they pretty much have to be outside. Then I'm thinking about how it's mud season. And then I look down at the three-inch heels on my suede boots. "You could have told me it was going to be outside."

Cole pulls into the parking area. I'm not sure what else to call a bare yard with twenty cars in it. The fire is ahead of us, across a plowed field studded with patches of snow. "You don't have to be outside. They party in the house too."

"With Dobber's dad?"

He takes the key out of the ignition and turns to me in one fluid movement, pointing it at my nose. "Stay away from Dobber's dad. A'ight?"

I stare at him in the light from the fire. "If the guy is such bad news, why are we even here?"

Cole looks at me like I asked why we breathe air. "What else are we gonna do?"

I have no answer for that, and anyway, he's already getting out of the car. I claw the blanket off and fumble for the door handle—only then realizing that's another part of the car that doesn't work.

Cole comes around to let me out. "Sorry. That's next on the list. Just waiting for my paycheck."

"You have a job?"

"Not really. I just do some work now and then at the mine—landscaping, running errands, random stuff." He runs his hand over the hood of the car. "It pays for parts."

I wrap my scarf up around my mouth. There's a breeze rattling the naked tree branches and the damp crawls right through my clothes and condenses on my skin. "So, you're fixing your car up yourself?"

"Yeah." We're walking toward the fire. As he turns to me, the shadows catch in his dimples and I wonder what it would be like to run my finger over them. "I've been working on it since I was fifteen. Daddy and I rebuilt the engine first. It didn't even run when I bought it. Cost me six grand."

"Are you kidding me? Six thousand dollars for a car that didn't run?"

"Well, yeah!" He snorts dramatically and jerks his thumb back at the car. "That's a '65 Mustang!"

"So…it's old."

"It's a *classic*?" He says it like a question. One I should know the answer to.

"Right." There's a long silence telling me I'm supposed to say something else. "Well, it looks great. I can't wait to see it when it's done."

He smiles. "You think you're gonna be here that long?"

A thousand things run through my head—my old school, Iris, Georgetown.

But then…MFM calling from the police station to say she'd been arrested. Withdrawing every cent from my college account to pay the lawyer's retainer. Living with Iris until MFM's plea hearing. Then, packing up the apartment alone, dealing with utilities, movers, and storage companies alone. And finally the bus ride to Granny's.

Where I'm no longer alone.

"Absolutely," I say. "I live here now."

SIX

"You wanna go inside?" Cole asks.

I'm shivering already and don't think even the bonfire would do much to warm the chill that's settled against my skin. "Yeah. If you don't mind."

"No. I can tell you're cold." He takes my hand and smiles at me. I'm kind of melting as he pulls me toward the house. "Your nose is running like a leaky faucet."

Great.

He turns and heads for the house, my hand still clutched in his, pulling me after him. I stumble along the uneven ground, past piles and piles of cast-off junk.

As we climb the steps, I realize the house isn't a house at all, but a trailer with a shingle roof built over it. A wood deck stretches down the side and dead-ends into an RV that's been welded to the end of the trailer...like an addition. The deck is cluttered with furniture that wasn't technically designed to be outside and one rusty appliance (I think it might be a stove) lying on its side. The music is so loud, Cole has to shout for me to hear him.

"Stick with me, okay?"

"Sure." I don't bother pointing out the obvious, that I don't know anybody else.

The air is so smoky it seems nearly solid, and by the smell, I can tell there's more than just tobacco here. There are about twenty people inside, standing in groups of threes and fours, red cups and cigarettes in hand.

What I wouldn't give for Iris's wit right now. She'd say something clever, and everybody would laugh and love her right away. Me? I stand here, holding Cole's hand, looking around like I'm super interested in the decor.

"A'ight, y'all," Cole says. "This is Liberty. She's going to Plurd now." He pulls me forward and tucks my hand under his arm. "Y'all say hi."

A couple people do. Most go back to their conversations where, judging by the glances directed at me, I seem to be the new topic. One of the girls—long, blond hair, dark eyes—gives me the once-over, complete with raised eyebrow and frown. I know the look. It says, "You don't belong here." Or maybe it's, "You don't belong with him."

I dislike her immediately.

I put my free hand on Cole's bicep and smile at her. It's catty, I know, but nobody tells me where I belong. Or with whom. And if she thinks *she* can just because I'm new, she can kiss my—

"Well, hello, Lady Liberty!" says an oily voice.

The crowd in the living room parts as a man swaggers down the hallway from the back of the trailer. He's got a bottle of whiskey in one hand and, by the way he's hanging onto the walls, it looks like the empty half is in his bloodstream. Cole pushes me behind him and I realize…

This is the infamous Dobber's Dad.

The fact that I actually stay behind Cole is a pretty good testament to the *scary* this guy gives off. His jeans are filthy, a couple sizes too big, and tied around his skinny waist with some kind of twine. Black hair hangs like yarn past his eyes. He's not wearing a shirt, unless you consider four tattoos and some half-healed sores clothing.

Topping it all off, a square box is strapped to his ankle. House arrest monitor.

"Looka here." He leans toward us, grinning through scabbed lips and pitted, brown teeth. "Shit, girl. You look just like your mama."

Cole puts his hands up, but stops short of actually touching the guy. I feel the tension in his shoulders and realize he's afraid. "Hang on, now. Aren't you supposed to be in your shop?"

Mr. Dobber's still staring at me. "I took your mama to the junior prom." His laugh sounds like a Doberman's bark. "Betcha didn't know that."

No way! This man's the same age as my mom? He looks ancient. But it figures MFM would've been hooked up with this whacko. She always was a crappy judge of character.

A guy the size of a tree lumbers past me and, laughing, wraps an enormous arm around Mr. Dobber's neck. "Daddy! What you doing out here? Don't make me hurt you."

Cole points. "That's Dobber."

"I gathered that," I say.

Mr. Dobber pulls and pushes against his son who's dragging him down the hall toward the RV addition. "I just come out to get some water, jackass."

"A'ight. You and me'll go back in your shop. Cole'll bring you some water. Won't ya, Coley?"

"Sure thing." Cole and I head for the kitchen.

"House arrest?" I whisper.

Cole nods.

"What'd he do?"

"Attacked a guy in town." Cole looks over my head to make sure Mr. Dobber is out of earshot. "Tried to strangle him. It took four men to pull him off."

"They didn't think he might be better off in jail?"

"Guess not." He rinses out one of the red cups in the sink and fills it with water from the tap. It's bright orange here too.

"Is he going to drink that?" I ask.

"It's fine, Lib. Just got a little iron in it."

He pushes his way through the crowd toward the hallway. As I try to decide whether I'd rather stand alone in a room where everybody's staring at me or go with Cole and brave another encounter with Mr. Dobber, somebody bumps into me.

Hard.

I step aside as the pretty blond girl from before pushes past me to the sink. "I bet where you're from, tap water's clear, ain't it?"

I can't tell if she's making conversation or lining up for the kill. "Generally, yes."

"Well then." She turns, her arms crossed over her chest. "Maybe you should go home."

"Maybe I am home."

"Yeah?" She glances around, and just for a second, the tough mask slips and her eyes go desperate. Like all the dreams she ever had winked out at once. "Too bad for you."

* * *

Given the choice between cold and mud or Dobber's dad and the bitchy blond, I decide the bonfire doesn't sound so bad after all. Cole gets the ick blanket from his car, and we slip-slide our way across the mud field. My boots will never be the same, but Cole keeps his arm around me, which kinda makes up for ruined suede.

The crowd at the bonfire is more laid-back. Three girls sitting at a picnic table pass around a bottle of pink wine. Some guy with a banjo is picking it quietly while another guy follows along on a harmonica. I haven't heard banjo music since Granddaddy died. I remember him playing it after dinner while Granny danced in the kitchen. I'd try to keep up with her, but her footwork was so fast. Like hummingbird wings.

Cole and I take an open bench close to the fire and he pulls the blanket across our backs. We have to sit close for it to cover us both. That's when I decide bonfires don't suck.

His face is really close, and I can smell the orange Tic Tacs we ate on the way from the car. The fire's turned his skin gold and thrown his dimples into sharp relief. He is. So. Beautiful. I wonder if his lips are soft, if his skin smells like soap, if his mouth tastes like oranges.

"So," I say, to cover the lust bunnies hopping around my head.

"So?" His voice is different. Deeper. "What?" It's a rhetorical question, since we're both already leaning toward each other. When our lips touch, warmth shoots through my body. I don't feel the wind. I don't feel the fire—just Cole's lips and his tongue, teasing mine. His hand slides up, and I tense, thinking he's going to grab my boob, but he touches my face instead, the back of my neck, pulling me into him.

I relax and melt against him, relieved he's not moving too fast. Just fast enough, as Iris would say. The warmth of his hand, the fire, his lips—I'm lost in this moment. This orange-candy-flavored, soap-scented moment. Just as I'm sliding my arms around his neck, something heavy lands on my back.

"Coley, my brother!" Dobber's behind us with a hand on each of our shoulders. "You gonna introduce me to your new friend?"

Cole looks like he'd rather punch him in the face. We untangle ourselves as Dobber laughs and sits down next to me on the bench.

"Sorry about him," Cole says to me. "Dobber learned his manners from goats."

"Manners?" Dobber snorts. "What manners?"

"Ain't that the truth. Liberty, this is Dobber. Dobber, Liberty."

Dobber holds out an enormous hand and I shake it. "Very pleased to make your acquaintance." He's so tall I have to lean back to look up at him. His dark hair is a little long, but not stringy like his dad's. His eyes are light, maybe blue. He's nowhere close to cute, not like Cole. His teeth are crooked, and his face is wide. But he's charming. Way charming. Maybe that's why Cole told me to stay away from him.

"It's nice to meet you," I say.

"So, where you from?" Dobber asks.

"Far, far away," Cole says. "Where I wish you were."

"Did I ask you, butthead?" Dobber turns to me, waiting.

"DC," I say. "But Kat Briscoe is my granny." I'm not sure why I add that. Maybe to prove I'm not an outsider.

"Is'at right?" He looks surprised. Or impressed. Or maybe he's just being nice. I can't read him at all. "You just visiting or you staying for a while?"

"I'm staying." Funny how that gets easier every time I say it.

"Sweet! We could use another pretty girl 'round here." His smile has gravity, tugging on me like the moon on the tides. I suspect he has half the girls in town wrapped around his giant little finger. "How you liking Ebbottsville so far?"

Cole groans. "Come on, man. Can't you get the 411 some other time? We were kinda in the middle of something."

Dobber laughs loud, and everybody around the fire jumps. "A'ight, fine. Go back to your previous activities." He stands up and the bench springs a little. "Be safe though." Winking at me, he adds, "You know what I'm talking 'bout, right?"

"Ignore him. He's a dog," Cole says as Dobber walks off. He's smiling though, and I can tell they're good friends.

Dobber walks over to the three girls near the picnic table. The wine bottle is empty now, sideways on the ground. The girls are huddled together, smoking. Now that they're standing, I can tell the girl on the end is pregnant. Really pregnant.

"She shouldn't be smoking," I say.

Cole snorts. "She shouldn't have done a lot of things."

"Well…yeah, I guess."

"Casey's like a public telephone. Half the county's dialed her up."

"Cole!" Maybe it's true, but the way he just discounts her…It makes me not like him so much.

"I'm sorry," he says. "That was mean."

"Yeah, it was," I say. "She made a mistake. Maybe a lot of mistakes." Cole's leaning away from me, and I'm desperately wishing my mouth would stop moving, but for some reason, I'm driven to defend this girl I don't know. "She's still a human being, you know." The minute MFM's words come out of my mouth, I stop cold.

Cole's eyebrows are pulled together as he looks at me. I'm still reeling from my brief mind meld with MFM. At the same time, I'm expecting Cole to tell me off or say I should find someone else to take me home. Instead, he stares at me and says, "You're different, Liberty. Different from people 'round here."

Unexpected, that. Is it a good thing? Or a bad thing? "Different how?"

But then his arms slide around me and his lips are on mine again, and I can't remember what the question was.

SEVEN

"You can't be serious," I mumble from under the comforter.

"Serious as a heart attack," Granny says. "Get your skinny butt up and get dressed for church."

I listen as her flip-flops shuffle down the hall. It's not like I hate church. I'd just rather keep replaying in my mind the kisses from last night. At the fire. In the car. At the front door. Mmm. Cole's a great kisser. Way better than Ryan Miller, the drool machine.

"Liberty! I don't hear no movement in there!"

"All right, you cranky old—"

"You sure you wanna finish that?" She's back in my doorway, this time with a rolled up newspaper.

I fling the covers back and sit up. "Happy?"

She just grunts and walks away.

* * *

Unity Baptist Church hasn't changed much since the last time I was here. The pews are still hard, it still needs paint, and despite those things, it's still packed full. Granny takes her usual seat, outside aisle of the second row.

I recognize Granny's friend Myrna Lattimer sitting just ahead of us.

She takes my hand. "Libby darling, when you walked in, I coulda sworn you was your mama."

Ergh.

"You are the spittin' image!"

I try to smile around my gritted teeth. "It's nice to see you again."

"How is Jamie?"

Clearly, Granny hasn't told anybody about MFM's arrest. I wish I could have gotten away with that in DC.

Luckily, Myrna doesn't wait for an answer. "Lordy, I can still see her, stomping around the courthouse with that sign of hers. What was she so fired up about, Kat?"

Granny snorts. "Which time?"

"Ain't that the truth? She was a serious little thing. Always trying to save somebody," Myrna says. "I had her in kindygarten. It was her job to hand out the cookies, 'cause I knew she'd make sure ever'body got the 'xact same amount."

I can't listen to this anymore and start scooting out of the pew. Granny grabs my arm before I get two steps.

"D'you do something new to your hair, Myrna?" she asks. "Looks real nice."

"Thank you. I'm so tickled you noticed."

I'm pretty sure Myrna's hair looks exactly the same as it did five years ago, except grayer. Actually, the whole congregation is looking pretty gray. And a little scary. There are enough people breathing off oxygen tanks that I'm starting to worry about the lit candle over by the organ.

Glancing around, I see a few people from the party last night, including my new blond frenemy, looking very Taylor Swift with her big, brown eyes. Banjo guy is there next to the organ, but playing a guitar today. Pregnant Casey's here too, and Cole's in the back row with some guy I don't recognize. I start to get up, thinking I'll go sit with him, when Granny grabs my arm again.

"No way, Jose," she says.

"I was just going to go sit with—"

"I know exactly what you was gonna do," she whispers through a fake smile for the benefit of the church ladies. "But this here's church, not a dating service."

"I was just going to *sit* with him."

"And now you're not." She shoves a book into my hands. "Find me hymn fifty-three. Them daggum page numbers is so little, I can't tell the eights from the sixes."

Shaking my head, I flip to the right page and hand the hymnal back.

I never loved church, but sitting here now while a hundred voices harmonize on "The Sweet By-and-By," I can see why Granny comes. It's peaceful. Whether it comes from the presence of a Holy Spirit or just knowing that this—the service, the people, the singing—will never change, I don't know. But I like it. Even the sermon, which always lasted forever when I was little, flies by, and before I know it, the preacher is announcing the final song.

"We're gonna wrap up with hymn one-oh-three this morning. I'd like to dedicate the song to our brothers and sisters in Christ who couldn't be with us today, being sick or laid up." He takes a sheet of paper out of his bible. "Please join me this week in praying for…"

The names go on, about sixteen in all, which seems like a lot for a small church. But there are a lot of old people here.

The preacher folds his list, says amen, and then we're singing "Swing Low, Sweet Chariot." I've always liked that song, and I actually join in, despite the fact that I'm completely tone-deaf. Granny puts her arm around me and says in my ear, "Sing it loud, girl. God don't care about the notes!"

* * *

I check my messages in the churchyard while Granny chats with her friends. There are a few texts from Iris, which I return. And a voice mail from MFM that I delete.

I'm texting Iris, party last night with the cutest guy ever, when Cole walks up.

"I didn't take you for a churchgoer." He leans against Granny's car, next to me, so close, I can feel the heat of his arm even through my coat.

"I wasn't given an option." I hit send and slide the phone into my pocket.

"Me either. Mama even makes us come when we're sick."

I laugh, which is lame because that wasn't all that funny. "Well, it's Christian to share, right? Even germs."

"I reckon." He glances across the parking lot. "How come your mama didn't come?"

I knew there'd be questions about that woman. "She's not living here. Just me."

"She stayed in DC?"

I nod.

Cole frowns. "I don't get it. If she's living there, seems like you'd wanna stay at your fancy school." He stares at me for a second, then smiles. "Unless you got kicked out."

I'll take any opportunity to steer the conversation away from MFM. "Something like that."

He slides one arm around me. "Dang girl. You don't seem like a hell-raiser. What'd you do?"

"I'd rather not talk about it." I'd rather focus on how his thumb is resting right on my hip bone.

He half smiles, staring at my mouth.

With a spasm somewhere near my bellybutton, I realize he's going to kiss me. I snuggle into his arm and tilt my head up, just a little, hoping Granny's looking the other way.

"Gagging!" My new blond frenemy is standing in front of us. "Really, Cole? Is she the best you can do?"

"Go to hell, Ashleigh."

Ah. A name. I bet she spells it with two *E*'s. Maybe three.

"Nice language," she says. "I see church made a big impression on you."

Cole mumbles something and plants a quick kiss on the side of my head. "I gotta go," he says quietly. "I'll call you."

"Okay. See ya."

I watch him walk away, acutely aware of Ashleigh's eyes boring into the side of my head.

"He won't," she says.

I wait a few seconds before turning to her. "Won't what?"

"Call you." She smiles, and I hate the fact that she's drop-dead gorgeous. "So don't get your hopes up. He'll shit on you just like he shit on every other girl he's dated."

"Like you?" I return the poison smile. "I'm not every other girl." But I'm wondering just how many other girls there were.

"Right. You're special. You were born somewhere else. Someplace rich. Someplace you can drink the water without getting sick."

"Wait…what?" That's the second time she's mentioned the water.

Before Ashleigh can answer, Granny flip-flops up beside me.

"Ashleigh, shug, how's your granddaddy?" she asks. I've seldom heard her voice so gentle; it's like she's talking to a baby.

Ashleigh turns to Granny, looking more like a blond cherub than the glare-y witch I've grown to know and not love. "He's hanging in there. Thanks for asking."

Granny pats her arm. "You tell him I asked after him. Y'all is in my prayers."

"Thanks, Mrs. Briscoe." Ashleigh smiles and I have trouble believing this is the same girl who just bitched me out for being born in a different town. "I'll tell him." She heads across the parking lot without so much as a parting sneer for me, which seems weird. It's not like her to miss an opportunity for meanness.

"What's wrong with her granddad?" I ask, staring after Ashleigh. No answer.

I look over at Granny, and she's glaring daggers—no, more like Uzis—at me. "What?"

"Didn't I tell you church ain't no dating service?"

"Huh?" It takes me a minute to realize she's talking about Cole. "We didn't do anything. He was just standing here."

"Get in the car." She pulls open the passenger door, which squeals like a garbage truck, and flops down.

"So I'm not even allowed to talk to him?"

"Just get in the car."

"Is that just at church? Or everywhere?"

"Get in the dad-blame car, Liberty!" And then she's coughing again.

"Nice language." I slam her door and walk around the car to the driver's side. Inside, I fumble through her purse, looking for the water I put in there this morning. "There is nothing wrong with me standing next to Cole or sitting next to him at church." I open the bottle and hand it to her. "This isn't 1950."

"It ain't Worshington, DC, neither."

I look across the churchyard, past the old people, at the squared-off top where Tanner's Peak used to be and think about what Ashleigh said about the water. Then I look at Granny, trying to rub the little drops of blood off her hand before I see them. A spasm of worry shudders through my chest.

No, I think. *This is a long way from DC.*

EIGHT

"The school bus stops at the end of the driveway," says Granny.

"Great," I mumble around my toast.

She comes to stand behind me, her tiny hands on my shoulders. I feel like a giant compared to her. "You nervous, sugarplum?"

"No." Why would I be nervous about starting at a new school where Ashleigh's probably the homecoming queen? I can feel the concentric red rings appearing on my back already.

"Well, you just be yourself. Them kids'll warm up to you soon enough."

Hm.

"I better go," I say, dropping the crust of my toast into the trash. Stooping down, I kiss Granny's cheek. It's warm and dry and smells like Jergens.

"Have a good day," Granny says.

"Not likely."

"Well, try anyways."

"I gotta run." And I do, because I hear what sounds like a bus rumbling up the road.

"Love you, sugar pie," she calls after me.

"Love you too," I yell back. Her cough follows me down the drive and I cringe, remembering the blood.

My messenger bag bangs against my hip as I run and try to avoid the muddy parts. The bus honks. I turn the last bend and run straight into a spider web of colossal proportions. Suddenly, I'm limboing backward, trying to get the sticky stuff off my face and out of my hair. My bag falls off my shoulder and lands with a splash, but all I'm concerned about is whether the spider that built this natural wonder is crawling into my shirt.

Judging by the laughter coming from the bus, I'm a pretty entertaining sight. Once I've pulled off the worst of the threads, I pick up my bag, duck the remainder of the web, and make my way onto the bus, where in the very front seat I'm unpleased to find my favorite bitchy blond.

She raises one perfectly shaped eyebrow. "Quite an entrance."

"Shut up." Taking an empty seat in the middle, I try to imagine what my hair looks like, post–spider dance. There's mud on my jeans from where my bag rubbed against them. I'm a mess, but that's not why everyone on the bus is openly staring at me. I might as well have *Outsider* tattooed across my forehead.

* * *

Plurd County High School is a fortress of brick. Flat, square buildings, low walls, and one tall chimney, all done in standard terracotta red. It's state-of-the-art 1950s, complete with giant flagpole. But there are a lot of big trees in front, dotting an expanse of what's probably grass when it's not mud season. I stick to the sidewalk, avoiding the red clay.

This is way different from Westfield Academy, located two drugdealer-infested blocks from Dupont Circle without a tree in sight. I'm thinking that here, in the spring, it must be nice to lie on the grass in the shade. Maybe with Cole, sharing a kiss or two. I feel the corners of my mouth turn up just as a hand claps me on the shoulder. I spin around, prepared for Ashleigh's angry angel face.

"New girl!" Dobber says. He gives me the full benefit of his smile, and I think, again, that he could probably charm the pants off most any girl here. Maybe even me, if it weren't for the Olympic cuteness that is Cole standing right behind him. I swear Cole's teeth are putting out sunrays.

"Hi." I try to smile at both of them, but I'm pretty sure my eyes don't leave Cole's face.

Dobber puts his arm around me and pulls me away. "So tell me, beautiful, how you liking Plurd County High?"

I don't remember anybody calling me beautiful before. Once, when Ryan Miller was trying to undo my bra, I asked if he thought I was pretty and he said, "Mm-hm," but it wasn't quite the same. I start to think Dobber's just as dangerous as his daddy, but in a totally different way.

"You'll have to ask me tomorrow," I say.

Dobber grins. "Is 'at a date?"

"Dobbs." Cole's voice is quiet and calm, but even I catch the undertone of warning.

"A'ight." Dobber's arm snakes back toward his own body. "Ain't nothin'."

Dobber steps away from me. Cole steps in and puts *his* arm around me, right where Dobber's was just a few seconds ago. I feel like a piece of meat getting tugged back and forth in the middle of an alpha-wolf challenge.

I don't like it.

"You know what?" I say, pulling free of Cole. "I have to check in with the guidance counselor before class, so I better go."

"Oh." Cole's smile goes flat.

I kiss him fast on the cheek. "See you later though? At lunch?"

"Sure." His smile is back. "You want to sit with us?"

"Yeah, great." Thank God. The "where to sit at lunch" issue is the absolute worst part of a first day at a new school. "See you then."

He winks and smiles. "Bye."

"Bye. Bye, Dobber."

"Later." He doesn't even look at me.

I head for what looks like the office thinking that, aside from the emotional whiplash, my first day at Plurd doesn't totally suck. So far.

* * *

"So? How's things?" Cole asks at lunch. He, Dobber, and I are sitting at a table alone. I wonder if it's normally just the two of them or if their other friends bailed because of me.

I poke at the über-basic salad I cobbled together: iceberg lettuce, grated cheese, and canned black olives. "So-so."

The counselor had bad news about my schedule. There's no Comparative Religion, no Anthropology, and no German III. There's no German at all, actually. Instead I'm taking Literature, something called Life Skills, and starting a whole new language—which should be interesting halfway through the year.

"Can't ask for better than so-so," Dobber says. "Not at school, anyway."

I don't tell him that I've always liked school. Or that I'm hoping I'll like it here. Eventually. After I make some friends. I glance across the cafeteria to where Ashleigh sits at a table with some other girls. Seeing their smiles and whispers makes me homesick for Iris.

I fold open my chocolate milk, drop in a straw, and suck down half the carton. I haven't had milk since I got here, just hot tea and water. Which reminds me…

"Hey, what do you guys know about the water situation?" I try to keep a casual tone. "Why's it orange?"

Cole shovels in a fork full of baked beans. "Well water's just weird."

"It's not usually orange though," I point out.

"Sometimes it is," Dobber says. "Like that summer we had that drought and ever'body's wells got low?"

We visited Granny that summer, and I remember it. "Yeah, but that was rust-colored. This is like…Crayola."

"D'your granny have her water tested?" Dobber asks.

I nod. "She said the report was okay."

"Then what're you worried about?" Cole asks.

"It's just weird," I say, impaling my last black olive with my fork. "Granny said it changed color after Tanner's Peak was blasted. Is that when you guys noticed it?"

Dobber shrugs.

Cole pushes his tray away and lays his arm across the back of my chair. "We have city water."

"Oh." His arm against my back feels warm and nice. I could sit like this for the rest of the day. "I think I'm going to look into it."

"Into what?"

"The water."

Cole scoffs. "What for?"

"Maybe there's something wrong with it. I mean, what if the water is what's making Granny sick?"

"Waste of time," Cole says. "If the county said the water's fine, then the water's fine."

I wish I had his faith in the system.

The bell rings and Cole groans.

"What's wrong?" I ask.

"Class from hell next."

"I see. And what are they teaching in hell these days?"

"Es-pag-no," Cole says.

"Huh?"

Dobber shoves the last half of his corndog into his mouth and pulls out the stick. "Thpanith."

Great. Now I'm covered in a light dusting of wet corn bread. "Spanish One?"

Cole nods.

I gather up my trash and stand. "Cool. You can show me where it is."

His brown eyes widen in the cutest way. "Really?"

I nod. "I had to take a language, and they don't have German here."

Cole grins and grabs his books. "Es-pag-no is now my favorite class of the day."

"That's sad, man." Dobber shakes his head as we walk out. "Ain't no girl cute enough to make Spanish good."

NINE

By the time the bus drops me back at Granny's, it's after four o'clock. I'll have to drive fast to get her to her appointment at four thirty.

Luckily, she's all ready to go.

That's an understatement, actually. She's dressed up, hair fixed, lipstick on, sitting in the car.

"What took you so long, slowpoke?"

I throw my bag into the back and settle into the driver's seat. "The bus," I say. "It goes all over the county before it drops me off."

"You better haul ass. We got twenty minutes to get there."

"Yes, ma'am." I put the car in gear and paint the sides with mud, speeding down the driveway.

"Holy Ghost in heaven," Granny yells as she bounces across the seat. "Easy on them potholes, Richard Petty."

"You said *haul ass*. I'm just doing what you said."

"That's a first."

Traffic is pretty light, meaning there aren't any tractors or coal trucks on the road, and we're pulling up to the clinic right on time. We walk in, and I tell the receptionist we're here.

"It'll be about thirty minutes," she says.

So much for hurrying.

The waiting room is dark and sounds like a TB ward. At least half the people in here are coughing like Granny. I start to feel a little better. It sounds like something's going around. Maybe that's what Granny's got.

We sit down in mismatched folding chairs and thumb through *People* magazines from two years ago. The waiting room slowly empties until, forty-five minutes later, a nurse sticks her head around a door and calls, "Katherine Briscoe?"

"That's me." Granny stands up and says, "'Bout Goddern time."

I mumble, "Sorry about that," as we file past the nurse.

Granny hears me and looks over her shoulder. "Where you think you're going, missy?"

"I'm going with you."

"The heck you are," she says. "I been seeing doctors by myself for fi'ty years, and I don't need no chaperone now."

"Too bad," I say. "I'm coming with."

"Like hell! You march your—"

"Oh quit bitching at me, you old bat." I push past her and plop down in the chair in the exam room. I'm bouncing my foot and glaring at a poster of the human nervous system when she shuffles in and sits down on the exam table.

"The doctor will be in shortly," the nurse says before closing the door.

"That was rude," says Granny.

"I'm sorry. It was a long day, I have a ton of homework to do when I get home, and the longer you stand there yelling, the longer we'll be here."

"That ain't no reason to be disrespectful." She sniffs. "Old bat, my ass."

The doctor is young, maybe thirty, and exhausted looking. "Okay, Mrs. Briscoe, what seems to be the problem?"

"Nothing." She gives him a blazing smile. "I'm fit as a fiddle."

"Really?" He puts his stethoscope into his ears and steps close to her. "That's great news, but let's just take a listen, shall we?"

Obviously, he's dealt with mountain people before.

"What'd you say your name was?" Granny asks.

"Dr. Lang."

"You been doctoring long?"

He smiles. There's a gap in his front teeth that makes me like him. "Long enough."

After checking her blood pressure and taking her temperature, he listens to her lungs in like eight different places.

"Did you have a long drive today?" he asks.

"Naw," Granny says. "Just down the hill. Speed Racer here made the trip in record time."

He looks at her fingernails and inside her nose. "You're on the east side of the mountain, then."

"Yessir. Been there almost forty years."

"That's a long time." Finally, he leans against the sink in the corner. "Well, Mrs. Briscoe—"

"Oh, now. You can call me Kat."

Oh my God. My grandmother's flirting.

"Well, Kat, I'm a little worried about your lungs. It sounds like you've got some fluid in there. Have you been coughing?"

Granny smiles. "No, not really."

"You have too!" I say.

He glances at me then back to Granny. "And when you cough, do you bring anything up? Mucus?"

"Nothing at all," Granny says.

"Bullshit. You've been coughing up blood for at least two days."

"That weren't blood," Granny snaps. "That was just some lung guck."

"Which is Granny-speak for blood," I say. Dr. Lang has pulled out a prescription pad and is scribbling away.

"Blood or guck, I'd like to get a better look at those lungs," he says. "I'm sending you in for x-rays." He tears the top sheet off and hands it to Granny. "The nearest imaging clinic is in Charlottesville. Will you have any trouble getting there?"

But Granny's worried about other things. "How much them x-rays gonna cost me?"

"I'll get her there," I say.

"I ain't got no insurance, 'cept for Medicaid."

"I understand, Mrs. Briscoe." And, rubbing his tired eyes, he looks like he does. "But I'm concerned you might have something more serious than a respiratory virus."

"Like what?" Granny and I both say at the same time.

The doctor waves us off. "Let's just see what the x-ray's show."

"How about you tell us *now* why you want them," I say.

"I ain't paying for nothing till I know what it's for," Granny adds.

The doctor gives us a weak smile. "I don't want to worry you until we have more data."

"Data?" Granny says. "I ain't a damn lab rat." Raising her voice starts her on a coughing fit.

He pats her on the back. "I understand that, Mrs.—"

"I'm already worried," I say. "She coughs up blood, for God's sake. You think that doesn't worry me?"

Granny's hacking up a lung, so I dig through her purse to find her water.

"There's no reason yet to think this is anything other than a lingering cold," he says.

"Right. And you always prescribe x-rays for colds, do you?" I hand Granny the water.

"Of course not." He's getting irritated with us. "I just want to rule out that it's not anything more serious."

"Such as?" I ask.

Sighing, he tilts his head back and stares at the ceiling.

"Well?" I say.

"Fine." His voice is quiet now. "I'd like to rule out the possibility of cancer."

"Cancer?" I feel my eyes widen. "Lung cancer?"

"Yes."

Granny is surprisingly silent. I put my arm around her. "Is that really a possibility?"

"A distant possibility. Her lungs have some fluid and her mucous membranes are a bit blue. Her fingernails are starting to club." His frown deepens. "And you live on the east side of the mountain."

"So?" Granny and I say at the same time.

"There've been…" He pauses, choosing his words. "We've seen a lot of health issues cropping up in that area in recent years."

I stare for a minute, my thoughts racing. "What are you saying? That it's a…" I try to remember the term we learned studying Chernobyl. "A cancer cluster?"

He blows out a puff of air. "Cancer. Heart disease. Kidney disease. Birth defects. It's a cluster, all right."

Granny holds up her hand and starts ticking off fingers. "Ben Willis had cancer. Died last fall. My friend Mary Nell had a heart attack a few months back. Jason and Tracy Easter's baby got stillborn. Her sister, Tanya, her baby got a cleft palate. Virgil Nelson had his gallbladder removed. That's been a year or two."

The doctor shakes his head. "I'd be surprised if there's a functioning gallbladder in the whole valley."

"What's causing it all?" I ask.

The doctor chews his lip for a minute then shrugs. "No way to tell conclusively." His mouth twists on the last word, like it tastes bad.

Granny stares hard at the doctor, then slaps the paper-covered exam table. "You want I should have that x-ray, Doc, I'll go have me a x-ray."

"I'm glad," he says. "But in the meantime, let's hope for the best."

"We'll be praying," Granny says. "Like a Baptist in a boat on fire. Won't we, Liberty?"

I nod, but my mind's fixed on something else—something abnormal in the valley. Something that might be causing all those health problems. And that *something* is bright orange.

TEN

We schedule the x-ray, but the clinic is busy and the earliest they can work us in is the middle of March. Three weeks away. I try not to think about how much tumors can grow in three weeks.

"Earth to Liberty. Come in, Liberty."

My head snaps up from the book I'm reading to find Cole standing next to me. "Hey." I wrap my arm around his waist. "Did the bell ring?"

"Five minutes ago." He takes the chair next to me, dropping his backpack on the table. "I've been looking for you. What're you doing in the library?"

"Literature class was last period. We had to pick out a novel for a movie trailer project."

He turns over the book in my hands to read the spine. "*Mountain of Coal*. This is a novel?"

"Um, no." I rub my eyes. "It's a...sort of a history of coal mining."

Cole drops the book onto the table. "Sounds gripping. That'll make one helluva movie trailer." He smiles at me, white teeth and sparkly eyes, and I almost forget about the book.

"It's not for class. It's for Granny," I say. "We went to the doctor yesterday. They think she might..." I'm not ready to say the *C* word. Saying it might make it true when maybe, hopefully, it's not. "She's pretty sick. The doctor ordered an x-ray of her lungs."

"Aw, Lib." He wraps his arms around me, smashing my face into his shoulder. I turn my head and rest it against him. It feels so nice to have someone to lean on. I wrap my arms around him and sink in. "I'm sorry. I'm sure she'll be fine."

"I hope so," I say as I pull away. "But it sounds like a lot of people on the east side of the mountain are getting sick. So I'm just wondering if it doesn't have something to do with the water."

"You're not on about that again." Cole shakes his head. "It's been tested."

"I know. It's just…orange. And lots of people are sick," I say. "Seems like too much of a coincidence."

"People get sick, Lib. Everywhere. It just happens." He leans forward and kisses my forehead. "I'm sorry about your granny though."

"Thanks." I lay my head on his shoulder, staring out the windows at the weak afternoon sunlight.

"I gotta run. You want a ride home?" he asks.

"No," I say. "I drove Granny's car today."

"A'ight then. See you tomorrow." His kisses are absolutely the best thing about this place—all soft, warm, and Tic-Tac-y. "And, Lib?"

"Yeah?"

"Don't go around talking about the mine. It ain't a good idea."

I nod once, very slowly, as he picks up his backpack and heads for the door. Cole's clearly of the belief that *rex non potest peccare*: the king can do no wrong. And by king, I mean Peabody Mining Company.

* * *

The school library didn't have much to help my research. So on Saturday, I go to the library in town, which I'm minorly creeped to see is called the "Peabody Community Library." Inside, next to the public message board, is a framed photo of Robert Peabody. He reminds me of an aging movie star—chiseled jaw, fake tan, faker smile. I don't think I like him.

His library is a far cry from the marble-and-glass temple of information we had in DC, but it does have a couple ancient PCs in one corner with a dial-up Internet connection. I sign up for thirty minutes of computer time and pull up Google.

"Mountaintop Removal Mining" turns up a gazillion pages, mostly environmental groups posting interesting statistics about MTR communities. Interesting meaning scary.

> *Children born in communities near mountaintop removal mines are 42 percent more likely to be born with birth defects.*

> *People living near mountaintop removal mines have cancer rates of 14.4 percent, as opposed to 9.4 percent for people living in other parts of Appalachia.*

I'm staring at the numbers on the computer screen, but I'm seeing the kids at Granny's church, the ones with leg braces and harelips, the baby we prayed for last week who was stillborn.

I read further.

> *Statistics for coal-mining areas of Appalachia show that these regions have had the highest mortality rates for every year from 1979–2005.*

> *People living near mountaintop removal mines have an average life expectancy five years lower than for people living elsewhere in the United States.*

Clicking through the data, I come across some photographs that could have been taken in Ebbottsville. They show the same boarded-up stores, the same chewed-up landscape, even the same sludgy containment pond.

I'm wondering why there's not more press on this. I mean, until I moved here, I'd never even heard of mountaintop removal mining. But it's been going on a long time.

In 2000, a containment pond in Martin County spilled 300 million gallons of toxic sludge into two rivers and killed everything downstream for hundreds of miles. The EPA called it the worst environmental disaster ever to occur in the southeastern U.S.

How can an environmental disaster thirty times bigger than the *Exxon Valdez* oil spill happen a few hundred miles west of the capital of the free world and *not* make the news?

Glancing at the clock, I realize my half hour is almost up. I fish ten cents out of my backpack to print the statistics. The librarian looks hard at the copy before she hands it across the desk and frowns at me. I can't decide if it's because she doesn't approve of the subject matter or that's just her normal sunny treatment of strangers.

As I drive home, I wonder why the hell nobody's worried about the water. It's bright freaking orange—not like any rust I've ever seen. But Granny said the county tested it and found it safe. And numbers don't lie. But after what I've read…I'm just not sure.

I slow down and take a right onto Oak Street. It's March already but half-frozen drizzle is clicking against the windshield. Even with the heater going full blast, there's a chill in the car that keeps my teeth chattering. Winter and spring seem to be battling it out. Today, winter is kicking spring's butt.

There's a girl walking across the Kroger parking lot as I drive past, and it takes me a second to realize it's Ashleigh. It takes me another five seconds to work up the guts to turn in. I pull up in front of her and roll down the squeaky window.

She pulls out an earbud and frowns at the car. "Nice ride."

I stare at the three heavy bags of groceries she's hauling on foot. "Yeah, you too." At least I have a ride.

She shifts them to her other hand. "What do you want?"

What I really want is not to be talking to her at all. I'd love for there not to be a reason I need her input, but I do. "The water," I say. "What do you know?"

I can't see her face in the shadow of her raincoat hood, and for a minute, she says nothing. But her mouth is moving, like she's chewing her words before she spits them out.

"Why?" she says at last.

I don't want to tell her Granny's sick. It's none of her business and I don't need sympathy. I just need information. "You keep talking about it like it's poison. I'm just wondering if I should drink it or not."

"Yes, you should." She plugs the earbud back into her ear. "Absolutely. Drink lots." She walks around the back of the car and heads for the sidewalk.

That went well. I turn off the ignition and climb out of the car as fast as the thousand-foot-wide door will let me. "Wait. Ashleigh, wait."

She stops but doesn't turn.

"Look, let me give you a ride home," I say. "We can talk."

"I'd rather walk," she says over her shoulder. "On hot coals."

But she isn't walking. She's standing in the rain, waiting. For something.

I cross over and stand in front of her. Now I'm chewing my words. How much does she know? And how much do I need her?

"My granny might be sick," I say. "I need to know about the water."

Her face softens a little, like I saw at church. She hands me one of the bags and heads for the car. "Don't think this makes us friends."

I swallow some unchewed words and follow her. Ashleigh's tugging on the passenger door handle. "You have to yank it," I say. "Unless you want to ride in the back."

"Funny."

I'm pulling back onto the street when Ashleigh says, "I'm sorry about your granny." She's staring out the passenger window. "I like her a lot."

"Thanks."

"My granddaddy's sick too."

"What's wrong with him?"

"Gallbladder."

"I'm sorry." I feel like I ought to leave it there, to be polite, but I need to know. "Was it the water?"

She shrugs.

"Do you know anything about it?"

"It's orange."

I snort. "Yeah, no shit."

Her baby doe eyes go all death glare. "Why're you such a bitch?"

"Me? You've been on full snark since the minute I met you."

"So? Am I supposed to fall down at your feet and declare my BFF-ness just 'cause you're new?"

"No, but you could at least be polite. Or if that's too hard, just try for something below raging hag."

"Right. 'Cause you're from somewhere else and therefore deserve my best behavior."

She's back to staring out the passenger window. We're nearing the edge of town and I realize I have no idea where I'm going.

"Where do you live anyway?"

"Turn left up there," she says. "It's a half mile past the concrete plant."

We ride in silence as the wet trees and dripping rocks roll by. The heater isn't doing a thing to alleviate the chill in the car, though now I don't think it's actually weather related.

"Look," I say. "Everything I've read says mountaintop removal mining causes all kinds of health problems—lung problems, tumors, brain cancer, emphysema." I pause for effect. "Gallbladder problems."

"And?"

"*And?* What do you mean, and? If that's the case, we need to let people know."

"You think it matters if people know?"

"Are you on crack? If people know, they'll stop drinking the water. And Peabody will stop mining. And they can fix this mess, so no one else gets sick." I realize about halfway through my soliloquy that I sound like MFM. It makes me itch, like I have mosquito bites all over the inside of my skin.

"Pull over," Ashleigh says.

"Here?" We just passed the concrete plant and there's not a driveway in sight.

"Here," she says. "Right now."

I slow the car down and pull off on the narrow gravel shoulder. She grabs her bags and uses her shoulder to bang open the door. The rain is coming down steady now, filling the ditches on each side of the road.

"What is your freaking problem?"

She ignores me and tries to get her bags balanced while not slipping in the mud.

"You're going to get hypothermia," I say, half hoping she does. It would serve her right.

She leans down before closing the door. "Here's the thing, Erin Brockovich. You don't understand anything about this town. You come waltzin' in here, trying to save us like we're a third-world country or something."

"I'm just trying to help."

"Why? You think we're too stupid to notice the water's orange? Too ignorant to know mines can be dangerous? Did it occur to you there might be a *reason* nobody says anything?"

My eyes blink while I try to make sense of that. "What possible reason could there be *not* to do anything about poisoned water?"

"It's complicated. We're not just a cage full of lab rats. And FYI? You should be a lot more careful who you talk to about Peabody Mining."

"Really? Why is that?"

"Robert Peabody's my uncle, dumbass." She slams the door and starts walking.

Oh.

Shit.

ELEVEN

I make a clumsy U-turn in the middle of the road and head up the hill. There's no way I could have known Ashleigh was related to Peabody, but I still feel really, really stupid. Halfway home, I pull off at an overlook where I know I can get a cell signal and dial Iris.

"Hey, it's Liberty." I feel like I need a friend right now, and Iris is an excellent sympathizer. Unfortunately, she's not picking up.

"Call me when you can." I end the call and then click over to my text messages. One from Iris earlier—jazzing about some internship she applied for. Then I check my email though I'm not sure why. The only person who ever emails me is MFM. Sure enough, there's a new message. This one with the subject line "Progress." I delete it without reading. I don't care how much closer she is to being declared guilty or innocent. Either way, it doesn't affect me.

I stare across the parking lot where I've pulled off and watch the fog roll around the tops of the hills. It swirls and drops, deeper into the hollers, filling them with pillows of white. It's beautiful but I wonder…if the water here's poisonous, is the fog dangerous too? Is it going to turn bright orange, like some funky breed of mustard gas, killing everything as it creeps through the valley on little cat feet?

Funny. But not.

* * *

Granny's napping on the couch when I get home. I let her sleep and start putting dinner together, which calms me. I like to cook. When we lived in DC, I used to pull recipes out of *Food & Wine* to try

out on the weekend. I'd make a huge dinner with a fancy dessert…
which I usually ate by myself because MFM ended up not coming
home from one of her rallies or protests or special projects.

I know all about her special projects now. Thanks to the reports
from the DC Police Department.

Staring into the cabinet with my stomach gnawing at my spine,
I'm wishing for a *Food & Wine* feast. Instead, my options are ramen
or canned soup, which I'll serve with frozen broccoli and a piece
of toast. Not the healthiest of meals, but at least I'll have invoked
some green matter. When I think about all those dinners I cooked
and ate alone—paella, gazpacho with homemade croutons, scallops
Alfredo—I wish I could have a do-over, so I could share them with
Granny. She deserves scallops.

Each week, I do my best to stretch the food stamps and the little
cash we have, but it doesn't cover shellfish. Not that they sell shellfish
here. This week was even harder. Thanks to Shark Week, I had to buy
a box of tampons that took almost a fifth of our food money. So, no
apples, no Mountain Dew. And we'll be eating ramen a lot between
now and Saturday.

"Liberty?"

I leave the water simmering and poke my head around the corner. "Hey there. How are you feeling?"

"I could stand a drink a water."

I get a bottle from the fridge and sit down next to her. "I'm making dinner."

"That's sweet of ya, sugarplum, but I ain't terrible hungry just
now."

She never is anymore. It's all I can do to get her to eat one decent
meal a day.

"Maybe you can eat a little ramen. Just a few bites?"

Frowning, she says, "You gonna fly them bites into my mouth like a airplane?"

I don't want to argue with her. When she gets riled up, she starts coughing. "Only if you say pretty please."

"Your mama called," she says as I walk into the kitchen.

I ignore her.

"She said you ain't been answering her emails."

The water for the broccoli is boiling now, steaming up the window over the sink. I stare through the mist at the darkening gray hillside in the backyard. Anything I say to Granny about MFM will cause a fight, and I don't want her expending a bunch of energy arguing with me. Because there's no point.

I pull the bread across the counter and undo the twist tie. The counter is gritty with dust again.

"Liberty? You hearing me?" Her voice is getting louder.

"I am, Granny. But I don't want to talk about it right now. Let's just have a nice, quiet dinner."

"She said she ain't heard from you at all."

"Do you want to eat in there or at the table?"

"Here on the couch suits me. But don't go changing the subject on me. I ain't done with you yet."

Once everything's ready, I take Granny's tray to her then go back for mine. After we say grace, Granny starts in.

"Now then."

"Eat," I say.

"I been listening to that cockeyed 'I-ain't-got-a-mama' story o' yours since you got here. And I ain't said nothing 'cause I know she hurt you, real bad. But she's paying for her mistake. And it seems to me, if the police and the courts are willing to let her do some kinda penance, then her own flesh and blood surely oughta be able to forgive her."

Staring at the rain pouring off the roof, I wish it could be that easy. "I don't care about the crime. She can blow up whatever she wants to. All I ever wanted was for her to be a mom. But there was always something more important. Everything, in fact, was more important."

Granny reaches for my hand. "She loves you, Liberty. Problem is, y'all two is just too much alike."

"What?" I turn so fast some ramen sloshes out of my bowl. "There is absolutely no way in which we are alike. None. Zero."

"Mmhm." She picks the noodles up with her napkin. "Your mama—"

"Stop calling her that!"

"Blessed baby Jesus! Fine! *My daughter* says you ain't said word one to her since you left DC."

"So?" I think back to the last phone conversation I had with MFM.

I was alone in the apartment, packing up all our crap so the movers could take it to the storage place the next day. The last thing I needed was to waste time listening to her justify things. Not that that stopped her.

"Lib, I'm so sorry about all this," she said. "It wasn't supposed to go down that way. Perry went off book and screwed the rest of us." She sighed. "If I could go back and undo it, I would. I totally would."

I dumped the silverware into a box, thinking, *Duh*.

"And, Lib…I feel really bad about your college money."

That was a stake through my heart. Thanks to her incredibly stupid decisions, the money Granny and Granddaddy squirreled away, dollar by dollar, year after year, for my college had been magically transformed into something called a retainer, cashed out and handed to a trial lawyer from Upper Marlboro.

"I promise I'll make it up to you. I'll pay back every cent."

That's when I flipped out. "Oh really? You'll pay back the money. Great! How do you plan to do that from prison?"

"I'm innocent," she says. "The judge will see that."

"Right. And what about the rest of it?"

She paused, not understanding as usual. "The rest?"

I wanted to yell at her, to say, "Yeah! The volleyball games you missed. The teacher conferences I went to alone. The dentist appointments I made for myself. The plays I starred in that you never saw. And the dinners. What about all the dinners?" I wanted to scream that at her and see if she had even an ounce of remorse. But I didn't. I just hung up and kept packing.

Granny is looking at me with concern. "Is it true you ain't even writ her once?"

"It's true. Are you done with your dinner?"

She nods. "You're at least reading her emails, ain't ya?"

I put her still nearly full plate onto my tray. "No, Granny."

"Aw, now. That ain't right. It costs money for her to be sending those."

"Then tell her to stop emailing and send us the money instead. God knows we could use it." I take her tray into the kitchen and start cleaning up.

Before I moved here, I had no idea how bad Granny's finances were. The little bit of Social Security she gets barely covers her own expenses, much less the extra food and school stuff for me.

That's been worrying me more and more. All these medical bills will be adding up. If Granny's cough is something serious, like cancer, we could be looking at thousands, even tens of thousands of dollars. There's no way she could pay that off, and Medicaid won't cover it, not all of it.

The only thing of value Granny has is this house. I don't know the rules—can they take it and sell it? Kick her out? Kick *us* out? Would they? What would we do then?

I watch the orange water swirling down the drain. I have no answers.

TWELVE

After a few weeks in Ebbottsville, I'm embarrassed to admit that lunch is now my favorite thing about school. Thanks to the Plurd County School District and some generous funding from the U.S. government, kids from poor families get free lunch. For some of us, it's the only meal of the day. I guess I'm one of the lucky ones. Our canned-soup dinners aren't exactly square, but they're something.

Cole winds a strand of my hair around his finger. "Are we doing something tonight?"

I nod, my mouth full of fish stick. I never expected to enjoy processed seafood, but four days of ramen can readjust a person's taste buds. So can an empty stomach. I'm seriously considering eating the cardboard lunch tray. And the milk carton. And maybe the spork.

"What's on the agenda?" I ask. "Any parties?" Specifying parties is a bit stupid, since there's never anything *else* going on. There's no theater, no clubs, no museums or decent restaurants. No…nothing. Just windy roads, hormonal teenagers, and acres of unsupervised mountains. It's no wonder the senior class boasts seven expectant mothers.

"No parties," Cole says. "I thought we'd just go to my house. Maybe watch some TV?"

"Oh. Cool." I haven't been to Cole's house yet. We've mostly just hung out after school and, obviously, at parties. Baseball season started last Thursday, and I stayed late to watch the first game. But that pretty much covers the landscape of our relationship.

"Pick you up at seven?"

"Seven's good," I say. "That'll give me time to go by the library and make dinner for Granny before I go."

"The library again?" says Cole. "C'mon, Lib. When are you gonna admit you're wrong about the water?"

Despite the research I've shown him, Cole refuses to believe the mine has anything to do with people getting sick. Maybe it's because his dad works there. Maybe it's because Cole's odd jobs at the mine pay for the missing parts of his car. Whatever the reason, he's absolutely sure I'm falling prey to some liberal media conspiracy. I've found it's easiest to change the subject.

"It doesn't make sense for you to come and get me tonight," I say. "I'll just drive Granny's car over."

"I don't mind."

I should probably let him. He always seems to have money for food and gas. But inefficiency bugs me. "No," I say. "You'd make four trips instead of me just making two."

Cole shrugs. "Whatever you want."

He turns to Dobber and starts talking about yesterday's practice. His fingers are still wound into mine though. I run my thumb across his knuckles, listening to the baseball talk and thinking about other things.

The appointment for Granny's x-ray is Monday. I wish I could fast-forward through the weekend and get the x-ray over with. I hate the not knowing. Plus, Granny's definitely been getting worse. She sleeps more, coughs more, eats less.

"I can't," Dobber says, interrupting my worry fest. "Daddy's gotta meet with his parole officer."

I've only heard a little about what Mr. Dobber did to warrant the bling on his ankle. But asking Dobber about his law-breaking father seems unfair, considering I wouldn't want him asking about MFM.

"You're missing practice, then?" Cole asks.

"Yeah, I gotta drive him into town." He glances at me then down to his log pile of fish sticks. I wonder if he pays extra for those or just flirts with the cafeteria lady. "Ain't you gonna ask?"

"What?" I'm trying to recall what they were talking about as two very ambrosia-looking fish sticks disappear into Dobber's mouth.

"Come on, new girl," he says. "Somebody goes to jail, what's the first thing ever'body wants to know?"

If Dobber only knew how well I knew the answer to that question. "You mean your dad. Do you want to tell me?"

"He beat somebody up." He stares across the table like he's daring me to ask more.

I like dares, and he's the one who brought this up, so I ask, "Who was it?"

"Robert Peabody."

"Peabody?" I wasn't expecting that. "Why?"

Cole taps Dobber on the arm. "That's ancient history, man. Don't go dragging shit up. You got a future to think about."

Dobber shrugs. "I ain't dragging nothing. Just thought she might want to know." He downs the last fish stick and starts piling trash onto his plate.

I'm wondering why Dobber wants me to know this. I mean, I've heard some of it already. That Mr. Dobber attacked a guy and nearly beat him to death. The only new information is who it was. "What's your dad got against Peabody?"

"He's a shit," Dobber says quietly.

"That's enough," Cole says.

Dobber's eyes shift from me to Cole and back again. They're

lighter than his father's, but I can see some of the same anger there. It's the first time he's reminded me of his dad. It's a little scary, that kind of mad in a package that big.

"Lots of people are shits," I say.

"Yeah, but Peabody's a special kind of shit."

"Bullcrap," Cole says. "If it weren't for Peabody, this town would dry up and blow away. Mine jobs are the only jobs worth having around here. You know that, Dobber."

It's weird to see Cole and Dobber on opposite sides of an issue. "Did Peabody do something to your dad?" I ask.

Dobber leans forward, tilting his chair.

Cole says, "Drop it, Dob."

Dobber's chair thuds against the floor as he drops back. "Why?"

"'Cause you're wrong. And it doesn't do any good for you to be talking about it," Cole says.

"Don't do no good to *not* talk about it either. Does it?" Dobber stands up and sort of addresses the tables around us. "We been *not* talking 'bout this for years and ain't nothing changed." People pretend not to notice, but I can tell they're all listening. "He's still making his dollar. He's still shitting on the men."

Next thing I know, Cole's in Dobber's face, pushing him back into his chair. "Shut up and shut up now," he whispers. "They're already watching y'all. You'll end up with a rope dog if you're not careful."

The hairs on my arms are standing on end from all the testosterone in the air.

"Fuck you, Cole. I ain't afraid of Peabody."

I'm wondering what the hell a rope dog is as Dobber slams out the cafeteria doors.

"Well," I say. "That was interesting."

Cole turns to me, his eyes still angry. "Look, you need to back off this."

"Back off what? I'm not the one who started talking about—"

"That research you're doing, saying crazy stuff about the water—"

"It's not crazy," I say. "There are scientific studies that prove mountaintop—"

"Studies my ass. That's nothing but a pack of lies."

"Right. A million web pages, a thousand different sources all got together to fabricate and disseminate the same fake information. Just for fun."

"Just drop it, a'ight?" He flops into his chair. "It's for the best."

"Best for whom?"

"For you. For everybody. Especially Dobber."

"In case you haven't noticed, Dobber doesn't seem to care what Peabody thinks about him."

"Well, he needs to. And he knows it."

"Why?"

"Think about it, Lib. You and me are outta here in a couple years—college, careers. Probably neither one of us will be coming back to Ebbottsville."

I wish I could see that far into the future.

"You think Dobber's got the cash for college? You think he's ever getting out of here?"

"I don't know. I guess I assumed—"

"It's not happening. And if you're stuck in Ebbottsville, there's only one way to make a decent living."

Mine jobs are the only jobs worth having.

"Dobber's daddy might be on Peabody's shit list, but Dob's not. Not yet anyway," Cole says. "He's strong and he's smart. My dad's been putting in a good word for him, so he might have a chance at a job there after graduation."

"I don't think Dobber wants that job," I point out.

"Dobber *needs* that job. He just doesn't understand how bad."

"You can't orchestrate people's lives for them," I say. "No matter how well-meaning you might be."

"It's for his own good," Cole says.

He seems to say that a lot.

"How come Mr. Dobber's on Peabody's shit list?" I ask.

"I said to drop it."

"No. I need to know. And either you can tell me or I can start asking around." I glance around the cafeteria like there's *anyone* who'd give me the time of day.

"For God's sake. Fine." He pulls his chair closer and leans in. "Peabody fired Dobber's dad a few years back. Told people he was doing drugs."

"That's not hard to believe."

"It was back then. Dobber's dad wasn't always a meth head. He used to coach my Little League team. He's a great ballplayer. Was, anyway."

"What happened to him?"

"After he got fired," Cole whispers, "he couldn't get another job since everybody knew why Peabody fired him."

I'm trying to figure out where this information fits with the pieces I already know about the water and the mine. "Why *did* Peabody fire him? If it wasn't really for drugs?"

"I dunno, Lib. But there must have been a good reason. Anyway, Dobber's dad hasn't had a job for three years now. Things have been really bad for them. They lost their house. Everything. I guess Mr. Dobber saw Peabody in town and just went off."

Three years of a shattered life could make a person pretty pissed.

Three years of living in that trailer, with no money to change things and no hope for a different future…watching your son grow up the same way.

"If Mr. Dobber can't get a job, how do they live?" I've seen Dobber eat and there's no way he's surviving like Granny and me… on food stamps and twenty bucks a week.

"Disability."

"You've got to be kidding me. The state pays him disability 'cause he's addicted to drugs?"

Cole snorts. "'Course not. He gets disability because he's got cancer."

THIRTEEN

Cole's house is at the end of a cul-de-sac in one of the nice neighborhoods on the west side of the valley. I feel a little conspicuous parking Granny's beat-up El Camino in his driveway, but he doesn't even glance at the car.

"What took you so long?" he asks as he opens the door.

"Sorry. I got an extra thirty minutes on the computer so I stayed longer at the library."

He rolls his eyes. "Lib, I've been waiting for you for an hour."

"I know. I'm really sorry. I would have called but my cell battery's dead and Granny's phone is out." We couldn't pay the bill. This month's money ran out before the month did, but Cole doesn't need to know the specifics. "Forgive me?"

It takes a few seconds, but he finally smiles. "I guess."

"Good."

As he closes the door behind me, I look around at the blue walls with tiny sea horses and starfish and suddenly realize—I'm probably about to see his parents for the first time in five years. I'm wondering if that means anything. And if I should have dressed up.

"You look nice." Cole wraps his arms around my waist from behind. "Smell nice too." His fingers are linked across my stomach and his thumbs are caressing the skin just under the edge of my shirt.

I spin in his arms and stand on tiptoe to kiss him hello. Just a quick peck, since I know his parents might be watching. "You smell nice too."

He grins and pulls me closer. "Why'd you stop kissing me then?"

I whisper into his ear. "Potential parental interruption?"

"No worries," he says. "We have the house to ourselves tonight."

"Oh." So that's why we're here instead of out at some party. "Nice house," I say. And it is—clean, well kept, and plenty big. Cole's mom did a nice job with the decor. There's a landscape painting on the wall over the fireplace, cute pillows with screen-printed elephants, an antique buffet stacked with matching china—all the benefits of a job with Peabody mining.

Cole walks across the living room into the kitchen and opens the fridge. "You want a beer?"

"Um, sure."

I take the can Cole hands me and he pops the top, misting me with Wittbrau Light. "Thanks."

"Cheers."

We clink cans and each take a swig. Ergh, fizzy bread water.

"You wanna watch TV?"

"Sure." I settle on the edge of the couch as Cole grabs the remote from the coffee table. Something about tonight feels awkward. We've been out a lot and together at school every single day, and it's been great. But tonight, something seems different and slightly off. He plops down next to me, and I snuggle under his arm, trying to find the comfort zone.

He flips channels, stopping on Cartoon Network.

I raise one eyebrow. "Rocky and Bullwinkle?"

He grins as he drops the remote on the floor. "I hadn't planned on actually watching." Running his finger up my throat, he tilts my chin up. My lips part and his mouth closes over mine. His lips are so soft. I slide my hand around his neck and pull him into me. He tastes minty, like toothpaste, and hoppy from the beer.

Cole pulls his tongue across my lip, shooting tremors through my body. I sigh as his lips move down my neck, onto my chest. I lean backward…and accidentally dump my beer in my lap.

Gasping, I jump up as ice cold Wittbrau pours out on my jeans. I'm now wearing about half a can of lager. "Dammit!"

Cole runs to the kitchen for a towel, laughing.

"I'm so sorry." I blot off as much as I can. "Is there any on the sofa?"

"No, I think you soaked it all up." He grins. "How 'bout we get those pants off you?"

"What?"

"Rinse 'em out and put 'em in the dryer."

I'm not completely sure how to answer that. Am I supposed to stand here in his living room in my underwear for thirty minutes? Or is he proposing something else?

"You can't go home smelling like beer," Cole says. "Your granny'd kick my ass."

"That's for sure." She'd love a reason to ban Cole from my life. Of course, getting half-naked with him is probably an even better reason for banning than beer.

"I'll get you somethin' to put on." He jogs down the hallway and ducks into the first door on the right.

I feel stupid. Of course he wouldn't expect me to stand around half-naked. Who knows when his parents might get home? They wouldn't be any happier with that than Granny.

Cole comes back with a pair of cut-off sweatpants. "The bathroom's the first door on the right."

I close the door behind me and struggle out of the tight, wet denim. After cinching the shorts around my waist, I glance in the mirror, wipe away a smudge of eyeliner and head back to the kitchen.

"Okay." I'm looking seriously ridiculous in my wool sweater and his gym shorts. But when Cole turns around he's not looking at my clothes.

"Wow. Nice legs."

"Thanks."

"You run?"

"No. Volleyball."

He takes my wet jeans, and I follow him into the kitchen, where he rinses the beer out in the sink.

"I feel pretty silly like this," I say, tugging the shorts up. "I hope your parents don't come home soon."

"No worries." Cole shuts off the water and turns to me. His grin isn't all dimples this time. It's sexier, hungry animal dressed in Southern gentleman. Something in my stomach flip-flops, and I start thinking about what his hands would feel like on my bare legs.

"No worries about them coming home? Or that I look silly?"

"Both?" He walks his fingers around my waist and steps closer. "They went to Charlottesville to see my sister this weekend. She's at UVA."

"Oh. All weekend?"

Cole lays my jeans on the counter and puts one hand against my cheek, staring into my eyes. I'm all alone with the cutest guy in the world. I'm trying to think of something perfect to say, but all I come up with is, "I didn't even know you had a sister."

My jeans slide off the counter. I hear the buttons hit the floor, but Cole's hands are around me, doing a slide of their own—one up my back, the other, across my butt in the too-loose shorts. I feel out of breath, like I've been climbing the ridge trail. I can't think straight with his kisses covering my neck, my cheeks, my mouth.

We wobble into the living room, stumbling over each other's feet, and crash onto the couch. He's pressing into me. His hands are sliding across my ribs, pushing my sweater up. It feels so warm, his skin against mine. I want more. I want to feel the muscles in his stomach, to run my hands across his bare chest.

I'm tugging at the buttons on his shirt, wishing it had a zipper. So preoccupied am I with the treasure beyond the stupid freaking buttons that I don't notice my shorts—his shorts—are sliding down my thighs. Along with my underwear.

"Whoa," I gasp.

"God, Lib. You're so beautiful," he murmurs in my ear.

"But…" I can't think. It feels good, what he's doing. Oh my God. What *is* he doing?

"Aw, Liberty," he whispers. Now he's fumbling with his jeans. My hands are frozen on his shirt. I've never done this. Never come anywhere *close* to this.

His hips are against mine now. I can feel the heat of his body on my skin, his angles, hollows, and points. He's doing that thing again, that feels so good—but also scary. I'm way, way outside my comfort zone.

"Stop," I whisper.

Whether he can't hear me or whether he's ignoring me, I can't tell, but nothing changes.

"Stop. Cole, stop."

"Shh…you're okay," he says.

I scoot away from him, up the couch. The elephant pillows are hampering my progress. "Cole! Stop! Stop it!"

He groans, loud, and rolls off onto the floor, breathing hard. "Dammit, Liberty. You can't just cut me off like that."

"I'm not ready," I mumble. My logical mind says I shouldn't feel bad, but I do. And childish.

Cole says nothing. I pull my underwear and shorts back up, and sit huddled on the couch, watching him stare at the ceiling.

My half-empty beer sits in silhouette against the flickering television. A toy commercial has replaced *The Rocky and Bullwinkle Show*. I stare absently and wonder what exactly just happened here.

On the surface, it seems obvious. Cole wanted to have sex. I asked him to stop and he did. I have the right to decide what happens to my body. I guess he has the right to be pissed about it. But it's not like him to lose his temper.

I feel like I should apologize for something. But the only thing I can come up with is "Sorry I was late," which seems ridiculous. So I sit in silence, hugging my legs, half-naked and feeling totally exposed.

"I'm sorry," Cole says finally. "I wasn't trying to force you." He turns toward me. "You know that, right?"

I nod.

"You're just so beautiful. I can't help it."

I nod again. "It's okay. It felt good, but...I can't."

His turn to nod. "A'ight. It's okay."

He stands, pulling his pants up as he does, and heads into the kitchen. He's back in a few seconds with my wet jeans. "They're not dry, but at least they don't smell like beer."

The return of my pants seems to indicate an end to the evening. It can't be later than eight thirty, but there's some wicked-crazy tension in the room. Again, I feel like I've been tried and convicted of something, though I'm not sure what.

Cole takes my beer into the kitchen and dumps it while I get changed. As I pull on my pants, I think how glad I am that I drove.

He leans against the door frame. "Are we okay?"

He's the one asking the question, but I don't think I'm the one with the answer. "All square." I hope my face looks surer than I feel. I want him to hug me. To tell me everything's fine. Getting rushed out the door, I feel like I'm being punished.

"I'm doing something with Dobber tomorrow night," he says. "But I'll see you at church on Sunday?"

"Oh." We hadn't technically talked about Saturday night, but I sort of assumed we'd be together. "Okay. You and Dobber are talking again?"

"What? You mean that thing at lunch?"

I nod.

"That was nothing. He knew I was right. He just had to remember it is all."

"Oh." I want so badly to disagree, but it seems stupid to pick a fight in the middle of making up. "Well…good." I take my purse and keys off the table behind the couch, trying to think of some way to make things normal between us. "So, your parents won't be here, but you're still going to church Sunday?"

"Only if I get to see you." It's embarrassing how his dimples melt me, no matter what.

"I'll be there. No chance of skipping with Granny around."

"It's a date, then." He winks and wraps his arm around my shoulders as I head for the door, making me feel at least a little better.

"Hm. Don't let her hear you say that." If she knew what just happened here, she'd be making summer sausage out of Cole right now. With a chunk or two of me thrown in for good measure.

Cole grins. "It'll be our secret."

FOURTEEN

"Ms. Briscoe? Any ideas?"

My eyes fly up to the front of the class, where my calculus teacher taps an equation on the board. "Um…" I have no idea what he's asking. For the past twenty minutes, I've been replaying the conversation I had with Cole yesterday at church. The one where he acted like everything was totally normal. Sort of. "Um…no."

Mr. Patterson frowns and points his marker at me. "Pay attention, please. Jones, how about you?"

Jones offers up a suggestion as I fall back into my thoughts. After the service, Cole and I talked for a while; then he kissed me good-bye, much to Granny's horror. Basically, a perfectly normal Sunday… but something still felt off, and I've been worrying about it ever since. That, and everything else. Like flunking Calculus. And the water. And Granny.

Today's the appointment for her x-ray, and I've been wondering about the cost. Will it be a hundred dollars? Or a thousand? It doesn't really matter since we don't have either. Not even close.

Thanks to the quarter tank of gas I put in the car today, we have only twelve dollars for this week's groceries. Eight dollars less than normal doesn't seem like a big deal until I start trying to figure out what we're going to give up. Some food? Granny's Mountain Dew? Ironically, eight dollars is exactly what we spend per week on bottled water.

"You okay, over there?" Granny asks, as we're driving to her appointment.

"I'm fine. Just thinking. How about you?"

"I'm awright. Just, I don't feel too chatty."

"No, neither do I."

We're a couple miles from the clinic when she says, "You think I got it?"

"What?" I look over. Her face is drawn up with worry, like it's been stitched on. "Cancer?"

Her lower lip quivers as she nods.

What can I say? I don't want to worry her. But she'd see right through me bullshitting her, and that would piss her off. After a few seconds, I give her the truth. "I don't know."

She reaches over and squeezes my hand. "Me neither."

I'm pulling off the highway a few minutes later when she says, "Your family's your rock, Liberty. You remember that. Whatever happens to me, the good Lord says if you build your house on solid rock, you gon' be okay." There are tears in her eyes.

I roll up to the stoplight and turn to her. "Stop that. Right now! There will be no quoting from the Bible unless we find out something's wrong. Okay?"

She laughs, a croaking, baby bird sound that builds into a belly laugh that brings on a hoarse cough. "You tickle me. Awright, then. Drive on and let's get them pictures shot. I'm plumb tuckered out already."

The x-rays take all of fifteen minutes, and then we're in the car, headed back over the mountain.

"Granny, how long's the water been orange?"

"Oh Lord, Liberty. You done asked me that fifty-leven times."

"Just an estimate. Like, a year? A couple months?"

"Been less than three, 'cause it weren't that way before Tanner's Peak got blowed off."

"Did you ever drink it?"

"I reckon I did. Toward the beginning. They told us it was safe."

"Who did?"

"The county."

I tap my fingers on the steering wheel. "Did you get some kind of report?"

"Yep. Came in the mail, all official looking."

"Do you still have it?"

Granny sighs. "Reckon I do. Somewheres."

"If they said the water was safe, what made you stop drinking it?"

"Well, it don't taste right."

"How long did you drink it before—"

"God almighty!" Granny says. "Am I on trial for my life? Stop asking me all these dang questions. I'm tired."

"All right, all right. You just rest. We'll be home in half an hour."

"Wake me up then," she says.

"What else would I do? Leave you asleep in the car?"

"I wouldn't put it past you."

* * *

When we get home, Granny heads for the couch, and I head for the old wood desk in the corner of the dining room. The drawers are stuffed with paperwork—letters, receipts, bills. Like Granddaddy, Granny keeps everything. Unlike Granddaddy, she doesn't organize any of it.

It takes an hour, but I find the water report buried in the third drawer. There's a cover letter from the county saying the numbers on the report are well within legal limits, and a second page from Quality Laboratory Services. I glance at the data listed, but it doesn't mean much to me. Random numbers follow various elements: coliform bacteria, nitrate-nitrogen, pH, iron, sulfate sulfur, chloride, etc.

I have to say it all looks pretty professional and well done. I'll look up minimum standards for drinking water next time I'm at the library. But the letter says they're within legal limits, which means our water is safe to drink.

I walk into the kitchen and fill a glass from the sink. *It's safe*, I tell myself, staring at the bright orange liquid. According to the county, I can drink this and not get sick. That'll save us eight dollars a week in bottled water. That's 40 percent of our grocery bill. We could get almost twice as much food—meat, vegetables, maybe even some fresh fruit!

I put the glass to my lips.

It's safe. The county paper says so.

Just a little rust. Everybody says so.

I'm thinking of strawberries and oranges and rib-eye steak. My mouth is watering like Niagara Falls, but then Granny starts to cough. It goes on and on until she's hacking up what I know are tiny clots of blood. Probably wiping them on the inside of her T-shirt so I don't see them, so I won't worry, so I'm not reminded that she's dying.

Sighing, I dump the water into the sink.

FIFTEEN

The radiologist said it would be days before we get the results, so for the rest of the week, we go through the motions. Granny rests, worries, and prays. I worry too, but I try not to let her see. MFM sends new emails that I regularly delete without reading. The application I requested from Georgetown arrives. The early-action deadline isn't until November, so I put it aside. But I wonder if it's even worth filling out. Even if they accepted me, I still don't have any money.

Other than that, it's life as usual. I go to school and hang out with Cole. Things are back to normal, I think, but I never mention the mine, and I only go to the library when I know he's busy with other stuff, like during baseball practice—which is where he is when I finally get to check those water numbers.

It's just like the county claimed; all the levels are well within the legal limits. It appears Granny's water is just as safe as the water we had in DC. My mind spins out a dozen different conspiracy theories. Maybe the testing company lied about the results. Maybe the county altered the data. But none of them really make sense. Neither the lab nor the county would want people drinking bad water.

"Hey, beautiful."

I jump ten feet and click "home"…trying to leave the water quality web page before Cole sees it.

"Hey." I stand and turn to him, blocking the computer. Its dial-up connection is slower than glaciers. "I thought you had practice."

His eyes stare past me, toward the screen. "We got done early."

"Nice." I put my hands on his shoulders, hoping he'll look at me instead. "So, what are you doing here?"

"History project." Instead of looking deep and romantically into my eyes, he leans down and starts reading the web page.

There's silence. Then he stands up, frowning at me. "You're still tryin' to make trouble for the mine?"

"Not trouble," I say. "I just want to—"

"All the stuff Mr. Peabody does for this town. All those jobs he creates."

"Okay, hang on." I try to keep my voice level, because I want him to really listen to me. "You keep saying that MTR creates all these great jobs. But all the numbers indicate that a mountaintop removal mine uses thirty percent fewer workers than the old way. So Peabody actually cut jobs."

Cole rolls his eyes. "Where'd you get that? One of your bleeding-heart websites about saving salamanders?"

"No, it's a fact," I say. The librarian's giving me a pretty furious *shh* signal, so I lower my voice. "Think about it. Half this town used to work for the mine. Now there's only a handful of jobs. People are living on welfare. Businesses are bankrupt."

"That's not Peabody's fault," Cole says. "That's because of the economy."

I'm baffled that someone as bright as Cole could be so deluded by the mine's propaganda machine. "No," I say gently. "It's not."

"Look, Liberty…" He kneels down and puts his hands on my knees. "I understand you're upset about your granny. But…" I can tell he's trying to pick just the right words. "Sometimes cancer just happens. It's not Peabody's fault. It's not anybody's fault."

"But what if, in this case, it *is* somebody's fault? And what if that somebody is the mine?"

"What if it's not? I mean, think about what you're doing. If you're wrong and people end up losing jobs over this…Peabody Mining's the only game in town. If he shuts down, there'll be nothing."

"And that's worse than people dying?"

"Lib, I don't understand how somebody as smart as you can buy into all these smoke and mirrors."

Oh my God.

"Look, just trust me on one thing. You have to stop stirring up trouble. For you own good."

"My own good? What's that supposed to mean?"

"I'm worried about you. You wanna fit in here, right? But if you keep pointing fingers at Peabody, you're just gonna piss people off."

"But people are *dying*," I say.

"Not because of the mine."

"You don't know that!"

He runs his hands through his sweaty hair and hooks his fingers behind his head. "Look, can't we just…what's the term? Agree to disagree?"

"Sure." I can agree to disagree—without agreeing to drop my research.

He leans forward and kisses me on the forehead. "I just want you to be happy. Take my advice and leave the mine alone. Okay?"

I just smile and bite the hell out of my tongue as he heads for the history section.

* * *

Saturday morning, spring's made a full frontal attack on winter. The dogwoods are budding out and the last little bite in the air is gone. There's always a point between the cold and warm of the year when I step outside and just know, somewhere in my bones, that winter's over. It's probably some kind of caveman instinct, but it makes me feel hopeful. Or it would, if I didn't have to re-create the miracle of the loaves and fishes at Kroger today. Another week's worth of food to buy and eight dollars less to do it with.

After breakfast, I fire up the El Camino and drive down the mountain with Granny's SNAP card and twelve dollars in my pocket. Forty-five minutes later, I'm holding two packages of frozen vegetables and staring at the cases of bottled water in the cart. I already put back Granny's Mountain Dew, but I'm still three dollars short. My choices are (a) have no vegetables this week, or (b) put back one of the cases of water. Which means, we'd run out of water around Wednesday. Which means…

I drop the broccoli and corn back into the freezer bin. One week with no veg won't kill us. I can't say the same about drinking the tap water.

After a month in Ebbottsville, I don't even think twice about using the SNAP card. I've seen more people with them than not, and I'm just so glad we have it, I stopped caring what other people might think. If it weren't for SNAP, I don't know what Granny would eat, but she definitely wouldn't be able to afford bottled water.

My phone rings as I'm loading the groceries into the car.

"Hi, Cole."

"Hey. Lib, I got some bad news."

For some reason, I think instantly of Dobber. "What is it?"

"I can't go to Jason's party tonight."

"Oh." I try not to sound like the highlight of my week has just been canceled. "That sucks. Why not?"

"Mom says it's family dinner night. She springs that on us every once in a while."

"It sounds nice actually." I bet they have pot roast with potatoes and carrots. Or fried chicken and mashed potatoes. And some kind of pie for dessert…apple or maybe cherry. My mouth is watering like crazy and I have to swallow before I can speak. "No worries. I guess I'll see you at church tomorrow?"

"Abso-damn-lutely."

"Okay. Have fun tonight."

He snorts into the phone. "Unlikely. I'll be missing you."

"Aw. I'll miss you too."

"You better."

I swear I can hear his dimples, and it makes me smile. After I hang up, I get in the car, put the keys in the ignition, and just sit there. I do *not* want to be one of those needy girls who has no life outside her boyfriend. I don't. So why am I so bummed about this? It's one freaking night, not the end of the world.

I start the car, not wanting to admit the truth. That he is my world. It's not like I can go hang out with my girlfriends instead. Cole's the only game in town for me. My throat closes a little at the realization that that's exactly how he described the mine.

On the drive back to Granny's though, the air feels great and the sun lights up the green-gold tree buds like neon twinkle lights. I blare the music as loud as it will go until I lose the signal in the rocks. Then I sing to myself—songs from TV commercials, Lady Gaga, whatever I can think of. Windows down, I'm belting out "Swing Low, Sweet Chariot" at the top of my lungs when I pull up in the yard and see, of all people, Dobber sitting on the front porch with Granny.

Head. Steering wheel.

"Well, you gotta give her a A for effort," Granny says as I climb out of the car.

Dobber jumps the porch railing and drops into the front yard in one easy movement. Guys are so hot when they do that stuff. I don't think they have any idea. "Need some help?" he asks.

"Sure." I hand him the cartons of water and grab the other two bags myself.

We get everything put away in the kitchen and Granny says, "I'ma let y'all set on the porch and talk while I take a lil' rest."

"Really?" If it were Cole on the porch, she'd be out there with a garden hoe and a can of pepper spray.

I hold the door open for Dobber and watch Granny settle on the couch with her blanket. "You need anything?" I ask.

"Naw, sugarplum. You go on outside with your friend."

I have no idea what's going on in her head—if she just likes Dobber better than Cole or if it's a matter of boyfriend versus friend. Either way, Dobber is standing on my front porch, staring across the mud lawn that's just starting to sprout green, like he belongs there.

"Nice day," he says. He's wearing a sweaty T-shirt that's maybe two sizes too small, meaning it's perfect, and a pair of cut-off sweat-pants that remind me of the debacle at Cole's house last weekend.

"What are you doing here?"

There's that smile...totally dangerous. "I was out for a run and found myself in the neighborhood. Thought I'd stop by."

"Welcome the new girl?"

"Somethin' like that."

I'm well aware Granny's listening to everything we say, so I head down the steps. "Walk with me?"

"A'ight."

I head for the ridge trail because it's the only path I know well. Walking single file uphill, we don't have a chance to talk until we reach the top. Tanner's Peak looks just as raw and wounded as it did when I first saw it, and it makes me think about our conversation at lunch the other day.

"What Peabody did to your dad...it's so unfair."

"No shit."

"Why'd you want me to know all that?"

He stares across the valley at the acres of bald mountainside. "Your granny's sick, ain't she?"

"She's..." I still can't bring myself to use the *C* word. "We don't know really."

"But she ain't well?"

"No," I admit. "She's not well."

He nods and turns back to the mine. I think there's another whole set of roads over there now. Like they've been clearing farther and farther to each side. I wonder if they have a limit or if they could just keep on going—blasting the top off the next mountain and the next and the next—all the way to Tennessee.

"My daddy ain't well neither."

"Cole told me. I'm sorry."

"You think it's the water making people sick?"

I pause. Up to now, I've been the one asking questions about the mine. It feels weird to be on the other end. "Maybe. It's happening in a lot of other places with that kind of mine nearby."

"The people from the county though, they come out and tested our water."

"They tested Granny's too and said it was safe to drink."

"Y'all drink it?"

"No, but Granny did for a while."

We're standing side by side staring at the ant-size men working across the valley. I'm conscious of Dobber's elbow nearly touching mine and wonder if Cole knows he's here. Or if Dobber will tell him. Or if I will.

"Liberty?"

"Hm?"

He's staring at me now, his gray-brown eyes squinting against the sun. "Be careful. A'ight? That there"—he jerks his thumb toward the mine—"that ain't nothing to be playing with. Peabody'll hurt you if you get in his way."

"I'll be careful." Trying to lighten the moment, I say, "Besides, I've got you and Cole to keep me straight."

His shoulders go stiff and his forehead creases with frown lines.

It's so uncharacteristic—Dobber frowning. "What?" I ask. "What's that face for?"

"Just…what I said." He turns and walks toward the trailhead. "Be careful. Real careful."

As he ducks into the thicket, I get the impression he's telling me to be careful of more than just the mine.

SIXTEEN

I stare across the valley until I'm sure Dobber's gone, then hike down the trail myself. Granny's sitting in her chair on the porch, wrapped in her fleece, and…GAH! Smoking.

"What the hell are you doing? For God's sake, your lungs are bleeding."

"My lungs ain't bleeding. That's just some red guck." But she stubs the cigarette out on the porch railing. Sparks fall to the ground and dust her dirty white tennis shoes with ashes.

"Are you going somewhere?" I ask.

"Thought I'd take me a walk. It's such a glorious day…be a shame to waste it setting inside."

Granny and I used to walk all over the farm, all sixty-three acres. There are corners of it I haven't seen in years. "Mind if I come with you?"

"I'd be pleased for the company, sugarplum, but ain't you got a date to get ready for?"

"Change of plans," I say. "Cole's family is having some together time tonight." Though after Dobber's reaction when I mentioned Cole's name, I'm wondering if there's more to that story.

"Together time, huh?" Granny struggles out of the chair and lays the fleece across the rail. "That Quentin sure is a nice boy."

"Who?"

"I ain't see'd him in a few years. He surely got big."

I realize Quentin must be Dobber's first name. How weird I've never heard it before. Even the teachers call him Dobber.

"He's nice," I say, remembering how Cole insisted I not mention that first party being at the Dobbers' house. Now, I'm wondering why. "Do you know his dad?"

"I do. Been ages since I see'd him though." Granny takes my arm and we start down the driveway. Silkie and Beethoven take off ahead of us, panting and chasing noises in the woods. Old Goldie trails along behind us, nudging our hands for the occasional scratch. "They used to come to church," says Granny. "The Dobbers. That was before she went off."

"She?"

"Quentin's mama."

"Oh. I thought his mom died. She just left?"

"Ran off. Or got sent away." Granny shakes her head. "There was two schools of thought on that."

"Sent away by who?"

"The sorry piece of crap she was having an affair with. Robert Peabody."

I stop in the middle of the drive. "She was having an—"

"I just said that, didn't I?" Granny pulls me along. "One morning, she took Quentin to day care and just never came back. There was a rumor she ran off to be with some builder man in Louisville. But I don't believe that myself."

"What do you think?"

"I believe she got herself knocked up with a little baby mine boss." Granny has her head bent close to me, like she's telling FBI secrets instead of wagering on small town history. "When Peabody found out, I'm thinking he run her out of town. Last I heard, she was living over in Clay County. Had a daughter couple years younger'n you."

"Did she at least keep in touch with Dobber? I mean, she's his mom."

"Not such that I know of. I expect Peabody warned her off

keeping any ties back here. He was married his own self. Wouldn't want that story getting back to his wife."

"Poor Dobber." If Granny's right, Peabody took away both his parents.

Just past the haunted birdhouses, we turn left into the woods. I vaguely remember this trail winding down to the creek and Granddaddy's secret crawdad hole. He paid me a dime for each one I caught and a quarter if I ate one.

"Granddaddy got a deal," I say. "I bought some crawdads at our fancy food market once, and they were fifteen dollars a pound."

Granny laughs. "Maybe you oughta start up a export business!"

But I'm thinking about something else. "Or maybe I'll just catch some for dinner." My mouth is already watering. Why haven't I thought of this before? "I could boil them with rice, Old Bay, and some wild onion."

"Oh my, that does sound like a de-light!"

My stomach is growling like crazy. "Wait right here," I say. "I'll go get the buckets."

I run back to the house and rummage around in the shed until I find two old metal pails, one large, one small, and some gardening gloves. It's been a while since I fished for crawdads and the idea of grabbing them barehanded creeps me out. I toss the gloves into the buckets and head back to where Granny waits in the woods. She's leaning on the old split-rail fence when I get there.

"You okay?" I ask.

"I'm just waitin' on you, slowpoke. What took you so long?"

"Your shed's a disorganized mess, that's what." I shake the buckets at her. "Let's go catch us some dinner."

We follow the overgrown path toward the sound of a rippling creek. It gets damper and greener the closer we get. Around the last turn, a huge boulder appears and below it, a small, sandy beach. "This is it," I say. "Granddaddy's secret crawdad hole." I'm more excited about these crawdads than I was about the regional volleyball tournament last year.

"I declare, it looks just the same as I remember it."

It does, mostly. Except the water's really muddy and there's some weird foam caught in the rocks on the far side. Somebody must've soaped up in the creek, upstream.

"You see any crawdads in there, Libby?"

"I can't see anything." I kick my shoes off and roll up my jeans. "But they're there, all right. And I'm going to find them."

Goldie stretches out on the sand. The other two dogs are long gone, chasing squirrels. Granny sits down on a log in the sun, and I feel like I'm ten years old again.

"Beware, creatures of underwater land. I am the crawdad slayer. Prepare to be captured!"

"You get 'em, sugarplum."

I wade into the water with the small bucket, wearing the garden gloves. "God, it's freezing!" Avoiding the weird, foamy stuff, I creep upstream to where the creek narrows. The water runs faster here. I start at the edges, where it's shallower. Since I can't really see the bottom, I just scoop up a pail full of creek bottom as fast as I can. The first couple times, I just turn up mud. But as I pick up the third one, I see something darting around in my bucket. I reach in and feel around until I pin something wiggly against the side of the pail. A nice, big crawdad.

"Woo-hoo!" I grab it below the front claws and show it to Granny.

"Oh, that's a nice one, Liberty." She holds out the larger bucket. "He'll be good eatin'!"

"Heck yeah, he will." His shell clatters as I drop him in. "Put some water in there so he can breathe."

"I know what to do with a crawdad. You just go on and catch us some more."

I wade back upstream and try again. There are tons of crawdads in the creek, more than I've ever seen. Maybe people don't fish for them anymore. I definitely can't imagine Ashleigh eating one.

"We're gonna have us a veritable feast, darling!" Granny says, looking into her pail where four fat crustaceans are scrabbling around. I'm thinking about how good the claw meat will taste drenched in butter. But as I hand the fifth one to Granny, I notice something. Something not right.

I freeze, the crawdad hovering over the mouth of the bucket.

"What's wrong?" Granny says. "Drop it in."

"Granny." My watering mouth is now trying not to gag. "Look. His head."

Really, that isn't grammatically correct. Because there isn't just one head. There are two. A Siamese twin crawdad. Like the fish I saw pictures of on the *End Mountaintop Removal Mining* website. Two heads. Two tails. Too many fins. Too many eyes.

Mutants.

I fling the crawdad across the creek and run onto the beach, pulling the garden gloves off and scrubbing my hands on my jeans. "Gross."

Granny stares into the bucket. "These fellers look all right. Reckon they're safe to eat?"

"Probably not. They mutate because the water is polluted. Even the normal ones are bad." I take the bucket and dump our dinner back into the creek.

Granny sighs. "That's a right shame. I had a awful hankering for a crawdad boil. Reckon we can have some other kinda feast?"

I sit on the wet sand, staring at the creek. My stomach is gnawing on itself and I don't have the heart to tell it, or Granny, there's nothing for dinner but plain rice.

Maybe that one crawdad was just a freak. Maybe everything else is okay. Maybe if I caught a fish—

The bucket crashes against the boulder behind me and I look up to see Granny, red-faced and shaking. "He ruint it," she says. "Ruint our farm. Ever' blessed bit of it."

Tears roll down her cheeks. I jump up and put my arms around her. "It's okay, Granny. We'll be okay."

But she isn't listening to me. She's sobbing. I hold her tighter, squeezing her together, because it feels like she's coming apart. She's the strongest person I know, but I can feel her breaking. And no matter how tight I hold her, she just keeps crying and saying the same words over and over.

"Goddam Peabody."

SEVENTEEN

Granny goes straight to bed when we get back to the house and falls right to sleep. I spend the afternoon cleaning—mopping up the dogs' muddy footprints in the kitchen and wiping away the dust that somehow gets in even when the windows are closed. Another benefit of being downwind of a mountaintop removal mine. I do a load of laundry and, despite the obscene amount of bleach I add, the whites all come out slightly peach colored. Again.

Around six, I dump a can of tomato soup into a pan and heat it up. After my dreams of a crawdad feast, I just can't face plain rice. Not that tomato soup is any sort of substitute for sweet, crabby crawdad meat dipped in garlic butter, with some crusty bread…

Sigh.

I fix a tray for Granny with crackers and the last Mountain Dew as a treat. I'm just about to take it in to her when my phone rings. Maybe Cole got done with family stuff early. That might salvage the night from total crapitude.

"Hello?"

"Hi. This is Dr. Lang. From the clinic?"

My heart leaps into my throat and I choke out, "Yes?"

"I came into the office to pick up some work and found the results of Mrs. Briscoe's x-rays had been faxed. Is this…Are you her granddaughter?"

"Yes. Liberty." I want so badly to know what those results say, but I'm also afraid to ask because the answer could change our lives.

"I'd like you to bring your grandmother in to talk about the results."

"Can't you just tell us over the phone?"

"No, it would be better if you came in. I have some time Monday afternoon. About five thirty?"

If it were good news, he'd let us know, right? But maybe it's just doctor rules that keep him from saying. I tell myself it means nothing that we have to go in. "Sure. Five thirty's fine." But I can barely hear my voice over the pounding in my head.

"I'll have the nurse put you on the appointment calendar."

"Okay. Thanks, Doctor." But he's gone.

The tray rattles and tips in my shaky hands as I take Granny her dinner. I decide not to tell her about the doctor's call until Monday. There's no sense in both of us worrying all weekend long.

* * *

Over breakfast Monday, I break the news.

She pauses in the stirring of her tea. "Why can't he just tell us on the phone?" she asks.

"I don't know, but he won't."

She stares into her mug for a few seconds, not moving. "He's trying to milk us for another office fee."

I doubt that's the case. "I bet you're right." Grabbing my books, I hug her and say, "Have a good day."

"You too, sugarplum. Drive careful."

Granny didn't need the car today, so I'm driving in. Saves me the two-hour tour of Plurd County after school. I scoot out the door without letting the dogs escape, toss my backpack into the back, and drive into town.

The morning is cool, but the sun is bright and the sky is cloudless. If the weather stays like this, it'll be perfect weather for Cole's baseball game Thursday. I'm thinking about what to wear as I pull into the parking lot and totally depressing myself. Half the things I brought are so stained from the orange water, I can't wear them. The other half I've worn so often I'm sick of them. Unfortunately, there's no money in our budget for clothes, and if there were, it'd go toward some underwear for Granny. She's flying commando most days.

Cole and Dobber are leaning against Cole's car. They look to be in a serious conversation, but Cole smiles when he sees me. I park next to them and lock up the car.

"Mornin', sunshine." Cole wraps his arms around me and kisses me hello.

"Hi, you. Hi, Dobber."

Dobber holds out his fist. "New girl."

I bump it with my own. "Are you ever going to stop calling me that? I'm not new anymore."

"You seen anybody else newer?" His smile isn't at the full hundred watts this morning.

"So that's it?" I say. "I'm the new girl until somebody else comes along?"

"Somethin' like that."

Cole takes my backpack and slings it onto his shoulder. "I missed you this weekend." The three of us start walking toward the side entrance, Cole and I holding hands.

"Missed you too," I say. "How was family night?"

"Miserable. Hours of Monopoly. Mom got mad at Dad for charging her rent after she cut him a deal. They ended up not speaking—"

"I gotta go," Dobber says. He veers off toward the gym.

"That was abrupt," I say. "What's up?"

"Nothin'. He prob'ly just knew I was going to do this." Cole wraps his arm around me and pulls me in for a kiss. He's all soap and orange Tic Tacs. His other hand rests against my ribs, and I remember the touch of his bare skin against mine. I feel dizzy and out of breath and I'm wishing there was a building or a tree or something to lean against because I'm having trouble remembering which way is up.

"Meet me after school?" Cole whispers.

"I can't," I groan. "I have to take Granny to the doctor."

His arms loosen. "You're killin' me." He grins and pulls me along, up the steps.

"Tomorrow?"

"Can't," he says. "I got some work." I notice he doesn't add "at the mine."

We've been careful to avoid the subject completely.

"Bummer." It probably shouldn't bug me so much that he works for Peabody, but it does, more and more lately. It's not just that he doubts the research I've turned up. He refuses to even look at it. That blind belief in the almighty Robert Peabody is über-creepy. "How about after work?"

"Maybe." The bell rings and he kisses me quick. "If you're nice."

"I can be nice." I'm thinking of all the nice things I'd like to do with him, some things I've never done before, and my cheeks feel hot.

"I bet you can." He winks and disappears into his class. I turn into first period, brain foggy from the steam rolling off my thoughts, and run straight into Ashleigh. Our elbows smash together and her books fall to the floor.

Instead of yelling at me, she smiles. Not in a nice way—more like she's imagining me being stuck with pins. "Nice weekend?"

"Um…okay." Why is she talking to me?

"Hm." She picks up her books and pushes past me. "Interesting."

"Why?" I say to her back. Maybe it's my imagination, but she seems like she's in an awfully good mood. That worries me. As if I didn't already have enough to worry about.

* * *

The waiting room is just as crowded as the last time, with the same battered magazines. We don't wait long. Dr. Lang calls us just a few minutes after five thirty. Right away, I can tell by his face the news isn't good.

"The results of your x-rays, Mrs. Briscoe, show a number of masses in your lungs."

Granny smashes her lips together.

"Tumors?" I ask.

Dr. Lang looks at me and nods.

I reach for Granny's hand. It's balled into a fist in her lap. "Are you sure it's cancer?"

"I'm afraid so."

Words like *radiation* and *chemotherapy* run through my head. "Okay then. What do we do?"

"Well…" He sits down on his little rolling stool. "We could try to attempt treatment. But I'm afraid with this type of cancer the rate of success is very slim. And the treatments are so hard on the body, I'm not sure it's worth it."

"So…" I raise my shoulders.

"You have to understand, this cancer has been growing for some time."

"Then take it out," I say. "Get rid of it and do chemotherapy or whatever."

"Surgery isn't really an option. There isn't one tumor, but lots of little ones, spread all through the lung tissue."

"What *are* our options then?"

"Let's back up a little." Dr. Lang rubs at the dark circles under his eyes. "Your grandmother has what we call stage four lymphoma."

"How many stages are there?"

For the first time, he can't look me in the eye. "Four."

A tremor runs through Granny. She hasn't said anything since we sat down. I put my arm around her, wishing there were somebody else here. I feel like I'm falling, literally falling, down a deep hole and there's nothing to grab on to. Granny sits rigid, barely breathing.

"What do we do?" I ask.

He hands me a sheet of paper from his notebook. "Contact information for hospice."

"Hopsice? But don't they come in when people are..."

"She could have months," he says to me. "Or possibly just weeks."

I choke. Weeks. *Weeks!* A week is no time. She could be dead before my next report card. I think I'm holding Granny, but I can hardly tell. My whole body is numb and buzzing. Granny must be crying because Dr. Lang hands her a box of tissues. The lameness of that strikes me as ridiculously funny. She's dying and all medical science can do is help her wipe her nose.

I fold the hospice information and tuck it into my pocket. I'm not ready to make decisions about my grandmother's life or death. But it appears she isn't either. She's staring mutely at the nervous system chart on the wall, tears seeping into the wrinkles on her face.

Dr. Lang looks at me and says, "Call them right away. I know they have a lot of patients in your area so they may have to work you in."

I think of Ashleigh's granddad. And Dobber's dad. And all the people on the church sick list. The two-headed crawdad. The foam in the creek. The orange water in the sink. And I begin to wonder what's going on in my own lungs. Are the little tumors starting already?

Granny's settled back into what's become her mantra the past two days. "Goddam Peabody." Her voice is clogged with tears.

The doctor stares at the floor, not knowing what to do for us.

I start to shake...with fear or grief or rage, maybe all three. In a perfect world, I'd have a parent or two to deal with this. But my world's far from perfect and my one parent went AWOL, taking all my money and, with it, our only chance to escape this fucking toxic mountain. My fight-or-flight mechanism tries to kick in, but we can't afford to run, and as much as I'd love to kick somebody's ass right now, I can't battle Granny's cancer. There's no one to fight.

"Goddam Peabody," says Granny.

Then again...maybe there is.

EIGHTEEN

I call in to school in the morning, pretending to be Granny, and tell them I'm sick. I have a lot to get done. In addition to calling hospice, I have a list of people Dr. Lang thought I could contact about getting the mine shut down.

A voice in my head keeps whispering to me that taking down Peabody won't fix anything. Granny's already sick, after all, and so are a bunch of other people. But I can't sit around watching her waste away without doing *something*.

I make Granny a bowl of oatmeal, which she doesn't eat. Then I sit down with the phone and start dialing. The meeting with hospice is easy to set up. Mrs. Blanchard says she'll stop by this afternoon for her first visit.

Next I call the EPA office in Tolesbridge to ask how to lodge a complaint against Peabody Mining. It takes a while to determine whether I'm reporting an environmental emergency or a violation. I get transferred to three different people until they decide the mine is not causing a *sudden* threat, and classify my complaint as a violation. Since I don't have Internet access at the house, they transfer me to a fourth person who gives me the number of the Southeast Regional EPA office where I can call and request the complaint form.

"How long does this all take?" I ask.

"The form isn't long, but it can take a while for it to be reviewed." I get the impression she has this same conversation thirty times a day.

"How long would it be before the mine can be closed down?"

Silence. Then, "What?"

"How long?" I repeat. "Just a ballpark guess is fine."

There's silence from the other end. "Look…" Her voice is softer now. "I understand you're concerned. And obviously the EPA will want to check into this. But I have to tell you, the likelihood of a mine's permit being revoked is very slim."

"Like how slim?"

"It's only happened once."

"Once? You mean, ever?"

"Yes."

I'm speechless.

"You would probably have better luck attacking this at the local level."

"Meaning?"

"Your city or county government might have more leverage in this situation. I'm sure they'd want to know about any health issues facing your community."

"Would they have the power to close the mine?"

"I wouldn't know. It's difficult to determine who has final say in cases like this. Sometimes, it's the state, but local ordinances and federal laws govern certain infractions. And every jurisdiction is different."

It sounds like nobody knows who's regulating what. "How do I find out which department is in charge?"

"It sort of depends on who's in charge."

I stare out the window. "Wait…what?"

She sighs. "Start with the county. You'll have to figure it out as you go along."

"Um…Okay." Dr. Lang did give me the name of the chairman of the county commissioners. "I'll try that. Thanks."

"Good luck," she says. Judging by her sigh, I can tell she's thinking, *You'll need it.*

I call the regional EPA office and request the complaint form. It's supposed to arrive in week or so. In two weeks, Granny could be gone. I try to ignore my brain as it whispers, *Where will I be?*

That's about all the good news I can handle for the moment, so I go check on Granny. I'm sure it's my imagination, but she seems smaller and weaker today. It's hard to believe she could make it to the dining room for lunch, much less down to the creek like she did yesterday.

I must have made a sound, because her eyes pop open. "How are you feeling?"

"Oh, just dandy."

I don't know how to deal with her sarcasm now. The possibility that she could go at anytime puts a different spin on things.

"I'm sorry, sugarplum," she says. "Come sit with me."

I perch on the edge of the bed. "Do you need anything?"

"Naw."

I push her red curls off her forehead. There's a stripe of white roots running down her part. Red and white. It reminds me of those round candy mints. "Does it hurt?"

She pushes herself up and settles into the pillows. "Not too terrible bad."

"But some?"

"Some, yeah."

"Do you want anything for the pain? The doctor gave you a prescription."

"Naw," she says. "I prefer not to take them chemicals."

"Right. They might give you cancer or something."

She smiles and shakes her finger at me. "I hear what you're saying, smart-ass. I'll take 'em if I'm hurting."

"I'm glad to hear that." I kiss her forehead, trying to get my mind around the idea that she could be gone next week while at the same time trying not to think about it. My brain's playing tug-of-war with itself. "I'm going to make some calls. You okay in here?"

"Yes, ma'am. Think I might read a little." She reaches for her Bible. As I close the door, she's opening the book to random pages and reading whatever her finger lands on. I hope whatever she finds brings her some comfort.

The county commissioner chair doesn't answer his phone, so I leave a message. "I'd like to talk to you about some health issues facing our community." I hope that's vague enough to pique his interest without setting off his "mine" alarm.

I spend an hour tidying up. Then I stare at my phone. The next thing I have to do is the hardest on the list.

I have to tell MFM about Granny's cancer.

Aside from the fact that I don't want anything to do with that woman, there's the whole issue of telling someone her mom is dying. Whatever our differences, I know MFM loves Granny. Granny stood by her when she got pregnant with me and helped her through it all. And the sad truth is, barring some miracle, Granny will be gone before MFM gets out of prison.

But nobody else is going to do it and while part of me might like to punish MFM by not telling her until it's too late, that's just too wrong.

Leaving Granny napping, I climb the ridge trail so I can get a signal and pull up one of her unopened emails. I promise myself I won't read it. That after a month and a half of me ignoring her, it'll be full of her telling me I'm a horrible person and explaining everything that's wrong with my behavior. I'm just going to open it and hit "reply" and then "delete all," so I don't have to read a single word.

But as I hit "select all," I see my name. And a few other words—miss you...sorry...love you...

And then I'm reading the whole letter. She misses me. Hopes I'm well. Her lawyers found a solid witness for her alibi and have scored some important meeting with the federal DA. I couldn't care less about the trial stuff, but I am surprised she isn't angry or hurt that I've been ignoring her. And it's kind of ironic, her ignoring the fact that I'm ignoring her existence.

But it doesn't change anything. It's too late for a second (or a third or a millionth) chance. She no longer exists, and if it wasn't for Granny, I wouldn't be contacting her at all. So, I delete her words and start composing my own. I try to be as brief and factual as possible.

"Granny's been sick since I got here. They ran some tests and the results came back that she has stage four lung cancer. They've given her only weeks, maybe a couple months, to live. I thought you should know."

I contemplate how to sign it and decide that emails don't really need signatures. I click "send" and off it goes.

Amazingly, a text from Iris comes in while I'm standing there. It feels like I haven't talked to her in weeks.

I have big news! Call me!

Biting my cheek, I stare at the letters. *Big news.* Something great, obviously. Maybe that internship she mentioned before. I should be happy. I should be dialing her number now, anxious to hear whatever wonderful thing happened. But I can't. My fingers won't move. They're bloodless, squeezing the phone.

I tell myself I'm just drained from writing to MFM. Still kicked in the gut from the news about Granny's cancer. But deep down I know—I don't *want* to hear Iris's news. My life sucks, hers is full of awesome, and I'm totally jealous. I suck as a friend.

Glancing across the valley at the mine, I mumble a "goddam

Peabody" for Granny and start back down the trail. Silkie and Beethoven come crashing out of the woods and escort me back to the house. I stop on the porch to scratch a dozing Goldie between the ears and go in to check on Granny.

She's asleep. I get her a new bottle of water and consider going to the library, but since I'm technically supposed to be in school, it seems like a dicey plan. Besides, I'm not sure more research is going to help me tackle the mine. Definitive proof that the water is dangerous and the mine is the cause—that's what I need. And that's not in the library. In fact, I'm not even sure it exists. I stare at the numbers on the water report, looking for something I might have missed. Something like "all numbers were completely fabricated by the testing company." But there's nothing.

I've been wondering if Robert Peabody knows what his company is doing to the people here. Does he think the orange water, the cancer cluster, the deformed fish came out of the blue? Or does he know it's his fault and is covering it up and bullying people into silence. As usual, I have questions no one will answer. They're all afraid of losing their jobs or getting on the wrong side of Peabody.

I toss the water report on the desk and stare at it upside down. That's when I notice it. On page two, the sheet that came from the lab—under "Sample collected by," it says Dewey Dobber.

Whoa. Dobber's dad?

Thoughts run fast through my head. *Huh, that's funny*. Then, *Wait…Mr. Dobber worked for the mine*. And, *Why would a mine employee have anything to do with the water test?*

For the first time, I've got a question somebody can answer. Somebody who's not afraid of Peabody. Somebody with nothing to lose. And thanks to his house-arrest ankle bracelet, I know exactly where to find him.

NINETEEN

I've been to Dobber's house a few times with Cole, dropping him off or picking him up. Still, I pass the road the first time and have to turn around. Their driveway is even worse than ours, and I take it really slow to make sure I don't lose the muffler. A minute later, I pull into the parking area, cut the engine, and stare at the trailer.

Mr. Dobber's in there somewhere. I think I see a curtain move, but I'm not sure. Now that I'm here, this seems like a seriously stupid idea. I doubt he remembers me, and on the off chance that he's not drunk or wasted, asking him anything about the mine is likely to piss him off. I have the key back in the ignition and I'm just about to leave when the front door opens.

There he is. A skinny, shirtless guy with scabby skin and stringy hair. He's holding a cigarette and leaning against the door frame, staring at me. I could still leave.

"Who the hell are you?"

I leave the keys in the ignition and open the door. "Mr. Dobber, my name's Liberty Briscoe? I met you a few weeks ago. I'm friends with your son."

He laughs and it sounds like his throat must be made of hamburger. "Lady Liberty. Look just like your mama." He flings the screen door open. "You comin' in?"

Every single cell in my brain is screaming, *Are you out of your mind? Of course we're not going in!* But somehow I walk to the steps and up on to the deck and finally, through the door into the darkness of Dobber's home.

It's actually not as bad as I expected. The kitchen is pretty clean, just a couple plates and a pot in the sink. Mr. Dobber opens the refrigerator and pulls out a beer.

"You want one?"

"No, thank you."

"Suit yerself."

I follow him into the living room and take the chair close to the door. It smells bad in here. Like old food and BO. But I can see places where somebody, I have to assume Dobber, has tried to make this place a home: a faded *National Geographic* world map print tacked up with push pins, a blanket on the couch, a candle in a wine bottle on the bookshelf.

"You here for drugs?"

"No." I fidget with my keys. "I wanted to ask you some questions about…"

It's a bombshell, that word. No matter what words you nest around it, in Ebbottsville *the mine* is always explosive.

"Aw shit." He pops open the beer. "This about Dobber?"

"No, it's—"

"If yer pregnant, there ain't—"

"What? No!" I must look seriously offended because he starts laughing.

"Naw, reckon you don't look the type. Too uptight."

"I wanted to ask you some questions about the mine."

His head snaps back and I get ready to run.

"What the hell?" His words are less slurred now. "Peabody send you?"

"No. I'm here because of my granny."

His eyes narrow. "Kat?"

"Yes. Kat."

He shakes his head and downs half the new beer. "Kat never had nothing to do with the mine. Your granddad didn't neither."

"Granny's got cancer," I say. "The doctor said she's got a couple months at the most."

"That's a damn shame. I like Kat," he says. "What that gots to do with me?"

I pretty much suck at cat and mouse and I can tell that, underneath the beer buzz and years of drug abuse, Mr. Dobber is still a smart man. And he's being very careful. So I go for the unusual tactic of honesty.

"I believe she got the cancer from drinking our well water. And I believe the well is bad because the chemicals from the mine have washed into the groundwater. I know you took the samples for the test the county did. What I'm wondering is…why was the mine involved in the water test at all?"

I watch Mr. Dobber's face as I reel that off. It goes from confusion to trapped animal in a matter of seconds. "That's a question for Robert Peabody. Not me. I was just doing what I's told."

"Did you collect samples from everybody's wells?"

"Ever'body who signed up." He twists the cuff on his ankle.

"Signed up? What do you mean signed up?"

With his gaze leveled at me, he suddenly seems completely lucid. "When the county started getting complaints about people's wells— some was running dry, some was getting orange—a couple folks in town said it was 'cause of the mine. Peabody paid to have ever'body's wells tested. Folks who wanted to signed up at the mine office. Not ever'body signed up."

"So, the company that might have caused the water issue was in charge of determining if they were to blame?" I feel a little sick. "Didn't anybody think that might be a conflict of interest?"

"Couple folks did." He taps his beer can on the arm of the chair and stares at the floor.

"Did they do anything about it? File a complaint? Anything?"

"They died before the tests was run, so...no."

"From cancer?"

"Naw." Mr. Dobber takes a long swig of beer and wipes his mouth with his sleeve. "Car wreck."

"Oh."

"Look here. This is all ancient history." The springs in his chair squeak as he leans forward. "You know what's good for you, you'll stop digging into this mess. 'Fore you get a car wreck of your own."

"Wait, are you saying Peabody caused the wreck?"

"S'pose he did?" Mr. Dobber asks. "That change your mind about all this?"

"I'm not afraid of Peabody," I say.

He half smiles before taking another swig of beer. "Damn, if you ain't just like your mama. She weren't afraid of nothing either."

That's one topic I don't want to hear about. So I stand up and walk toward the door, puzzling over what he's told me. Right away, something about the timing of everything triggers an alarm. "Mr. Dobber, did the water test have anything to do with you getting fired?"

The vein in the side of Mr. Dobber's neck starts to throb.

"I'm sorry," I say. "But if it did—"

"I believe we're done here."

But I have one more question and I need an answer. "Did you falsify the water samples? Take them all from a source you knew was—"

The can he's holding hits the wall behind me. "Get out!" Beer sprays everywhere.

I'm out the door by the time he's on his feet. Jumping the stairs, I open the car door as he comes out onto the deck.

"Look, I'm sorry I upset you," I say, my voice shaking. "But this water is killing people. Somebody needs to take a stand against Peabody."

"Take a stand?" He stomps down the steps as I slide into the car and lock the doors. "Look around. That bastard took ever'thing I had. What I got to take a stand for?"

"You still have Dobber," I yell through the window. "Don't you think he's worth it?"

He slams his hands against my window. "You wanna get yourself killed, you do it. The world could stand one less uppity white girl. But leave my boy outta this!"

I start the car and put it in reverse. The last I see of him, he's flipping me off, and I careen down the driveway, praying the muffler stays with me.

TWENTY

I'm in town before my heart stops pounding. The half-excitement, half-fear adrenaline my body's pumping has every hair on my arm standing at attention. I pull over in the Kroger parking lot to breathe and check my messages.

There's a reply from MFM and my brain switches gears. I stare at it for a long time, trying to decide whether to open it or not. It would be nice not to go through Granny dying alone. But I don't want MFM back in my life. Whatever happens with Granny, I won't go back to DC and live with MFM. Never.

I delete the email, pull back onto the road, and head home, heart rate mostly back in the normal range.

Granny's sitting on the couch watching a soap opera when I get back. "Where you been?" she asks.

"I went into town," I say, which is sort of true. "How are you feeling?"

"'Bout the same." She has a tissue crumpled in her hand. A few red spots stand out against the white, and I know she's been coughing again. "That hospice woman came."

Crap! I forgot about that. "What was she like?"

"Nice, I reckon. She says I gotta have a day nurse though."

"Day nurse?"

"Bunch a' malarkey," Granny says. "I'm just fine here on my owns."

"Right." *For now*, I think. But neither of us knows what to expect as she gets worse. And I have to be in school every day. "Did she say how I was supposed to find a day nurse?" Or who's supposed to pay for it?

"She left a phone number for some woman." Granny sniffs loudly. "Not that you need to call it."

I decide to call later, when Granny's taking a shower. Chances are, we won't need her for a while, but I'd like to have that base covered if something does come up. "Can I get you anything?"

"Naw."

I walk into the kitchen, open the refrigerator, and stare into the abyss wishing for…anything. Absolutely. Anything. I could eat.

"You had a couple calls while you was out," Granny says.

"From who?"

"One was that boy."

"Cole?"

"Yeah. Him."

I close the fridge and go lean against the doorway to the living room. "He has a name."

"Hm."

"You know, when I first got here, you didn't seem to hate him. You said he grew up cute."

"Things is different now."

"How? Did he suddenly become evil?"

"No."

"Did I do something wrong?"

"Not such as I know of."

"Then what's the problem?"

She frowns at me for a minute. "You ever see a moth at a candle?"

I nod, wondering where she's going with this.

"Moths is fine creatures. And candles is fine things. But a flame ain't what a moth needs."

"Am I the moth or the flame?"

"You don't belong here, darlin'."

I feel like she just punched me in the stomach. "Don't say that!" All of the sudden, I'm fighting tears. How many times have I heard that since I moved here? With Ashleigh telling me to go home, strangers staring at me like I have seven heads, none of the kids at school talking to me, even Dobber—who still insists on calling me "new girl." But hearing it from Granny cuts me to the quick. She's my everything. My everybody. My *only* body. If I don't belong with her, I don't belong anywhere.

"Aw, shoot." Granny struggles off the couch and puts her arms around me. "I didn't mean nothing. I love you, sugarplum, but…" She puts her hands on either side of my face and holds me steady. "I saw your mama go down this road."

"I'm not her."

"Shoot, you're like a carbon copy," she says. "Except where she's calm, you got fire."

I unclench my fists, just to prove her wrong.

"You got to trust me. This pond ain't big enough for you. Don't hook your boat to this tiny dock. You got bigger seas to sail."

"This is my home, Granny. I've got nowhere else."

"Your home for now. For a little bitty while." She shakes her head. "But not for good and always."

The meaning of her words hangs in the air like lead fog. *For now. For a while.* But for how long? Till next week? Next month? Where will I go when Granny's gone?

I can feel her pushing me toward MFM, back to DC, toward scholarships and college. Away from Ebbottsville, with its poisoned water and its poverty. I understand her analogy now. I'm the moth and Cole's the flame. Singeing my wings in Ebbottsville means getting stuck here forever.

I get it. But the sad fact is, aside from Granny, Cole's all I've got right now. The only game in town.

"I better call him back," I say. "I need to check on homework."

She sighs and shakes her head. "You'll do what you'll do, I reckon. That reminds me," she says. "Some woman from the county called too."

"Oh. Good."

"She said if you got business for the commissioners' meeting, you can call and get yourself on the agenda. The public hearin's next Wednesday night."

"Public hearing…" I had in mind something a little more private, like filling out some forms with one person in an office cubicle.

"What business you got with the county, sugarplum?"

"I wanted to talk to them about the water," I say. "The woman at the EPA said the county is my best shot for getting the mine shut down."

Granny's eyes turn into moons. "Shut down the mine?"

"Well…yeah."

"No." She totters back to the couch, shaking her head. "No, no, no."

"Granny, they've poisoned the water."

"Darlin'…" Her forehead wrinkles. "It ain't that simple. You shut down that mine, lotsa good people gonna lose their jobs."

"Granny, people are *dying*!" I feel my eyes flood with tears. "*You're* dying. I think dying's a lot worse than losing a job."

"'Course it is, but…" She shakes her head. "You ain't seeing the whole picture. People with no jobs die too. Families with no food die. Towns with no families die. See what I'm saying?"

I stare at the woman on the couch, who is normally kicking ass and taking names, now urging ridiculous caution. "So it's okay for Peabody to poison the town so long as he employs a few people in the process?"

"No. But Peabody ain't the only person who gets hurt if the mine goes away."

"How many people get hurt if it doesn't?"

She sags into the couch. "I get ya, but this ain't all black-and-white."

"It is! Killing people is wrong. And somebody has to do something."

"Well, it don't have to be you, does it?" she asks, pleading.

"Who else is it going to be?" Those words fly out before I think about it, but I know they're true as soon as I hear them. "Everybody in this town is so damn scared of Robert Peabody, they aren't going to risk saying anything."

"There's a reason for that. He's dangerous." Granny's voice has dropped, like someone might overhear her.

I'm deeply creeped at the hold that man has over everyone… even my own rock-solid Granny and the scarier-than-clowns Mr. Dobber. "He can't hurt me," I say.

"That's what you think."

"Really?" I snort. "Let's recap: You're dying. The woman you call my mother is in prison. He can't take away our money, because we don't have any. Neither of us have jobs to lose, and I'm a social outcast. What could he *possibly* do to make my life worse?"

Granny shakes her head and starts laughing. "We're a pair, ain't we?"

"Well, it's true. The only thing I really care about is you. And God knows if he took you, he'd bring you right back."

"Aw, sugarplum. I do dearly love you." She holds out her hand.

I take it and sink onto the couch. "There's nothing I can do to fix you. But maybe I can stop him from hurting everybody else."

"I knew I kept your mama's old picket signs for a reason." She squeezes my hand and I ignore the comparison. "If you're dead set on tilting at this windmill, I'm with ya. A hunnert percent."

"You're sure?"

"I'm sure I believe in you."

It's just starting to sink in, what's ahead of me, and I sigh. "I better call the county and get on the agenda for next Wednesday."

"Whatcha gonna say at the hearing?"

"I don't know. But I have a week to think about it." As I pick up the phone, I try not to wonder if Granny has another week.

TWENTY-ONE

Thinking is exactly all I manage over the next week, because when Wednesday morning rolls around, I still have no idea what I'm going to say at the meeting. Despite working on scripts all weekend, I haven't figured out how to hit the right note of concern without being accusatory. People have strong ties to the mine here. Cole's made that pretty clear. And coming out squarely against Peabody could backfire.

Ignoring my first three classes of the day, I manage to cobble together something I think might just work. I just have to finish the end during lunch, which is a problem because up till now, I've kept my plans for the county commissioners' meeting a secret from Cole. But since I have a test and two quizzes this afternoon, I'm completely out of time. I inhale my hamburger and salad in fourteen seconds so I can get back to my meeting prep.

"You want me to eat somewhere else?" Dobber asks. "Or make napkins outta these papers?"

"Sorry." I scrape my research copies into a pile next to me.

He drops his tray on the table and opens his straw. "My daddy said you came by last week."

"Ah...yeah."

His smile stretches all the way across his face. "That was brave."

"Brave or insane?"

"Some o' both, maybe. You sure did piss him off."

"Sorry."

"Naw. It's good." He jabs the straw into his juice box. "We talked 'bout stuff. I think I understand him some better now."

"Oh, well...good then."

Dobber leans over and reads the article on top of the stack. "'Agency Revokes Permit for Major Coal Mining Project.' What's all this for?"

I take my backpack off the chair next to me as Cole arrives with his lunch. "Um..."

At this point, there's no way I can avoid the subject—no matter how much I want to avoid an argument with Cole. And in this town, he'll hear about it by tomorrow anyway.

"I'm putting together a presentation for the county commissioners' meeting tonight. About the damage the mine is doing to the valley."

"You're *what?*" Cole slams his tray onto the table and applesauce splatters all over my notes. "Are you crazy?"

"Calm down," I say, mopping up the damage. "It's a public meeting. Anyone can speak, and the county needs to know what MTR mining does, so they can see what it's doing to Ebbottsville."

Cole snorts. "No way." He shakes his chocolate milk so hard I'm sure it's going to go Mount Vesuvius on us. "You are not doing this."

"Excuse me?"

"I'm not going to let you make a fool of yourself."

I nearly laugh in his face. "You're not *letting* me? I don't remember asking for your permission. And why do you assume I'd make a fool of myself, anyway? I happen to know what I'm talking about."

"All the facts and figures from your crazy liberal websites? Nobody wants to hear that shit." Cole opens his milk and takes a long drink. Dobber's staring at him with his forgotten burger halfway to his mouth. "So forget it. All of it. No more research. No more talk about the mine. This is the end of it."

I'm speechless. Does he honestly think he can tell me what to do? All I can do is stare while he shovels french fries into his mouth and avoids my eyes.

"You don't own me."

"You're my girlfriend," Cole says evenly. "That gives me the right to say when you're making a mistake."

"I don't take orders from *anybody*." The people at the tables near us look over to see what's going on.

"You're not going to that meeting," Cole says, still not looking at me. "This isn't up for debate."

"You're right about that. It's not up for debate." I'm absolutely dumbfounded that he thinks he can control me. "I *am* going to the commissioners' meeting and I *am* going to tell them what Peabody's mine is doing to this place. And I don't give a damn whether you like it or not."

The tables around us are quiet, and I get the impression that everyone's listening even though they're pretending not to. I glance at Dobber, who hasn't said a word. He's looking from Cole to me with narrowed eyes.

"Liberty…" Cole wraps his hand around the top of my arm and squeezes hard. Now his eyes are locked on mine. "I said no." His voice is quiet but his grip hurts. "I'm sick and tired of having to defend you to everybody."

"Then stop. I never asked you to do that." I try to pull away from him. "But I'm going to the meeting."

His grip tightens. "I said no."

"I don't care what you said." I'm trying to pry his fingers away, but he's too strong. "Cole, let go."

"Not till you agree you're not going to that meeting."

"Forget it."

"Then I'm not letting go."

"Cut it out, man," Dobber says quietly.

"I'm just trying to keep her from looking like an ass."

"Bullshit! You're trying to force me to do what you want," I say.

"It's for your own good," Cole says.

My arm is throbbing and my fingers are going numb. "Dammit, Cole. Let go."

"Not till you agree to drop the meeting."

"No!" The veins in my arm are standing out and my hand has turned bright red. I try to twist my arm away, but it doesn't work. "That hurts."

People are glancing over at us, but nobody seems to want to get involved, like it's not their business. Staring at Cole's face, I realize he knows he's hurting me. He just doesn't care.

Dobber's voice seems so far away. "Let go, Cole."

But Cole's hand doesn't loosen.

I'm starting to feel a little light-headed, and I'll be damned if I'm going to pass out on the cafeteria floor. It's probably crawling with bacteria. So I make my free hand into a fist, pull my arm back, and punch Cole square in the face.

My fist lands hard on his eyebrow and my ring finger makes a snapping sound. Cole grunts and lets go of my arm. As the blood swirls back into my hand and through my body, it carries waves of pain from my broken finger to my brain.

"Shit!" I hunch over, cradling my hand in my lap. "Shit, shit, shit."

"Goddammit!"

I look over at Cole. He has blood running over his eye and down his cheek. Looking down, I see my wounded finger swelling like a sausage around my class ring.

"What the hell?" Cole's voice isn't calm and quiet anymore. It's sort of hysterical and whiny.

Watching the blood drip off the napkin he's holding against his eye, I know I'll be in some big trouble with the school, but I'm having trouble caring. "You deserved that, shithead."

"The hell I did."

The whole cafeteria is staring at us, and one of the teachers is making his way toward our table.

"You're gonna regret this, bitch." Cole stands up, grabs his backpack, and walks out of the cafeteria.

My finger is throbbing like it has bongo drums in it and blood is seeping out of little crescent-shaped wounds where my fingernails cut into my palm. Dobber's standing over me, staring at my hand.

"I think you broke it," he says.

"No shit." I'd like to go to the nurse and get some ice, but my head is swimmy and standing up seems kind of dangerous.

Mr. Cheek, the PE teacher, stops at our table. "Everything okay here?" He too is staring at my Quasimodo hand, which is clearly not okay.

"Fantastic," I say.

"I think the nurse should take a look at that." And then, miraculously, he's gone. Broken fingers at Plurd County High…nothing to get worked up about.

"Good thing you didn't tuck your thumb in," Dobber says. "Most girls do."

"Do they?" I frankly couldn't care less about most girls right now.

"I'll get you some ice." Dobber heads for the kitchen, leaving me at the table all alone, in a room full of people staring.

Given that I just punched in the face one of the two people who actually speak to me, being alone is probably something I should get used to.

TWENTY-TWO

Twelve note cards, held together with a hair band, lie in my lap. Each is neatly printed with a topic and several bulleted notes underneath.

- health statistics in the valley (compliments of Dr. Lang)
- health statistics of MTR mining communities
- commonalities between the two

I toy with the green splint on my finger and try to concentrate on what I'm going to say. I need to be convincing but not inflammatory. I need to point out that jobs can't take precedence over people's lives. I need to sound less nervous than I feel. I need to breathe.

I look at the clock over the wood-paneled counter at the front of the room. 7:02. They should be starting, but the council is nowhere in sight. I'm sure I'm at the right place because there's a handful of people sitting in the room with me, each with his or her own version of notes. No one else has a bright-green splinted finger though.

Someone drops into the seat next to me and I glance up.

"Hey, new girl."

Dobber! I've never been so happy to see anyone in my entire life. "What are you doing here?"

He glances sideways at me, a half smile on his face. "Taking a stand."

I remember my advice to his father and grimace a little. "Does Cole know you're here?"

"Yep."

"How'd that go over?"

"'Bout as well as you punching him in the face. But dammit, Liberty, Peabody screwed my daddy over bad." His eyebrows pull together. "I gotta do *something*."

"I understand." In my mind, I see a frail old lady on a faded plaid sofa, clutching a bloody Kleenex. "We're in the same boat."

A door at the back of the dais opens and a group of men and women come through, the last two men deep in conversation together. The taller man, dressed in a suit I can tell was cut just for him, has Donald Trump hair and a lot of shiny, white teeth he manages to smile through even when talking. I recognize him from the photo at the town library. His library. Robert Peabody.

"Mother fucker." Dobber's hand tightens on the armrest.

"What's he doing here?"

"You think he knows why you're here?"

"No way. I didn't tell the woman from the county what my business was."

"That don't mean he don't know." Dobber frowns at me. "You were talking about it at school."

"Just to you and…"

We stare at each other, both wondering the same thing. Would Cole have told Peabody? Even with the black eye factored in, I just can't see Cole doing that. It'd be like tattletaling on me. So kindergarten.

"No way," I say. My voice sounds about as sure as I feel. Which is not very.

Dobber sighs. "Liberty, there's something you should know. Cole—"

A gavel bangs and everyone in the room stands.

I raise my eyebrows at Dobber. "What?"

"Later."

The meeting is called to order with the Pledge of Allegiance and an introduction of the commissioners. Robert Peabody takes a seat on the stage even though he's not on the commission. I don't like it at all. It's bad enough that he's *here*, but for him to be up on the dais, in a position of power, while I make accusations against his mine… "I think I might throw up."

Dobber puts his hand on my arm. "Don't let him scare you."

I nod, looking down at the agenda again, where "Liberty Briscoe" is listed as Item Number Four. I hadn't noticed before, but Item Six is Peabody Mining Company. I point that out to Dobber as an older guy makes his way to the public podium.

"Hm," is all Dobber says.

I watch Peabody while Items One through Three complain about their neighbor's fence, the trash burning ordinance, and property taxes. He completely ignores the people presenting and spends the time texting or checking his watch. His arrogance is obvious—at one point, the chairperson of the commission looks over at him and Peabody taps his watch. Immediately, Item Three is thanked for their comments and dismissed. Apparently, the county government runs on Peabody's schedule.

I hate him even more now that I've seen him.

"Item Number Four," reads the chairperson. "Liberty Briscoe?"

I stand and walk to the podium. I'm about halfway there when I realize Dobber is right behind me. I don't know what he thinks he's doing, but it's comforting to have him there.

"Hello." My amplified voice is high and shaky. I run my finger over the duct tape holding the microphone to the stand. "My name is Liberty Briscoe. My grandmother, Kat Briscoe, lives on the east side of the mountain, across the valley from Tanner's Peak. Well, where Tanner's Peak used to be."

I glance at Peabody. He's not texting now. He's looking at me with a half smile on his face. Turning my attention back to the commission, I start rattling off facts and figures, my voice warbling more the longer I talk.

Cancer rates in the valley: two hundred percent higher than normal.

Kidney disease: seventy percent higher.

Birth defects: twice as high.

I pause to let that sink in then deliver the punch. "All of these statistics match those seen in other communities with mountaintop removal mines."

My bombshell bombs. None of the commissioners are looking at me. They're shuffling papers, staring at their watches. One woman is digging around in her purse. But Peabody's still smiling at me, amused, like I'm a kitten with a ball of string.

That pisses me off. I didn't come here to be amusing. This is my best, if not only, chance to get that mine shut down. And I need these commissioners to listen to me.

"My granny has cancer." I hear the words before I realize I've gone off script. It works though. Every one of the commissioners looks up. "She's going to die. Any day now." I point behind me, to where Dobber stands like a stone wall. "Quentin Dobber's father has cancer. The 'pray for' list at my church gets longer every week. I bet it's the same at your church. You have to ask yourself, why are these things happening? Why here?"

The chairperson, Mr. Hennequin, looks over at Peabody, who casually cuts his hand across his neck before straightening his tie. His message is clear. Hennequin looks up at me and smiles. "We're gonna have to stop you here, Miss Briscoe, since we're running out of time. But I think we should all be proud of the job Plurd County High School is doing with our kids. That was a most professional-sounding presentation."

"What? This isn't some school project," I argue. "Those numbers I read off earlier, they're real! They have faces and families. They're people you know." The two women on the commission…I can tell I've gotten to them. One is nodding. The other is staring through me, like the sick people I'm talking about are hovering behind me.

Hennequin ignores me. "Let's give the young lady a round of applause for her school project."

The commissioners clap a few times, then look down at their agendas, ready for the next item.

"People in your county are dying! Lots of them! Don't you care?" My voice goes all high and shaky. I sound hysterical, but I can't help it. It's not that I expected them to shut the mine down tonight, but I thought there would at least be some discussion. That they'd show some shred of concern.

Hennequin motions to the cop standing at the back of the room and he heads toward me. I figure I've got about twenty seconds. "Weren't you elected to take care of this town? Isn't that your job?"

"Young lady," says Hennequin, "this commission does everything it can to protect our citizens. It may interest you to know we ordered tests to make sure everyone's water was safe to drink."

"Yeah, tests you let the mine have control over. Do you realize how easily they could have been tampered with?"

"Get her outta here."

The cop reaches out for my arm, but Dobber steps between us. He's a good six inches taller than the cop, and I'm sure Dobber could turn him into jelly in about three seconds.

"It's fine, Dobber. We'll go." I turn back to look at Peabody. The smile is still there, but his eyes are different. I'm no longer a kitten but prey.

"People I care about are dying," I say. "If you want to keep lying to yourselves about the cause, you do that. But whether you admit it or not, you're responsible for those deaths."

Dobber pulls me to the back of the room as the cop follows. Hennequin starts the meeting again. "Item Number Five: Tammy Edgerton," he says as the door closes behind us.

Dobber and I stare at each other in the lobby until the cop says, "Sorry, but y'all have to actually leave the building."

He follows us to the front door then says, "See ya, Dob."

"Later, man."

"You know him?" I ask.

"I know ever'body."

We walk to the edge of the parking lot, where Dobber's car is parked next to mine.

"That didn't go so good," Dobber says.

"Understatement of the year. That bastard has the whole commission under his thumb! Did you see the way Hennequin kept looking at him for guidance?" My teeth chatter over the words as I shiver in the damp evening air.

Dobber opens his passenger door and motions me to get in. "I saw. Problem is…" He pauses as he walks around to the driver side. After he climbs in, he closes the door and taps the steering wheel for a couple seconds. I can tell he's choosing his words carefully, trying to be gentle, I think. "Problem is, we ain't got no real proof that the mine's causing the cancer."

"No. But we will." I feel like a gauntlet's been thrown down. I came here tonight thinking the commission just needed to understand what was happening, that they'd do the right thing if they knew there was even the *possibility* that the mine was hurting the people of Ebbottsville. But now I know—Peabody owns them. "I'll find the proof, Dobber. Somewhere. I'll bet you a hundred dollars Peabody screwed with the water reports somehow."

"I'm with ya," Dobber says. "Like you said, we're in the same boat."

"We are." I barely see him, silhouetted against the streetlight across the road. His hair is sticking up like it always does and his cheekbones are more lumpy than chiseled. For some reason, I think of Cole, with his Greek god chin and perfect teeth, which reminds me… "Hey, what were you going to tell me earlier?"

"About what?"

"You said something about Cole."

"Oh." He fidgets like a five-year-old, tracing the spokes on the steering wheel. "It don't really matter now, cause y'all ain't together no more."

My stomach suddenly feels a little sick. "Tell me."

"Cole and Jillian Coffey…they been, um, hanging out."

I try to place a face to the name. I come up with a girl in our Spanish class, light brown hair, curvy, popular. "And by hanging out you mean…"

"Yeah. That."

Oh God. "When?" I ask. But I know already. Family night. The week before that, when he had to do something with Dobber. The Tuesday when he didn't call after practice.

"I'm sorry," says Dobber.

Ashleigh's words come back to me. *He'll shit on you just like he shit on every other girl.* Then I remember her asking me how my weekend was. She knew what Cole was doing. Dammit, the whole freaking school probably knew. Knew and talked about it all behind my back. My eyes start to burn and I count to five. "Why didn't you tell me?"

He slams his hand against the steering wheel. "I didn't know what to do. Cole's like my brother. Well, he was."

"But...how could you watch him being all boyfriend-y and not...just...God, Dobber!" I stare at the Kroger across the street, trying to get my mind around this latest bit of perfection. "He told me I was beautiful." I snort and start crying and laughing at the same time. "Bastard."

Dobber hands me a crumpled napkin from the cup holder. "Don't cry," he says. "He ain't worth it."

"You're right about that," I say, dabbing the corners of my eyes and trying not to worry about why the napkin is sticky. "Look. The meeting must be over."

The commissioners are filing out of the building. They call good-byes, get in their cars, and drive off. Everyone except Hennequin and Peabody, who must still be inside.

"You know what pisses me off most?" I say.

"That I didn't tell you?"

"No. Well, yes. That was seriously shitty of you."

"Sorry."

"But no, what pisses me off most is that I sorta knew, but I didn't do anything. Because I didn't want it to be true." I twist the corner of the napkin into a sharp point. "I guess pretending something isn't happening doesn't make it go away."

"Somebody oughta tell that to the county commissioners."

"Yeah. Good point." Still reeling, I dig into that swirling tornado of ick in my stomach and try to see what it's really made of. "The worst part is that everybody knew except me. Like I was the butt of a joke I didn't even know about and everybody at school was laughing at me."

"Not ever'body," Dobber says. "Not me."

"Great. That makes it all better."

"Well, it don't make it worse, does it?" He smiles and even in the dark I can see his face change. That smile is so magnetic. I think about the first time I saw it, at the campfire at his house, and how I thought he must be dangerous, charming, and cheap. Man, did I have him and Cole confused.

"Looks like the meeting was good for somebody." Dobber nods toward the courthouse, where Peabody and Hennequin are walking out together. They're laughing as they stroll toward their cars. I can't help but wonder if, like everyone at school, they're laughing at me.

"I guess Peabody got what he wanted. Wonder what it was."

"No idea…" He sits up straighter in the seat. "But I'm pretty sure I know what that is."

I look back at the men and see Peabody handing Hennequin an envelope. He opens it, and thumbs through it. Peabody smacks him on the arm and Hennequin slides the envelope into his jacket.

"Holy shit." I look back at Dobber. "Is that really what it looks like?"

"Let's get out of here," Dobber says.

But it's too late. Even as I sink down in my seat, Peabody looks around and sees Dobber's car. Whether he knows who it belongs to or can see us inside, I'm not sure. But he's coming this way.

"Dammit." Dobber fumbles with the key.

"Stop!" I hiss. "What are you doing?"

"Getting us outta here."

"If we run away, he'll know we saw that payoff."

"We did see it!"

"But he doesn't know that." Peabody's halfway across the parking lot now, with Hennequin a few steps behind. I'm thinking as fast as I can. Once he gets to the car, he'll know we're in here. How can we make him believe we weren't paying attention to them?

"Dobber," I say. "Kiss me."

TWENTY-THREE

Dobber's head turns so fast I think he might break his neck. "Huh?"

"Now." I reach across the center console and pull him toward me. "Pretend we're making out."

"Oh." He leans toward me, puts one hand on the side of my face…and the other hand over my mouth. Then he kisses his hand.

I look up at him, thinking, *Really? Would it have killed you to have actually kissed me?* I try to pretend that feeling squirming around inside me isn't disappointment.

Dobber's eyes are wide-open, staring past me. Peabody must be almost to the car by now. I put my arm around his neck and whisper. "Have they seen us?"

"Yep."

Someone knocks against the window. I jump so high I nearly hit my head on the roof. Dobber keeps his arm around me, but leans over to look up at Peabody.

"What?" Dobber yells.

Hennequin peers in at us, wrapped together, and says something quietly to Peabody. But Peabody shakes his head and keeps staring.

I can't tell what he's thinking. I mean, bribing a public official—that's prison time. And I'm a hundred percent sure Peabody doesn't want to go to prison. I'm wondering how far he'd go to keep us quiet.

"What's your problem?" I ask, rolling down the window. "Do you two get off sneaking around, watching people make out?"

Hennequin shakes his head, chins wobbling. "Oh for Pete's sake."

Peabody stares through me. I search his eyes for some idea of what's going through his mind. But they're just empty, like the glass ones in a mannequin. There's no humanity in the man.

"Watch yourself, Miss Briscoe." He smiles, lots of white teeth but no warmth. It's a jackal sneer.

I muster up my best impersonation of Ashleigh. "Is that a threat?"

He doesn't blink. "Only if you turn it into one."

"I'll be sure not to do that then." I roll up the window. My hands are shaking as they walk away.

"Dammit," Dobber says. "You think he knows we saw?"

"I think he's worried we did."

"That's just as bad."

"If he thinks we saw his payoff, maybe we can bargain with him," I say.

"Bargain? With Peabody?" Dobber snorts. "Ain't gonna happen."

"So he'd rather go to jail than stop the MTR mining?"

"Naw, he'd rather shut us up than risk us telling the cops," Dobber says. "Not that the cops'd do anything. They're in his pocket like ever'body else."

We watch the men as they walk across the parking lot, still talking.

"I better go," I say, pointing to Granny's car a few spaces down.

"Wait till Peabody leaves."

"Why? You think he's going to follow me home?"

Dobber doesn't answer.

Peabody gets into his car and pulls out of the parking lot. I'm rattled. Having stared into the depths of Peabody's soul, or lack thereof, I know our situation is bad. I start playing out different scenarios in my head. All of them ending in suspicious car wrecks.

"We're in danger, aren't we?"

It's a while before Dobber answers. "Naw," he says finally. "I reckon if somethin' happened to you and me after that meetin', it'd look pretty funny."

"But there were only five people at the meeting," I say.

Dobber grins. "Word spreads fast around here. You speaking out against the mine? That's gonna be all over town tomorrow."

"Fantastic." I can only imagine how that'll affect my popularity at school.

"It's good actually."

"How so?"

"If we turn up dead, Peabody'll be a prime suspect."

"Again. Fantastic." But I see what he's getting at, and it does make sense in a morbid sort of way.

Dobber laughs and the sound of it relieves some of the tension. "Lotta folks put up with Peabody 'cause they have to. But I reckon most all of 'em would draw the line at him murdering kids."

"Great. All we have to do to get people on our side is die. Brilliant plan." The lights on the Kroger flip off, closing up for the night.

"I ain't saying that's the plan. I'm saying it'll keep Peabody from hurting us."

"I hope you're right." It wouldn't be hard for him to come after me. Granny and I, alone in a house with no front door lock, two miles from the nearest neighbor, and no weapons except our sharp wits. I doubt even Granny's sarcasm would hold up against some thug with a baseball bat. Or worse.

"So, what *is* our plan?" Dobber asks. "Can we go to the state?"

I sigh. "Who knows?" I explain what the lady at the EPA said about the maze of agencies and regulations we have to navigate just to figure out who to talk to. "And even if the EPA does have jurisdiction, it's unlikely they'll revoke Peabody's permit. They've only done that once in the history of forever."

"Don't matter. Peabody don't live by the rules anyway," Dobber says. "We ain't gonna stop him that way."

I look over at him, lit only by the lights from the dash. "That's really quite deep. I didn't realize you were so smart."

He glances at me and grins. "What? You thought I was a ignorant redneck just 'cause I don't speak Shakespeare-like English?"

I'm uncomfortable with how close to the truth that is.

"I get straight As," he says. "I just don't go bragging on it."

"I had no idea. Okay, brainiac. You come up with a plan, then. How do we get the mine shut down?"

"Illegally."

"Illegally how?"

"I dunno. We need, like, a environmental group to come in and blow ever'thing up."

My stomach lurches sideways. "God no."

"What's wrong?"

"Nothing, just…nothing."

"You got something against environmental people?"

"No," I say. "Just bombers."

"Right." Dobber laughs. "How many bombers d'you know?"

"Just the one." I'm not at all sure I want to tell this story. But I look at Dobber and think about his dad. It seems only fair that I finally come clean. "She gave birth to me."

"Wait…Your *mom*?"

I nod in the darkness. "The woman *formerly* known as my mother." I stare at the dark windows of the grocery store, take a deep breath, and tell him the three words I haven't said to anyone here. "She's in prison."

He whistles quietly through his teeth. "Reckon we got somethin' else in common then."

"Reckon so."

"What'd she do?"

"One of her millions of political protests went wrong." I repeat the basic gist of what she told me. "Somehow their *controlled explosion* turned into a car bomb that injured five people."

"That sounds like a accident."

"Well, maybe. But why'd they use explosives to begin with? Why couldn't they just tell their side of the story? Petition the government. Write letters." I stop short of mentioning flyers. "Why was she there in the first place? Why wasn't she home with her daughter, acting like a mother for once in her freaking life?" I'm embarrassed by how whiny my voice is, but I can't seem to rein it in.

Dobber's quiet for a few seconds after my rant. "I see."

"See *what*?" I snap. "What, Dobber? What's that supposed to mean?"

"Just...I know what that's like."

That stops me in my tracks. Of course he knows. Complaining about my mom to Dobber is like complaining about being poor to Mother Teresa. "Crap. I'm sorry."

"Naw, I get it. It sucks. Sucks donkey balls." He plays with the loose cording on the steering wheel, wrapping it around and around, trying to tuck it into place. "He was a awesome dad. Before..."

I try to imagine Mr. Dobber cleaned up. "I heard he used to coach baseball."

"Yeah. I used to watch him play and I'd think, *When I grow up, I'ma be just like him.* But then Peabody fired him. He couldn't get a job. Found out he had cancer."

I want to ask *why* Peabody fired him, but the timing isn't right. "I'm sorry."

"Docs gave him some medicine to deal with the pain, but it didn't work so good. So he started selling his pain meds to pay for meth." Dobber's hands are quiet now, resting on the steering wheel. "I hate it, but there ain't much I can do. It's a big ole mess."

Yep. Another mess caused by Robert Peabody. I want to make him pay. For Granny. For the Dobbers. For everybody.

"Maybe your mama can help us," he says. "I ain't against blowing something up. So long as it hurts Peabody."

"*What?*" I back away, into the door. "No way!"

"He deserves it, Liberty. Look what he's doing to ever'body. Look what he's done to your granny."

"Yeah, but…" I stammer, trying to put the revulsion roiling in my gut into words. "I wouldn't ask that woman for anything. Not for advice, not for help, nothing. And in case you didn't hear me, she's in *prison* for what you're proposing. Her choices were wrong. She's got no moral compass. She's a waste of skin, frankly."

"Ouch."

I reach for the door handle. "She deserves that, trust me."

"Why? 'Cause she cares about stuff? 'Cause she gets riled up about stuff?" He shrugs. "That don't sound so bad. Kinda sounds like you."

TWENTY-FOUR

I'm lying in bed, staring at the ceiling, while all the things I wish I'd said at the meeting swim through my brain—along with all the things I wish I *hadn't* said to Dobber. After he told me MFM sounded a lot like me, I called him every bad name I knew plus a few I made up on the spot, like brainless wormhole. And fetid zombie carcass. And poop clown.

Dobber was pretty pissed off when he drove away, which I feel bad about. I'll have to apologize tomorrow at school, which is actually today, since it's 4:00 a.m. I stare at the clock ticking off numbers, ticking off minutes of my life. Of Granny's life. One of these could be her final minute, and I wouldn't even know. I wouldn't know my life had changed until I woke up in a different one.

* * *

At some point, I doze off. In my dream, I'm sitting on Tanner's Peak with Granny, watching the sunset. It's almost summer, and the honeysuckle is blooming in the thickets around us.

"I do truly love that smell," Granny says. "Your granddad used to make me a wreath of honeysuckle ever' year for our anniversary. It never lasted more'n a couple hours, but it surely smelled nice."

Behind us, I hear a motor of some kind, a car or a machine, I can't tell. And then the dogs are barking. I keep trying to shush them, but they won't be quiet, and I realize that part isn't a dream. I sit up fast and look around in the gray morning light. All three are at the door, yapping like crazy. Not their normal, morning I-gotta-pee bark but a loud, somebody's-out-there kind of bark.

I run through the house and open the front door. The dogs take off around the house, still barking. The morning air is thick with mist, pressing the smoke from our chimney down into the holler. It's acrid and stings the inside of my nose, making my eyes water. Trying to see anything through the fog is impossible, so I stand on the porch and listen. Aside from the dogs, I hear a ticking sound coming from the side yard. I walk to that end of the porch, listening. It's more of a crackle, actually, and about the same time I recognize the sound, I see the orange glow through the haze.

The shed's on fire.

I climb over the railing, turn on the hose and drag it as far as it will reach, my splinted finger hindering the whole process. Once I get close though, I realize it's too late. The structure is completely engulfed in flames. The roof caves in and showers of sparks fly out, sizzling when they hit the wet ground. Something inside explodes, the gas for the lawn mower probably, and I back up fast, not sure what else Granny might have stored inside.

Staring into the flames, I recognize this for what it is. A warning. This time, it was the shed. Next time, it could be the barn. Or the house. Keeping my mouth shut is payment for not waking up in an inferno.

"Fuck you, Peabody." It'll take a lot more than this to shut me up.

The flames are lower now, and my bare feet are turning to ice in the cold mud. There's not much left of the shed so I go inside to call the police. The same police who, according to Dobber, are owned by the person who set the fire.

This should be interesting.

* * *

It takes the cops about thirty minutes to show up. They ask what

- 148 -

happened, if I heard anything unusual, if I'm fighting with any of my friends.

"Robert Peabody," I say. "Not that he's a friend."

The older police officer shakes his head and wanders down the driveway, where the firemen are deciding whether to risk their truck on the muddy drive.

The younger cop pauses in his note taking. "You're the girl who stirred up all the trouble at the county meeting last night, aren't ya?"

News travels fast. "I presented some statistics. That's all."

The cop, who can't be more than a few years older than me, gives me a disapproving frown. "I heard you claimed the mine was poisoning people's water."

It would be pointless to get into an argument with this guy, so I just shrug. "It's happened at a lot of other MTR mines."

"Well, it ain't happening here," he says. "People need those mine jobs."

The complete lack of logic in his argument pisses me off. "What if it is happening here? What if the mine's giving people cancer?"

"It ain't."

"How can you be sure?"

"There's all kinds of regulations on that mine."

"Really?" I've been researching that for weeks, trying to figure out how the EPA keeps tabs on what the mines are doing. So I play along. "What kind of regulations?"

"They gotta send in samples and reports to the EPA all the time."

"Samples of what?"

"The containment pond. Water from creeks downstream. All kinds of stuff."

"How do you know so much?"

"My brother works in the mine office," he says. "Trust me. If they weren't following the rules, they'd get shut down fast."

"I guess you're right," I say. But what I'm really thinking is, *How's Peabody getting clean results for all those samples? Bribes? Threats?*

"Listen, I don't know who did this." Officer Smiley Face glances over at the smoldering black posts sticking out of the ground. "But you ain't making yourself any friends by bad-mouthing the mine. You get me?"

Oh, I get it all right. "Yes, Officer."

He hands me his card that says Stuey Hanford. I think Stuey's a pretty ridiculous name for a cop.

"If you have any other trouble, you let us know."

"Right." Because you've been so successful at tracking down today's bad guy.

Since the blaze is basically out, the firemen decide against risking the driveway. The police drive off down the road, and Granny and I are alone on the porch with the dogs. Around us, we have eleven acres of forest and the knowledge that Robert Peabody's angry enough at me to burn our buildings. The phrase "out of the frying pan and into the fire" seems creepily apropos.

TWENTY-FIVE

I look at the hills, wondering if our neighborhood arsonist is still lurking around up there, and if so, what else they might have been instructed to do. Maybe burning things isn't their only skill. "I'm not going to school today."

"The heck you ain't," Granny says. "You done skipped on Mond'y."

"Well, I'm sure as hell not leaving you here alone!" The day nurse is coming out to meet with us this afternoon. I wish now I'd asked her to come earlier.

"I ain't gonna have your grades slipping off just cause o' this here."

"Just because someone snuck in and destroyed part of our home, you mean?"

"Liberty, I been living in this house alone since your Granddad passed on. That's ten years of nobody bothering me."

"Well, they're bothering you now. I know who it is, and it's my fault."

"Your fault, my fault, Robert Peabody's fault—what difference does it make? I'ma be dead in a little bitty while anyway."

"Granny!" I stare at the tops of the trees, eyes wide, trying to dry the tears before they start. "Don't say that."

"It's true and there ain't no sense pretending otherwise."

"I know but…" I count to five, take a breath.

"But nothing," she says gently. "It's gonna happen and we gotta accept that."

"Accept that you're gonna die and it's Robert Peabody's fault?" Sad tears get replaced by angry tears. I count to five again. "I don't want to accept it," I say. "It's not fair, and I hate it. It's not fucking fair!"

Fair echoes up the holler five, six, seven times before it fades away.

"It is what it is," Granny says. "All people got to die some way. This here's mine."

"But this is Robert Peabody's fault. And when people are at fault for someone else's death, that's murder."

She chuckles a little. "You'd have a hard time proving that, darlin'."

I know she's right. Proving the mine is killing people is an impossible task. Peabody's got money, lawyers, resources—heck, he even has the police.

What do I have? A sick granny, a burnt shed, a big friend with a pissed-off, meth-head father, and...

Oh, the beautiful irony.

I've got a mother, in prison for fighting people just like Peabody.

Well played, Universe.

"What you thinking in there?" Granny asks.

"Nothing." Everything.

"Well, get on to school. You're already late."

I stand my ground for a minute, but the truth is I'm already way behind in everything, and if I miss today, I'll have two more quizzes to make up. "All right. But I'm calling you between every class to make sure you're okay."

"You do that," she says. As I'm opening the car door, she adds, "I'll be sure to turn off the ringer."

"I'm sure you will." I stop before climbing in. "I love you."

"Right back atcha, sugarplum."

"I'll be home after school."

"No baseball practice today?"

Being reminded of Cole, that the whole school knew about him cheating on me, gives me a sick feeling in my stomach. "No, Granny. No baseball." I can't deal with telling her the truth right now. She'll want the whole story and I don't have time. "Gotta run."

"Drive safe."

The drive to school takes no time at all, probably because I'm dreading today. The fire took my mind off everything for a while, but it comes flooding back when I see the low brick walls of Plurd County High. I count through my list of hellish blessings: no boyfriend, one friend, half the school laughing about Cole cheating on me, the other half talking about my speech at the county commissioners meeting. And, worst of all, potentially no Dobber.

It's halfway through second period, so I report to Calculus and attempt to do last night's homework while Mr. Patterson goes over the next lesson. The rest of the morning passes as normally as it ever does—no fires in my locker, nobody attacking me in the halls—and then it's time for lunch.

Yesterday at this time, I punched Cole in the face and reduced my friend pool to one: Dobber. But last night, I called him a dumb shit and an ignorant donkey head, so I'm thinking he may prefer to sit elsewhere, with someone less insulting. Or at least someone with wittier insults.

I take our usual table and enjoy the one bright spot in the day— Salisbury steak. Between gravy-covered bites of processed meat, I keep an eye out for Dobber. If I have to make a public apology on bended knee, I'll do it, but I'm hoping it won't come to that.

"I heard about last night."

I recognize Ashleigh's voice. "So?" I don't bother looking at her. I'm sure she's perfectly gorgeous and I don't need the demoralization—not with bags the size of army duffels under my eyes.

"Gutsy," she says. "Or just stupid. I haven't decided."

I'm not sure where she's going with this. "Whatever."

She doesn't reply, and after a minute, I look up. She's across the cafeteria surrounded by her typical gaggle of BFFs.

What the hell was that about?

Something heavy drops into the chair next to me, and I turn to find Dobber, his plate with double steak oozing gravy over the edges. My mouth waters at the sight.

"Hey, poop clown," he says.

For the first time today, I almost smile. "Yeah. Sorry about that."

"That's a'ight. I been called worse."

"Worse than poop clown? Really?"

He just grins.

"I'm glad you're not pissed at me. I need to tell you something."

"Sounds serious." His gray eyes crinkle around the edges. "You asking me out?"

"Somebody burned down our shed this morning."

His smile disappears. "No shit?"

"Absolutely none. No shit at all."

"Damn, Lib." He sits back in his chair and shakes his head. "I reckon we know who did it."

"Right. As a warning." I lean forward, my voice low. "I'm done screwing around, Dob. That fire could have spread to the barn or even the house. Granny and I could have died." Then I remember— Granny *is* dying. And so is Mr. Dobber. "I want to stop Peabody. Before he hurts anybody else."

"Count me in!" Dobber grins. "What's the plan?"

I toy with the splint on my finger, hesitating. It took me hours to make peace with this idea, and I still cringe when I say, "I'm going to email my former mother."

TWENTY-SIX

The nurse is coming this afternoon, and I promised Granny I'd be home when she arrived. But first, I have an email to send, so I stop at the overlook. I super do not want to write this email, but we need her advice. She's the closest thing to an expert that we have.

Dear Mom,

I type, then erase. *Way* too personal.

Dobber says I don't have to like her to ask her a couple questions. I guess he's right, but I'm afraid she's going to think me reaching out to her means everything is okay between us now. Which it's not.

Hi.

Type. Erase. Decide emails don't really need greetings.

I struggle over every word, making sure nothing can be misconstrued as respect. Or love or forgiveness. Plus, I'm not sure if her emails get screened. I don't want anyone at the prison knowing about some potentially illegal plans we might cook up. In the end, I send off a vague email that could have been written by a robot, and hope she can read between the lines:

Discovered the mine has poisoned the water here...

responsible for Granny's cancer. Mine owner is

untouchable. Ideas?

I hit send, then I race the rest of the way home to meet the nurse. Granny's sitting on the front porch, wrapped in a fleece even though it's about seventy-five degrees.

"Did I miss her?"

"No. Ain't nobody been by."

She looks pale to me, and tired. "How are you feeling? Do you want to lie down for a while?"

"If I wanted to lie down, I would," she snaps. "I still got a brain."

"Okay, okay. Don't yell." But it's too late. That little bit of venom in her voice starts her coughing. Her lungs sound full of stuff lately, and when she finally stops, the tissue she held to her mouth has a lot of blood on it.

"Looks like the red guck is getting worse," I say.

"Looks like."

I stand next to her, holding my backpack, feeling useless. "We're going to find a way to make Peabody pay for this."

She pats Silkie on the head and sighs. "Okay, darlin'. If that makes you feel better." She glances toward the yard and the black stumps of the shed posts. "Like I said, I'm with ya a hunnert percent."

It's a stake through my chest. *I'm with you, Liberty, even if my house gets burned down.*

The phone rings. I drop my backpack on the porch and go in to answer it.

"Hello?"

"Hi. This is Mrs. Lamar, the nurse."

"Oh, hi. I'm Liberty, Kat's granddaughter. We're expecting you."

"Yes, I know, and I'm so sorry but I just don't think I'll be able to make it."

"Oh." My radar goes up. "Do you want to reschedule?"

Pause. "Actually, I don't believe I'll be able to add Mrs. Briscoe to my patient list after all."

"But you said—"

"I know, but I've looked at my schedule, and…well, I'm afraid I just don't have time. And with you all living so far out, I'd be driving so much."

"But my granny needs care. What am I supposed to do? I'm in school all day—"

"I'm sorry. I wish I could help," she says. "You can call Mrs. Blanchard, the hospice nurse, and see if someone else might be available."

"I've already talked to her," I say, gritting my teeth. "She sent me to you because you had the lightest patient load."

"Well, I'm sorry I can't help," she says.

"Right. I'm sure you are." Just like I'm sure this has nothing to do with Peabody Mining.

There's a long pause. "I'm sorry, but that's just the way it is."

"Right." I don't bother with good-bye. I just hang up wondering what the hell I'm supposed to do now.

"Who's on the phone?" Granny calls.

I walk back to the porch. "The nurse. She…" How do I word this? "She's not coming."

Granny squints at me, reading my face like a book. "Not coming ever, huh?"

"Right."

"Hmpf. So much for that hippocrastic oath."

"Exactly what I was thinking."

Granny takes a deep breath. "Well, can't say as I blame her. Don't nobody wanna get on the bad side of Robert Peabody. Not that he has a good side."

"She said I should call Mrs. Blanchard back and find somebody else."

"Sugarplum, I'm just fine on my owns. You ain't got to worry over me." She wobbles her way inside, then collapses on the couch, breathing hard.

I stand in the doorway, watching. Just fine on her owns she might be, but for how much longer?

TWENTY-SEVEN

I call in sick to school Friday. It's a half day anyway, so I won't be missing much, and I need to find a nurse for Granny.

"Mrs. Blanchard?" I say into the phone. "This is Liberty Briscoe. I'm calling about my granny."

"Oh sure." The hospice nurse's voice is kind and reassuring. I realize not many people talk to me that way anymore. "How is Kat?"

"She's okay. Listen…" Without going into details, I explain that the day nurse didn't work out, and she gives me a couple more names.

"Call them soon," she says. "I know Kat seems fine now, but…"

"I understand," I say. Dr. Lang told us her health could deteriorate fast as she gets closer to the end. Plus, I hate leaving her alone with all of the strange things that have been happening around the house. "I'll call them today. Thanks!"

After hanging up with her, I call and leave messages at both numbers. Then there's nothing to do, so I straighten up the house. I'm slowly making progress in my war on the dust. There's less of it in the house every time I clean.

The fact that my triumph over the dust is the biggest success of the month makes me sad. This is the month I'd planned to start working on my early-action application to Georgetown. The reality: I haven't even opened the envelope. It's still sitting on the dresser in my room. Covered with dust. Maybe the dust won after all.

I'm just about to make some ramen for lunch when I hear a car coming up the drive. Dobber's rusted-out, beater Datsun stops in front.

I push open the screen door. "Hey there."

"Hey." He climbs out of the car holding a newspaper. "You sick?"

"No. I skipped so I could get some things done for Granny. What's up?"

"Nothing you'll like." Taking the front steps in one stride, he hands me the paper. Then he stands next to me and points at an article on the front page. His arm is hot against mine.

"Good news, is it?" I ask.

"I think you're looking at Item Six," he says. "From the hearing."

I read the headline. "County Commissioners Agree to Support Extension of Tanner's Peak Mine." The absolute asinine stupidity of it leaves me speechless for a moment.

Dobber points farther down the article. "It says they're gonna start mining on Dry Ridge."

"But that's right above Green Hills subdivision! There must be two hundred houses over there. What the hell are the commissioners thinking?"

"They ain't thinking. They just following orders."

I scan the article quickly. "Oh my God. It gets worse. He's applied to the state for an approximate original contour waiver."

"I saw that. What's it mean?"

"There's a state law that says after a mining company's done, it has to return the area to its 'approximate original contour,'" I explain. "Basically, they have to build the mountain back. If Peabody's asking for a waiver, it's because he wants to blow off the top of the ridge and dump it into the valley, just like he did Tanner's Peak." I fling the paper onto the porch rocker. "And the county commissioners are okay with that? Un-frigging-believable."

"It says they're expecting EPA approval next month," Dobber says.

"So what happens to the people living below the ridge? Do they have to move? Is Peabody going to buy their houses?"

Dobber shakes his head. "What d'you think?"

I look across the valley at the hilltops opposite, trying to imagine them with no trees, trying to imagine the top of the ridge dumped into the hollers below—trying to imagine the destruction soon to come. "We have to stop him before he gets that approval."

"D'you write your mama?"

"My *former* mother. Yes, I did."

"She write back?"

Good question. "Let's hike up to the ridge. I can get a signal up there."

I run in to get my phone and tell Granny where we're going.

"Have a nice walk," she says. "You'll be back in time to take that pie out of the oven?"

"Pie?" I stop and stare at her. "What pie?"

She squints at me. "You got a apple pie baking, don't ya?"

I snort. "No." Us having pie is about as likely as me being crowned prom queen. "No pie. Sorry."

"I coulda swore I smelled one."

"Wishful thinking," I say, bending down to give her a kiss on the cheek.

"Y'all take these dogs," Granny says. "They got some yayas to get worked out."

Silkie and Beethoven run out into the yard, tails wagging, waiting to see which direction we're going. As soon as I start for the ridge trail, they shoot ahead, barking at anything that moves. Sweet, old Goldie pads along behind.

"So," I say over my shoulder as we climb, "how's baseball going?"

What I really mean is how are things with Cole.

Dobber laughs…short and soft. "A'ight."

"Really?"

"It's a team, Liberty. I don't gotta like ever'body on it. Usually don't, anyway."

"Well, I feel sort of bad. It's my fault you guys aren't friends."

"Naw. It's his fault." We're both breathing hard from the climb. "Him grabbing your arm like that? That wasn't right. And all that other stuff…"

"Sounds like he did that other stuff a lot though. According to Ashleigh."

"It was different this time."

I reach the top first and turn toward him. "Different how?"

He looks at me then looks away, across the valley. "Dunno. Just different."

I wonder what that means as I pull out my phone. No voice messages. No emails. Nothing from MFM. Just a text from Iris.

Where are you?

It's been forever since I talked to her. I haven't even heard what her big news is.

I type a quick message back (Serious shit hitting fan. Call you tonight) and look over at Tanner's-No-Longer-Existent-Peak.

I run my phone across my lip, thinking. "Whatever's poisoning the water, it's happening right over there. In broad daylight."

"I know," Dobber says. "Funny, huh?"

Funny but not. "The cop told me the mine has to submit water samples for testing, to prove they're not leaking poisons into the environment."

"What're you thinking? That he ain't submitting the samples? Or he ain't taking 'em from the right place?"

"I don't know," I admit. "But if there's any proof to be had, it's at the mine." I give it a second's thought then turn and head down the trail. "Let's go."

"Go where?"

"Duh. To the mine."

TWENTY-EIGHT

We take Granny's car, since Peabody got a good look at Dobber's the other night. I let Dobber drive since he knows how to get there. It takes about twenty minutes, winding up a two-lane road, dodging dump trucks full of coal every other curve. Driving a little ways past the mine entrance, we leave the car in the trees and creep out to the edge of the clearing. Crouched behind a pile of rock, we have clear view of the operation.

It's enormous. I mean, it looks big from the other side of the valley, but I thought it was big like a mall. Up close, it's more like a city, comprised of multiple plateaus of dirt, each of which could hold the whole town of Ebbottsville. Steep roads slope in and out of giant craters, and above it all towers the dragline, the giant crane that scrapes the flesh off the earth and dumps it into the valley. Twenty stories tall, it's a warehouse on a rotating platform. The scraper bucket is big enough to park a couple buses in. The dump trucks that were just running us off the road look like fleas compared to the crane.

Even as far away as we are, the noise is deafening and I can feel the ground vibrating through my shoes. I'm not sure what I'm looking for, but so far I don't see anything, just a bunch of equipment and a lot of raw dirt.

"What'dya reckon they take samples of?" Dobber asks. "There's no water up here."

He's right. All the creeks and pools have been scooped up and tossed away. Aside from the containment pond, the place they dump the water laced with the sixty different chemicals they use to clean the coal, the site is dry.

I stare at the pond, halfway down the east side of the hill, remembering what I learned during my research. The carcinogens and heavy metals from the cleaning process sink to the bottom of the containment pond, enter the groundwater, and, rolling downhill, end up in the rivers and wells down in the valley. Granny's well. The Dobbers' well. Everybody's wells.

"Hang on," I mutter. "Not everybody's."

"Say what?"

I squint into the sun, past Tanner's Peak toward the west part of Ebbottsville beyond. "Oh my God. That's it!"

"What's it?"

"Not everybody is getting sick."

"So?"

"Why do you suppose the county commissioners let Peabody do what he wants, even if it's a health hazard?"

"'Cause he pays 'em?"

"You can't pay somebody not to care about getting cancer. Or not to care that their kids might get cancer."

"So what then?"

"They won't *get* cancer." I point to the sludgy pool. "That containment pond is on the east side."

Dobber stares. "Okay."

"And where does Peabody live? And the county commissioners? And all the other rich people in Ebbottsville?"

"Oh. In Summerset…on the west side of the mountain."

"Exactly. *Up*stream of the mine runoff. And where is the mine expansion going?"

"On Dry Ridge—south of the mountain."

"Which drains to the east."

Dobber shakes his head. "Like my daddy says, don't shit in your own backyard."

"Looks like Robert Peabody took that lesson to heart, which means he knew the mine would be dangerous."

"S'at give us proof?" Dobber asks.

"Not exactly. But if Peabody realized that mine would hurt people, and he went ahead with it anyway—"

"Then he deserves to get blowed up."

"No, I was going to say he's committing murder."

TWENTY-NINE

We creep back to the car and head down the mountain. This time, I drive.

"Maybe they had studies done," I say, taking a curve fast enough for the tires to squeal. "Topographic reports that show exactly where to locate the pond to keep the west valley safe. That would be proof of premeditation."

"Even if they did, them studies'll be in Peabody's office," Dobber says. "And there ain't no way we can get in there. They got..." He drifts off.

"Got what?"

We're just passing the mine entrance. I glance at Dobber, but he's not looking at the gates. He's looking at the car coming toward us, waiting to turn into the mine. The white Cadillac Escalade. The one with Robert Peabody behind the wheel.

"Shit."

I pull my green-splinted hand off the steering wheel. Tilting my head, I let my hair fall over the left side of my face. Dobber dives forward, bending nearly double to get his head below the dash.

Through my bangs, I sneak a peek at Peabody as we pass by, but all I can see is the reflection of the trees above on his windshield. One second later, we're past him. I watch him turn left into the parking lot. I have no idea if he's seen us or not.

Dobber raises his head just a bit, staring at his side-view mirror.

"Is he following us?" I ask.

"I don't think so."

"Should I pull off on one of these side roads?"

"Naw," he says. "Just slow down right up there."

I take the switchback curve with my brakes on slightly. Around the bend, the trees give way to a rock face and a clear view of the road directly above us. I'm crawling along at about twenty miles an hour, while Dobber watches for the Escalade.

But it doesn't appear.

I exhale. My chest feels like a balloon that's been stretched out too long. "Maybe he didn't see us. The glare on the windshield was pretty bad."

"Maybe."

"Plus, he doesn't know Granny's car," I say, feeling better with each second I put between us and Peabody. "And we weren't technically at the mine. This is a public road."

"I reckon," Dobber says. "'Cept there ain't nothing up there *but* the mine."

My safe feeling evaporates. He's right. Now that the top of the mountain is gone, the mine's the end of the road. Anybody up here is either on mine business or completely lost.

"Do you think he saw us?" I ask.

Dobber rubs his hand across his cheek, covered with half a day's stubble, and sighs. "Dunno, Lib. But I reckon we'll find out."

I erupt in a bad case of goose bumps.

* * *

Back at the house, Granny's fallen asleep. Dobber heads home after I promise to call him if I have any trouble. He doesn't specify what "trouble" might be and I don't ask.

The phone rings and I jump for it, hoping one of the nurses is finally calling back.

"Hello?"

"Hello. This is Dr. Lang."

"Oh." I take the phone outside, onto the porch. "Hi, Doctor."

"I wanted to check in on Mrs. Briscoe. How's she doing?"

"Okay, I guess."

"No sudden weakness? No nausea?"

"No," I say. "But the red guck is getting worse."

"That's to be expected, I'm afraid. How is she feeling? Any pain?"

"A little, but she's been taking those pills you gave her."

"Good. There's no reason for her not to be comfortable."

I'm struck by the irony of being comfortable and dying at the same time. "It's nice of you to call," I say. "Do you always check up on your patients?"

"Sometimes," he says. "Liberty…"

I'm impressed he's remembered my name…which is followed by a long pause.

"Yes?"

"This type of cancer…it spreads rapidly. With your grandmother in stage four, there's a good chance it's already done that."

"Spread?" What's he saying? She's going to die quicker? "Spread where?"

"Other organs. Potentially to her brain. If that happens, it could be very hard on her caregivers. On you."

"Oh." God. Oh God.

"Have you noticed any new symptoms?" the doctor asks.

"Um…" The words "brain cancer" are ricocheting around in my head like bullets, driving out all other thoughts.

"Confusion. Hallucinations of any kind."

"No…"

"Hallucinations can manifest in any of the senses."

I force my mind back to the last few days. "I can't remember anything. She's been just as cranky and sarcastic as ever."

Dr. Lang laughs. "Well, that's a good sign. It may not be an issue, but I did want you to be aware."

"Yeah. Thanks."

"I'll check in again," he says. "And Mrs. Blanchard will send me notes from her visits too."

"Okay. Thanks again for calling."

"Not a problem." And then the phone clicks. Someone really ought to explain the concept of "good-bye" to that man.

I sink onto the rocker, trying to remember if there is anything at all that might suggest Granny's brain is affected. But really, there's nothing. I drop my head and, clasping the phone with both hands, pray. "Please, God. Don't let her get brain cancer."

I'm pretty sure I couldn't handle that. Granny's the smartest of all the smart-asses I know. Seeing her mind go, having her forget who I am, maybe even who she is, that would be impossible to take. Granny stirs on the couch, and I drop the phone back in the charger.

"What time is it?" she asks.

"About five." I crouch down next to her.

"Lordy, I'm just so tired all a time."

"You need rest," I say. "Your body's going through a lot."

"Um hm." She looks hard at me. "And how 'bout you?"

"How 'bout me what?"

"What're you going through?"

I settle onto the floor cross-legged. "What are you talking about?"

"You wanna tell me what happened with that boy? Or you gonna keep it bottled up inside and let it fester?"

Brain cancer? I don't think so. She doesn't miss a thing. "I assume you mean Cole."

"Well, I don't mean Charlie Brown."

Sighing, I launch into a rundown of the cafeteria incident. "And then I punched him in the face."

"Um hm." She nods at my hand. "That how you popped your finger?"

"Yes."

"I knew that 'slammed it in the car door' story was bull the minute I heard it."

"Sorry."

"How's things stand between you now?"

"Um, I punched him in the face. So..." I give her the clearest "duh" face I can muster.

"So it's over?"

"Oh, it's over all right." I scrape at a spot of mud on the side of my boot. The ick tornado spins to life in my stomach again, as I think about all the people who knew Cole was cheating. "Apparently..." I can't bring myself to look at Granny. "Apparently, he was messing around with somebody else too."

"Oh Lord."

"My feelings exactly."

"What you mean by 'messing around'?"

"Um, well...like..." I thought I could tell Granny anything. I can't believe I'm having this much trouble saying one tiny word. "Sex."

"Sex?" Granny sits up fast. "Hold on, now. What kinda things did y'all get up to on them dates of yours?"

"Not me! Nothing. We never...no." I'm so damn relieved that's true, given the way things ended.

She slouches back onto the cushions. "Well, at least you punched him. Sounds like he deserved it."

"I guess."

There's that word again. Deserved. What Cole deserved, what Peabody deserves. We humans are awfully quick to decide what everybody else deserves. We just reach into our well of judgment and pull out a verdict. Actually handing out the desserts though, that's a different story. Cole may have deserved a punch in the face, but I ended up with a broken finger. Was that the universe's way of saying I was wrong to even his karmic score?

Then there's Peabody, sitting in his Jacuzzi on the west side of town, dealing out death every single day. What does he deserve? More than a punch in the face, obviously. But who's going to give it to him? And what will the universe have to say about that?

"Granny, what if Peabody did burn our shed?"

"Then he'll have to answer to his maker for that."

"I can't wait that long," I say. "He ought to be in jail right now."

"Did you tell the police you thought he done it?"

"Yes."

"They gonna arrest him?"

"Of course not." I wiggle my finger through a hole in the fabric of the couch. "They think he's some kind of God."

"Then I reckon you gon' have to wait."

But sitting here, in this broken-down house, with poisoned water and almost no food, watching the one and only person in all the world that I love die, I know I can't wait.

THIRTY

After dinner (ramen again), I take the phone to my room and call Iris. It's been weeks since I talked to her, and lately it's been as much my fault as hers.

"Where the hell have you been, girl?" she asks.

Hearing her voice is like finding a great pair of jeans I forgot I had. "I miss you," I say. My chin trembles. But I don't cry about happy stuff either, so I bite the inside of my cheek and count to five.

"Ditto you! So? How're things in rural America?"

I think about what to tell her, bite harder, count more. "Tough."

"Ohmigod. Are you biting your cheek?" she asks. "What's going on out there?"

I take a deep breath. "My grandmother has cancer."

"Oh shit!"

I pretend I'm acting out a scene, like all the things I'm saying aren't actually happening to me. Doing that, I can get through it without any tears. "It's terminal. They gave her weeks, maybe a couple months, to live."

"Liberty! I'm so sorry."

"I don't know what I'm going to do. I'm not eighteen, so…"

"God, I hadn't thought about that. When's your mom's trial?"

"It doesn't matter," I say. "I'm not moving back with her."

"What choice do you have?"

I toy with a necklace on my nightstand, my stomach churning at my only option. "Foster care."

Silence on the other end, then, "You have *got* to be kidding me. Even your whacko mom is better than foster care."

"Says the girl with the perfect nuclear family."

"Look, stay with your grandma until…well…as long as you can. After that, maybe you can stay with us until…well…"

Until what? I run through the options while the silence stretches on. Until I turn eighteen, get a minimum-wage job and an apartment I share with thirteen other people. Until my untimely death in a freak house fire. "Iris, there's something else."

"Something *else*?"

As quickly as I can, I explain about the mine, Peabody, the shed, my plans with Dobber.

When I'm done, Iris says, "I'm coming to get you."

That makes me laugh. My throat muscles barely remember how, but they get the hang of it pretty fast. It feels good. For those ten seconds, the weight lifts. "Thanks for that. I thought you'd…you know, forgotten me."

"No way! Aw, I'm sorry Libs. It's just, the play starts next week, so we've had rehearsals every day and—Oh man! I forgot to tell you. I got my internship with the *Washington Recorder*!"

Her dream come true. Iris's been applying to the *Recorder* for years, trying to get her foot in the door. I should have guessed.

"Yep. Is that perfect or what?"

"Perfectly perfect." I fight down a wave of jealousy.

"The guy I'm interning with said he might even let me write a little."

"That's so great. Iris, I'm really happy for you."

"You can celebrate with me in person," Iris says. "I'm coming to get you tomorrow."

The idea of going back to DC, back to Westfield Academy, leaving behind arsonists and orange water and dying grannies, makes me feel like I've got a helium balloon in my chest, lifting me up above all the crap. And then it pops. "I can't leave Granny."

Iris sighs. "Yeah, I know. But God, Lib. That guy setting fire to your shed? That's insane."

"I know." Glancing out the window, I realize it's gotten dark and close the blinds. God only knows who might be out there.

"Promise me you'll stay out of his way," Iris says.

Oh, how I'd love to. "Well…"

"Liberty, seriously. Stay the hell away from the guy!"

"I can't," I say. "I have to make this right."

"Your granny is dying. The mountain's trashed. The people in charge there just voted to screw themselves over even more. How can you make any of that right?"

"I don't know. But it's not fair! None of it."

Iris groans. "Oh no. Not Liberty Briscoe's infamous quest for fairness again."

"What?"

"I've been down that road too many times already."

"I don't know what you're talking about."

"Seriously? How about when Chester got credit for all our work on that team project?"

"What about it?" I say. "Chester shows up for half an hour and gets an A because we worked all night for two days?"

"It wasn't fair. I agree. But you went all vigilante on him."

"I did not."

"Throwing his homework away, for two weeks, when you were Mr. Murphy's classroom aid? That's vigilante. He nearly flunked."

"Well, he deserved—" My gut clenches at the word.

"And then that time Jason Mueller told Ms. Shatner that Tabitha

Warner cheated off his test, when it was actually the other way around."

"I remember." I'm still trying to scrub the word "deserved" out of my mouth.

"You stuffed a thong in his locker and his girlfriend dumped him when she saw it." Iris laughs. "Oh, and remember when that kid tied a firecracker to that stray cat?"

"Okay, I get it." The pattern of behavior she's describing sounds disturbingly similar to someone else I know. Someone I really don't respect. Someone who's sitting in prison right this second.

"I'm just saying, you have an interesting way of making things fair."

"Thanks for pointing that out." I feel icky inside now. I don't like being reminded that I did those things, even if, at the time, they seemed right and fair…and maybe deserved.

"Whatever." Iris sighs. "Look, I'm worried about you. Are you sure I can't come get you?"

"I can't leave Granny."

"I know you can't. Just promise you'll call if you need me."

"Promise."

"I'll call you this weekend, okay?"

"Okay."

"Love you, Lib."

"Ditto you."

I hang up the phone, missing Iris like crazy and not liking myself very much at all.

THIRTY-ONE

I open my eyes and stare at the ceiling, waiting for the sunshine to light up the far wall. It must be before eight. The house is still in the shadow of the holler. All's quiet—no scratching dogs, no Granny sounds in the kitchen. Just birds tweeting and the occasional rustle of a breeze. I wish I could go back to sleep, reenter the dream where I had friends, we weren't poor, and nobody was dying. But no matter how tight I close my eyes, it doesn't work.

It's Saturday—grocery day. My least favorite day of the week, partly because I won't get a nice hot lunch of fish sticks or a country fried chicken patty, and partly because I have to do the shopping. At least this week I don't have tampons eating into my budget, but I wish that meant I could get something special—a roast or fresh asparagus or a doughnut. God, I'd give my left suede boot for a doughnut.

I pull on a sweater over my pajama top. It's cold in the mornings still, and Granny keeps the fire in the wood stove as low as we can stand. Shoving my feet into slippers, I head for the kitchen to make some tea. I stop at Granny's door to check on her.

"Granny? You awake?"

No answer.

She had a rough night, lots of pain around eleven. I gave her a pill, but it didn't seem to do much. I heard her tossing and turning until way past one.

I put my hand on her forehead. She feels cold, so I pull an extra blanket over her. She mutters in her sleep but doesn't wake. It's not like her to sleep so soundly. She must have taken another pill at some point. That Vicodin really knocks her out.

After tea and no toast (the bread's all gone), I get dressed and make a list for the store. I look in on Granny again before heading into town, but she's still sleeping. It worries me a little but short of shaking her awake, I'm not sure what to do about it. Instead, I tell myself it's good for her to rest, and I climb into the car.

On the way to town, I see mud season is officially over. All the fields and yards have thick carpets of crops and grass. The rocks are sprouting moss. Everything's dressed in green, except the top of Tanner's Peak, which looms above us just as raw and red as ever. It's like the bloody stump of a mountain that never scabs over.

The grocery store is the same as always—full of stuff I want but can't have, full of people who stare but don't smile. By now, I recognize the regular Saturday morning shoppers. Not that they acknowledge me. I've gone from being a simple outsider to a trouble-making interloper.

So I push my cart up and down the aisles, pretending not to notice the stares and glares. Other people's carts seem so full, stacked with groceries, shrieking with kids, some double-parked while young moms whisper, heads bent together. My cart's just like my life. Empty. Silent. Alone.

* * *

On the way home, I stop at the overlook to check my messages. Finally, there's an email from MFM.

Dear Liberty,

Your last letter concerns me. I know Robert Peabody, just as I knew his father and many other

- 177 -

men of their ilk through the years—big company owners who stand on the shoulders of other
men with little or no regard for the other man's
well-being.

This is classic Mom. Rambly, stilted prose, forever circling the point.

I don't doubt that the mine is to blame for the health
issues. We've seen this same situation throughout
Appalachia. MTR mining is deadly to communities, socially, economically, and environmentally.

Like I haven't already figured this out myself.

You won't get anywhere with the EPA and I doubt
the county will challenge Peabody. Not when so
much of the economy depends on him and the
mine. You'll have to take matters into your own
hands. Protest the mine. Form a picket line. Make
flyers explaining the risks. Let the people know.
Once they realize their families are in danger, you'll
have some allies.

Seriously? This is her big plan? All that's gonna get me is another
couple house fires and maybe a broken kneecap.

I'm proud of you for taking this on. Peabody
shouldn't be allowed to get away with this kind of
destruction, carte blanche.

Let me know how things go. I love you so much,
Mom

P.S. Give Mommy a hug for me. She's in my
thoughts constantly.

Useless! I delete the email and restrain myself from throwing the
phone over the edge. Where's the woman who chained herself to the
Chinese ambassador's car to protest their human rights violations? I
want to make Peabody pay for what he did to Granny—an eye for an
eye, a tooth for a tooth sort of thing. And she tells me to make flyers?
Flyers?

I climb into the car and head home. The greens seem less bright
now, the sky less blue, and I feel more helpless than ever. Back at
the house, I haul in the cartons of water and put the groceries away.
I'm just setting the milk in the fridge when Granny steps into the
hallway.

"Hi, sleepyhead." I realize as soon as the words are out of my
mouth that something's wrong. Granny has one hand over her eyes
and she's leaning against the wall, moving slowly forward. "Granny?
What's wrong?"

"Just get me to the couch," she says.

I run over and take her arm. "What is it?"

"I feel so dizzy," she says as I help her to the sofa. "Ever'thing's all
catawampus." Her skin is pale and clammy.

"Did you take too much medicine?" I ask. "Vicodin can make
you nauseous."

"Naw. Just that pill you give me last night." She has both hands
on her head, like she's trying to hold it still.

"I'm going to get you some water." I go into the kitchen and open the fridge. I'm trying to get through the plastic wrapping on the carton when I hear...ergh...puking. I run back into the living room and hold Granny's birdlike shoulders as she shudders through heave after dry heave. When she's done, I get a towel and clean up the little bit of sick that came out. Small benefit of never having enough to eat: nothing to puke up.

"Sorry," she says. "I think maybe it's the bacon that made me so nauseated."

I pause, halfway to the kitchen. We haven't had bacon since I moved here. "What are you talking about?"

"That bacon you're frying. I smelled it all the way in my bedroom."

"I'm not frying—" And then I realize. The apple pie she smelled yesterday. The bacon today. They're not smells. They're hallucinations.

The cancer has spread to her brain.

THIRTY-TWO

I spend the weekend watching Granny sleep, barely leaving her side except to call the two numbers I have for day nurses. There's no answer at either place and, despite the numerous and increasingly desperate messages I leave, no one calls me back. I keep telling myself they're probably out of town or just busy, that it has nothing to do with my special new relationship with Robert Peabody.

Monday morning, I wake early and start mulling over my options. Which are (1) go to school and leave Granny alone, or (2) stay home with Granny and get further behind in school. Thanks to missed homework and bad quiz grades, I'm floating between Cs and Ds in every class except English. Flipping a coin seems like as good a solution as any, though I'm not sure I have a coin to flip. I'm just about to get out of bed and check my purse when this enormous boom shakes the entire house, rattling the windows so hard I'm afraid they may break. I hear another sound, a crash in the hallway. I leap out of bed and throw open the door.

My heart pounds as I stare through the semidarkness until I make out a picture lying on the floor with broken glass all around it. The explosion shook it right off the wall. Thanks to my research, I'm pretty sure we have Robert Peabody to thank for the explosion. In fact, we'll probably get to hear a lot more of these over the next few days. I know the EPA hasn't approved his petition for expansion, so they must be blasting deeper into the hole they already have.

Goddam Peabody.

Nothing's wrong. Nobody's breaking in, but I'm left with an uneasy feeling I can't reason away. Thankfully, nothing wakes Granny when she's on Vicodin. I leave her sleeping and head up the road to catch the bus.

Even after a week, I still totally suck at opening my locker with one hand. It takes three attempts before I manage to wiggle the handle with just the right amount of pressure to open the door without jamming it and losing the combination. As I pull out my math book, a slip of paper flutters out and lands at my feet. I reach down to pick it up, registering at the same time that it's covered with words cut out of magazines, like a ransom note:

STAY AWAY FROM THE MINE. WE'RE WATCHING YOU.

I glance around the hallway. Goose bumps creep across my skin and I have to fight the urge to dump my books, run to the car, and go home to check on Granny. The idea that somebody's spying on us is deeply disturbing. I wonder what they've seen me do—get dressed? Shower? Are they following me around? Or are they standing on the front porch at home right now? I try to tell myself they're watching me, not Granny, but I'm still worried. Ducking into the bathroom, I dial Granny's number. She answers on the fourth ring.

"Hello?" Her voice is slurred and sleepy.

"Granny, it's me."

"Mm."

"I wanted to make sure you were all right." I explain about the note. "Are you okay there alone? Maybe I should come home."

She sighs, a rattly sound from deep in her chest. "You can't be worrying about me ever' single minute."

"I can't help it."

"You being here ain't gonna change nothing," she says.

I guess she's right. Me skipping school to sit by her side isn't going to stop whoever's watching us. Most likely, it'll just land me detention or a possible repeat of junior year. Besides, I'd have to call a taxi to get home, and I don't have any money. "Okay. Just...keep the phone with you all the time. If anything weird happens, you call the police."

"Right," she says.

"I'll check in later."

The line clicks and I realize she hung up on me.

I read the cut-out letters one last time, make a mental note to keep the shade in the bathroom pulled down, then toss the paper in the trash. I wish it were as easy to get rid of the fear.

THIRTY-THREE

The bus ride home seems to take twice as long as normal. I sit alone, as usual, and worry about Granny the whole way. She seemed tired when I called her at lunch, so she's probably asleep. I hate leaving her alone. Tonight, I'm going to call-bomb those nurses every thirty minutes. They'll have to pick up the phone eventually, right?

When the bus finally drops me off, I race up the driveway. I'm breathing hard by the time I reach the house. Crossing the yard, I see the front door is standing open. It's pretty warm today, but still…it's weird. Granny's been so cold lately, she hasn't even wanted to open a window. On the porch, I notice her tennis shoes are gone and try to remember if I took them in for some reason.

My stomach starts twisting when I see Granny's not in the living room. I drop my books in the middle of the floor and run-walk through the house.

Bedroom—empty.

Bathroom—empty.

My room—empty.

Kitchen—empty.

I go back and double check.

I triple check.

Out in the yard, I search the old barn, calling for her. Silkie and Beethoven are gone, so I call them too. Goldie trails along behind me.

Nothing answers me, except my own voice echoing up the holler.

"Gran-ny-ny-ny-ny…"

My heart pounds as I run down the drive and through the woods to the crawdad hole. Nobody. I head back to the house, still calling, and take the trail to the ridge.

"Beethoven!"

She could have gone for a walk, I tell myself. She probably would have taken the dogs. It all makes sense. Perfect, logical sense.

I purposely ignore the fact that she can't make it down the hallway lately without resting. I also try not to think about the fire or the note in my locker. Or about Robert Peabody's cold, dead eyes.

"Silkie!"

Halfway to the ridge, I hear a bark. Sounds echo so much in the hills, it's hard to tell, but I think it came from below.

"Silkie?"

Another bark. I crash off trail, through the rhododendron. "Here, dog!"

She sounds louder each time so I must be getting closer. The branches are thick and the ground slopes hard downward. I can't tell where I am or where I'm going. I just keep calling Silkie and slipping, crashing my way down the hill toward her barks.

As the ground levels out, the shrubs start to thin, and I hear something scrabbling toward me. Pretty soon, a white ball of fluff flies at my ankles, barking and panting. It's Silkie. But no Granny.

"Good dog. Good girl," I say. "Where's Granny? Find Granny."

Silkie turns to the left and starts plowing through the brush. I follow as best I can, calling her back now and then, and yelling for Granny. After a few minutes thrashing through the thick green shrubs, I stumble into the sunshine…back at the house.

"No, Silkie! Where's Granny? Find Granny!"

But the little terrier is no Lassie. She just wags her tail and runs up onto the porch, barking to go inside.

I decide to call the police. If Granny's lost in the woods, I won't find her by myself. And the longer she's out there, the more hurt she could get. Plus, if she's *not* lost in the woods…I shudder at the thought.

In the house, I find the card the police officer gave me last week and call the number. He answers on the fourth ring. I tell him who I am and what's happened.

He tells me that until Granny's been missing for at least twenty-four hours, they can't do anything.

"She probably just went for a walk," he says. "But if she don't turn up by tomorrow, you call me. We'll come right out."

"Great. In twenty-four hours…" I stop myself from finishing the sentence. "You do remember what happened here last week, right?"

He scoffs into the phone. "I'm sure your granny's fine."

"You better hope so," I say. "For your sake."

I hang up and dial the one and only person I can call. Dobber answers right away.

"Hey, new girl."

"Dobber, Granny's disappeared."

"Say what?" His voice is full of concern. Unlike Officer Smiley Face, Dobber's taking this seriously.

"I came home from school, and she's gone. I've looked everywhere. The dogs were gone too. I found Silkie in the woods but—"

"Be right there."

While I wait for Dobber, I check the house again. Silkie curls up on the couch and goes to sleep.

"Useless dog."

Dobber pulls up not five minutes later. He's out of the car before it even stops rolling. "You find her?"

"No."

"Where'd you look?"

I tell him where I checked and explain where I found Silkie.

"A'ight, I'm gonna check the fields behind the barn. She'd probably stick to flat ground. You look down the driveway."

"Dobber, you don't think…" I can't even say it.

He shakes his head. "Peabody's got no beef with Kat." He wraps his arm around my shoulder and squeezes. "We'll find her."

"Okay." I hope he's right.

We head off in opposite directions. I scan the damper parts of the drive for footprints, but find nothing. Dobber's voice drifts through the trees as he calls for Granny. At the end of the drive, I turn and head back to the house, walking slower, checking the ditches on both sides for footprints or…whatever.

"Granny? Beethoven?"

A short distance off the road, there's a break in the hackberry hedge and a nearly invisible path. I'd have missed it, but the grass is flattened at the edge of the ditch like someone recently trampled it.

There's an old springhouse somewhere down that trail. I went there once with Granddaddy to get some of the peaches Granny'd put up. I jump the ditch and push through the prickly shrubs.

"Granny?"

I pick up a stick and hold it up in front of me in case of spider webs, but there aren't many. Someone's definitely walked the trail recently. I just hope it was Granny and not some hired thug from the mine.

"Beethoven?" I call.

There's an answering bark not far ahead. I start crashing through the bushes as fast as I can and nearly take a header into the old stone wall of the springhouse.

"Granny? Are you in there?"

I creep around to the front, skirting the moss-covered walls. The wood door is hanging by one hinge, and it groans as I push it open. Waves of cold, damp air hit me. I step inside, trying to get my eyes to adjust to the blackness. Something warm and furry jumps up on my legs, tail wagging.

"Good dog," I say, scratching Beethoven's head. "Granny?"

I hear a weak cough from the corner. In the dim light, I can barely make out a lump of something…maybe human…lying on the wet floor.

"Oh no." I kneel down and fumble around in the dark until I get my hands under her arms. Then I lift her up and drag her out into the sunshine. She moans a little when I lie her down on a flat spot covered with dry leaves. Her sweatpants are coated with mud, and her T-shirt and hair are damp enough to drip. We'll be lucky if she doesn't have pneumonia.

"Dobber!" I yell. "Dobber, I found her."

"Where you at?" he yells from way up the drive.

"Springhouse. East side of the driveway, near the road."

Granny shifts on the ground.

"Granny, wake up." I kneel down and take her hand. It's icy cold and covered in mud.

Her eyes are closed but moving fast like she's in REM sleep. I hear Dobber's running footsteps on the gravel.

"Look for a path on your left," I yell.

After a couple minutes, he's kneeling next to me. "We better get her back to the house."

"Do you think you can carry her?"

"Shoot, I bet she don't weigh nothing." He slides his arms under her and picks her up. "Like a lil' old bird. I'll get her to the driveway. You fetch the car."

I go first, holding the branches out of the way for them as best I can. Once we get out of the woods, I sprint for the house and drive straight back.

Dobber leans over the back of the El Camino holding Granny and lays her down in the bed. I lean over the side and brush some dirt off Granny's face.

Her eyes flutter open.

"Granny!"

She stares at the trees above, then focuses on our faces hovering over her. Her eyes dart from me to Dobber and back again.

"How are you feeling?" I ask.

Her eyes go wide and her chin starts to tremble. "Who the hell are you?"

THIRTY-FOUR

I sit next to Granny's bed on the chair I dragged in from the dining room. It's seven o'clock. She's sleeping now, but the last three hours have been hell. My body aches. My heart aches. Something deeper that I think might be my soul aches.

Dobber helped me bring Granny into the house and then left, saying he had something he had to do. Alone, I attempted to get her into a hot bath and then some dry clothes. Attempted being the key word.

She yelled at me the whole time. "Get outta my house!"

"Granny, it's me! Liberty!"

"I'ma call the po-lice!"

I wrestled her onto the bed and tried to pull off her wet T-shirt. "Stop that!" she screamed. "What're you doing?" Her cough started up again, and I struggled to pull off the sticking shirt while she hacked up copious amounts of lung guck and continued to scream.

"Granny, look at me! You have to get out of these wet clothes. You're freezing!"

"I don't know you!" she yelled. "Get outta my house."

I couldn't bear it. Finally, I just wrapped her in a robe and told her I would leave if she got under the covers. So, wet clothes, muddy shoes, and all, she climbed into bed. All I can do is hope that when she wakes up, she'll know who I am.

Staring at her dirty face, I call myself every horrible thing I can think of. How could I have left her? She needed me. Truly needed me. *And I left her.* I'm just like MFM.

I stare at the ceiling. "God, if you're up there, please let Granny wake up knowing me. I won't leave her alone again. I'll drop the whole thing with the mine and forget about Peabody. I'll quit school. Whatever it takes, I swear. Just please, please let her recognize me."

After ten minutes of promising God I'll take better care of Granny, there's a knock at the door. I assume it's Dobber, but when I look through the peephole, I see a woman.

I flip on the porch light and open the door.

"Can I help you?"

The woman is in her fifties, with short hair that's purplish brown. Her eyes are gray, just like Dobber's. "Quentin says you need a day nurse."

"I...yeah."

I step back as she pushes her way in. She closes the door behind her and takes a hard look around the room. "Kat got Medicaid?"

"Yes." She looks enough like Dobber that I think they must be related.

"You'll be the night nurse?" she asks after peering into the kitchen.

I nod, half-afraid if I open my mouth I'll scare her away. Though... she doesn't look easily scare-able.

Her inspection seems to be over, and she stands in front of me, half a head shorter but somehow still imposing. "I bill Medicaid directly."

I chance a question. "So you're related to Dobber?"

"He's my nephew."

We stare at each other a bit longer. I get the impression she'd rather not be here, that maybe she's heard about me and the mine. But she *is* here, which is more than I can say for the other two nurses I've called. Dobber must have really twisted her arm to get her to agree to this.

"Thank you." The words come out just like I want them to. Deeply grateful and maybe a little humble.

Her no-nonsense eyes soften a little. "I'll be back in the mornin'. About eight. I'll stay till three."

I think arriving at seven would be better, but she doesn't really invite any difference of opinion. "That's great. The hospice nurse, Mrs. Blanchard, comes on Wednesdays."

"I know Poppy Blanchard," she says. "I'll check in with her tomorrow."

She turns for the door, her giant pink purse bumping on her hip.

"Oh wait," I say. "I don't know your name."

"Trudy Philpott."

"Thank you, Mrs. Philpott."

Then she's gone and I'm alone with Granny. A muddy Granny who may or may not know me from Johnny Cash. Listening to Mrs. Philpott's car start up outside, I think she's not the sort of nurse who would put a patient in bed with muddy shoes. I need to fix that before she comes back tomorrow.

I run a warm bath, complete with bubbles, then go in to get Granny. She's still sleeping, so I take advantage of the situation and get her shoes and pants off before I wake her up.

She groans and pulls her legs up when the cold air hits them. Her skin is white like a fish's belly and crepey. It doesn't exactly surprise me that she's not wearing underwear. I do the laundry, and I know she only has three pairs. But it's upsetting. My grandmother naked is not something I've ever seen. I'm not sure how to deal with this. It all feels wrong.

Covering her legs with the blanket, I shake her awake.

"Granny?"

Her eyes open, blurry with sleep, struggling to focus on something.

They land on my face and I hope, hope like a dying wish, that she recognizes me.

"Liberty, darlin'. I got a terrible thirst."

My body relaxes, like at the end of a marathon, relieved to be known. I hand her a bottle of water from the nightstand, and she chugs the whole thing.

"You need to take a bath," I say. "You think you can manage?"

"I believe so."

But it's clear by the way she can't even fight her way out of the blankets that there's no way she'll get down the hall and into the tub alone.

"I'll help you." With my arm around her, I lift her to her feet.

"How come I got no britches on?"

"They were muddy."

"Muddy?" She tugs on the bottom of her T-shirt, trying to make it cover everything.

"You went for a walk to the springhouse." We have a little scrum at the door, both of us trying to get through at the same time.

"You're joshing me," she says. "I ain't been to the springhouse in ages."

At the bathroom door, I turn sideways so we can fit through together. "Hold on to the sink and I'll help you get your shirt off."

"I can take a bath by my own damn self," she says.

God, how I want that to be true. I want to close the door and go into the living room and work on my homework, happily oblivious to whatever cleansing rituals are going on in here. But she can't manage this by herself. Not anymore.

"Get in the tub," I say. She seems happy enough to sit down in the coverage of the bubbles, but when I try to take off her T-shirt, she hits the roof.

"Cut that out, dammit! I don't want you seeing me naked. You try that again and I'll rip your arms off and beat you with them."

"Trust me, I don't want to see you naked, you cranky old bat."

"Then get outta here."

I take a deep breath, lower my voice. "You can take a bath by yourself," I say. "I just want to help you get your T-shirt off."

"I told you, I can do it myself." She pulls at the hem of her shirt, now soaked from the bath water. After a few weak tugs, she looks up at me, half–rabid dog, half–wounded puppy. "This how it's gonna be, then?"

I bite my cheek. Count to three. "This is how it's gonna be."

She sets her jaw, raises her arms over her head, and waits. I lean over her and pull the T-shirt off, keeping my eyes on the soap dish, the shampoo bottle, my pink razor, anything but her. "Call me when you're ready to get out."

"I'll do no such thing."

"Fine. I'll just check back every thirty seconds."

"Goddamit! Aw'right! Just get out."

"Make sure you get behind your ears," I say.

She mumbles something I can't make out completely, but I'm pretty sure it ended in "bitch." I leave her to her bath and go start a load of laundry. I doubt Mrs. Philpott tolerates muddy sheets either.

THIRTY-FIVE

Granny's still sleeping when I leave for school the next morning. She wasn't happy when I told her about the nurse, claiming she was just "fine and dandy on my owns." But she settled to the idea a little when she found out it was Mrs. Philpott. I guess they know each other from church, though I don't remember ever seeing her there. In any case, I feel better leaving her knowing she won't be alone.

Last night, trying to fall asleep, I thought of a bunch of things I should have told Mrs. Philpott—important things (like how much medicine Granny can have and that the cancer seems to have spread to her brain) and unimportant things (like what shows she watches and how she likes her ramen with a little bit of the uncooked noodles crumbled on top like croutons.) So I got up and wrote Mrs. Philpott a note. Which turned into a three-page letter that took until 2:00 a.m. to finish.

I am exhausted.

I barely remember the drive to school, except to note that I'm nearly out of gas. I'll have to put some in tomorrow if I can find some money, or ride the bus the rest of the week, which I can't do, because Mrs. Philpott leaves at three o'clock, and the bus doesn't get me home until after four.

As I pull into the parking lot, I see Cole standing with a bunch of guys from the baseball team. We've done a pretty good job of avoiding each other. It must be a lot harder on Dobber. They were friends with all the same people, and it seems like Cole got them all in the divorce.

Still, Dobber hasn't complained. He sits with me at lunch. We talk about the mine and what we can do to get it shut down. At least, that's what we used to do.

"Forget it," I say as I shovel iceberg lettuce with a pound of faux bacon bits into my mouth. "I have to take care of Granny."

"You are," he says.

"Not very well." In my mind, I see her shivering in the muddy gloom of the springhouse.

"You're doing fine," Dobber says. "We just gotta come up with a way to get that mine shut."

"Why? So Peabody can burn some more of our farm? Keep your dad from getting a job? Keep *you* from getting a job?" I scrape around in my ranch dressing, looking for more cheese. "It's not worth it. Granny needs to be my number-one priority."

"Ain't she?" he asks. "Ain't that why you're doing this?"

"Getting the mine closed won't make a single bit of difference to Granny."

Dobber tilts his head to one side. "A difference?"

"Yes, Dobber. A difference. That's the point, isn't it?" I instantly regret snapping at him. "Sorry."

He nods at me for like an eon, then says, "Come with me after school. I got something to show you."

"I can't. I need to get home—"

"I'll get Aunt Trudy to stay with your granny a little longer today," he says. "There's something you need to see."

"Why?"

Dobber frowns and says, "Trust me."

I think of how many times Cole said that and the answer was always no. But with Dobber, it's different. "Fine, but if I run out of gas, you have to tow my car back to Granny's."

After school, I follow Dobber to his house, my eyes on the gas gauge as much as they're on the road. We pull up in front, and I realize I haven't been here since that time I talked to his dad. I hope Mr. Dobber's not here right now. I can't imagine he'd be too pleased to see me again, the uppity white girl.

Dobber opens the door for me and we go inside. He heads straight for the back of the trailer, where his dad's "workshop" is.

"Wait," I say. "Where are we going?"

"Back here," he says. "C'mon."

I hesitate.

"It's a'ight. Really."

I follow him, my heart speeding up with each step. What's he trying to show me?

At the end of the hall, Dobber pushes open a door and steps into a dark room. Someone inside groans.

"Daddy, y'okay?"

I hover at the doorway, feeling a little sick with dread. I don't think I want to see whatever's inside. Dobber flips on a light. My eyes go wide and I take two steps back.

There's a mattress on the floor, half-dressed in dirty sheets. A towel has been stapled over the only window. Overflowing ashtrays sit everywhere, and in the middle of it all is Dobber's dad, literally writhing on the bed.

He's wearing a pair of sweatpants and nothing else, tossing and turning. His ankle bracelet's rubbed the skin off his leg and his arms are covered in scabs, some oozing, some still bleeding. When he looks up at Dobber, his eyes are so bloodshot, I wonder if everything he sees is red.

Dobber kneels down next to him. "Hey, Daddy."

"Mm."

"How'd today go?"

"Weren't no day at the park," Mr. Dobber croaks.

I'm wondering why in the name of God Dobber wanted me to see this. Is it supposed to be some kind of incentive—stop Peabody before this happens to me?

"You need anything?" Dobber's voice is low and gentle.

"Naw, just shut that light."

"A'ight."

Dobber creeps out of the room, turning off the light before he closes the door. He says nothing as he passes me and walks into the kitchen. I follow him, waiting for some kind of explanation as to why I needed to see this.

He leans against the sink, crosses his arms, and stares at me. "You know what that was?"

"No idea."

Dobber smiles—not like his usual "charm the pants off you" smile. Something different. Something more like...I don't know... pride? "That's my dad getting clean."

My eyes go wide and flit back toward the door. "Oh." That's what getting clean looks like? "Wow. He looks..." I want to say he looks great, but the truth is anything but.

"Terrible, I know," Dobber says. "He can't eat. Got body cramps. Migraines. He sees things that ain't there, like spiders crawling all over him."

That explains all the scratches.

"The first day was the worst. I had to strap him down. But he ain't had no drugs or alcohol in four days."

"Dobber...that's...wow." It never occurred to me there was enough human left inside Mr. Dobber to remember what sober was like, much less attempt it.

"That there's your difference."

"My what?"

"Your difference." This isn't typical Dobber, the class clown Dobber. This is a Dobber I didn't know existed, serious and intense. In some ways, he reminds me of his dad…but in a better way. "You said taking on Peabody couldn't make no difference. But you already did."

"Look, if something I said made your dad want to get clean, that's awesome. But that doesn't mean anything else would change. That stupid mine is too woven into this town." The comparison strikes me out of the blue, grimly apropos. "Like a network of tiny tumors scattered all over somebody's lungs."

He starts to reach for me, then drops his hand. "Look, Liberty. I'm sorry about your granny. I like her a lot, but…" He winces like whatever he's about to say hurts him to think. "I'm sorry, but what can you do about her cancer?"

"Nothing," I say. "The doctor said there's nothing—"

"Exactly!" He grabs me by the shoulders and bends down, staring into my eyes. "There ain't *nothing* you can do about the *cancer.*"

I'm struggling to find the revelation he's clearly expecting me to have.

"So? Is'at what you're gonna do?" he asks. "*Nothing?*"

The way he says it, the word is loaded, the antithesis of nothing. It's all bad things—death, decay, torture—boiled together in a poisonous orange stew. And it makes sense, the analogy, because Peabody's brought all those things to this valley.

"You gonna sit back and do nothing?" he asks.

I want to explain again that taking care of Granny isn't nothing, that she's my first priority and fighting the mine isn't going to help her. But my blood is pulsing against my eardrums, screaming for action. My gut yearns for some kind of justice. My brain leaps at the possibility of bringing down Peabody. And the voice that speaks in the deepest part of my soul, that cannot be quieted, is telling me what I'm capable of. And, more importantly, what I'm not.

"No," I admit quietly. "I can't do *nothing*."

THIRTY-SIX

Mrs. Philpott is waiting on the porch when I finally get home. She's all business, handing me a neatly written page showing what Granny ate and when her meds were given. The nurse is clearly better at persuading her to eat than I am.

"I'll be back at eight tomorrow."

"Thanks," I say.

She stops halfway down the steps and turns to me. "I appreciated your letter."

"Oh, right." I can't believe it was only last night that I wrote it. Seems like a month ago. "Well, I thought you might need to know some of that stuff."

"It was very helpful."

I watch her get into her car. The driver's side sinks when her butt hits the seat. She nods at me before she backs out. I get the impression that she doesn't dislike me as much as she seemed to yesterday. Or maybe it's just that I'm less of a new girl now that she's waded through three pages of my heartfelt chicken scratch.

Granny's asleep, so I walk down the driveway to check the mail. There's a fat envelope from the EPA office addressed to me. Inside is the complaint form I requested two weeks ago. The timing is perfect, and thanks to my discovery about mine employees being involved in the water testing, I actually have a specific valid complaint to file.

I spend the evening ignoring my Mount Everest of homework and instead fill out the EPA forms. It's much more satisfying than conjugating Spanish verbs, since I get to imagine the look on Peabody's face when the EPA shows up asking questions. The idea of bringing him down almost eclipses the rays of worry about what he'll do once he sees my name at the bottom of the complaint. Almost.

After another ramen dinner, I fold the forms into an envelope and scrounge enough stamps from the desk in the dining room to get it back to the EPA. Granny mostly sleeps through it all. I get her to drink the nutrition shake Mrs. Philpott left for dinner, though I'm wondering if we have to pay her for it. I've seen them in the store and they're expensive. I can get seven ramens or three cans of soup for the same price as one shake. Around nine, I give Granny a Vicodin. She's asleep again before I get done writing down the dosage and the time.

I wander back to the living room, eat some dry ramen noodles that I fail to convince myself are potato chips, and fall asleep.

* * *

"Shouldn't you be at school?"

My eyes fly open, registering Mrs. Philpott's tan-colored panty hose and the fact that it's way too bright to be 6:30 a.m.

"Crap." I untangle myself from the couch and run for my bedroom.

Being an hour late for school, I can't very well catch the bus. So fifteen minutes later, I'm pumping two dollars worth of next week's grocery money into the El Camino, unshowered, unmakeupped, and unfed. That last part is making me really cranky.

I sign in at the office, but before I can get to English, I'm intercepted in the hall by Mr. Stoddard, the vice principal.

"Miss Briscoe, I've been meaning to talk to you about your absences."

"I'm on my way to class now," I say. "Can I make an appointment for later?"

"I just wanted to say, you are dangerously close to repeating this school year. If you miss two more days, the district policy says you will not be able to advance with your class."

I almost laugh. "My class." There's nothing about the Plurd County High junior class that's mine. But laughter probably wouldn't go over too well just now. "I'm sorry, sir. It's just that my granny's sick—"

"I'm familiar with your situation." Mr. Stoddard is a huge guy. As big as Dobber, with a soft voice and an accent that tells me he came from some wealthier part of the South. More Charleston than Chickfield. "I'm sorry about your grandmother, Miss Briscoe. But your schoolwork is important too. I'm sure she doesn't want you falling behind."

Sometimes adults baffle me. "You realize she's dying, right?"

His neck turns red as he nods just once.

"And I assume you know she has no one, *no one*, in the world besides me?"

Stoddard tugs on his collar. "I merely meant to impress upon you the seriousness of your situation. I suggest you go on to class now."

He's gone before I can express the seriousness of my pissed-off-ness. Really? He's threatening to fail me in the face of all the shit that's going on in my life?

Steaming, I walk down the hall to English and hand Mrs. Staley my tardy note. It's not till I'm sliding into my seat that I remember I didn't do any of my homework last night. The seriousness of my situation hits me pretty hard.

Two hours later, I've failed an English test and a Spanish quiz and I'm inhaling my lunch while trying to talk Dobber out of his salad.

It's not too hard since he got three extra pieces of garlic bread to go with his spaghetti and meat-ish sauce from his cafeteria aunt. Where does he get all these fairy god-aunts?

Even with the salad, I'm still hungry.

"I figured out a plan," Dobber says.

"Let's hear it."

Dobber leans close. I smell garlic and spices and, beneath that, soap. "We blow up that green pond. If it's gone, no more poison, right?"

I polish off the last piece of grated carrot and listen to my stomach growl. "I'm pretty sure that won't work."

"Why not?"

"One, you don't have any explosives. Two, you don't know anything about blowing stuff up. Three, if you did manage to blow it up, all the water from the pond would flood the valley. Four, poison contained *in the pond* is better than poison flowing in the creeks and rivers. Five—"

"A'ight. Plan B," he says. "We blow up the diggers."

"Are you listening?" I ask. "Same first two issues as before. Plus, he'll just buy new diggers."

"Plan C, we blow up his house."

"I'm not even going to dignify that with a response." I eye his tray hungrily. Maybe if I sneezed on Dobber's last piece of garlic bread, he'd let me have it.

"Fine. What's your plan, Einstein?"

"My plan's already underway." The last piece of toast disappears into Dobber's mouth and I sigh.

"Since when?"

"Since last night, when I filled out a formal complaint to the EPA."

"'Bout what? Orange water?"

"Nope. About mine employees taking the samples for the water quality test. Peabody shouldn't have had anything to do with those tests. It's a total conflict of interest." I watch Dobber chew and try to remember what it was like to feel full. I really can't remember. It must be a wonderful feeling. Euphoric, even.

Dobber frowns. "My daddy took them samples."

"I know. I saw his name on the report."

"You saying he faked 'em or something?"

"Well…no." This is dangerous territory. I don't want to piss off Dobber by pointing a finger at his dad, but I can't deny I've been wondering that very thing. "Just that it was inappropriate to have the mine involved at all."

"Hm. I reckon." His gray eyes unfocus and stare into the space between us. "That was right around the time he got fired, I think."

"It'll be a couple weeks before the complaint gets filed. So we just have to wait. Peabody'll think I'm actually leaving him alone, which should keep us all safe." The bell rings and I gather up my books. "At some point though, they'll send someone out to investigate. If they find Peabody did anything wrong, they'll fine him or better yet—" I turn and stop just short of running into Cole. His eye is still yellowish green and his face is so twisted and angry I completely forget what I was about to say.

He glares at me, then at Dobber. "Y'all just don't know when to stop, do ya?"

My heart pounds as I wonder how much of our conversation he heard. "I don't know what you're talking about."

His eyes narrow and his mouth presses together in an ugly smile, no dimples, no white teeth. "Don't say I didn't warn y'all."

THIRTY-SEVEN

I hear her whimper in my sleep, and my exhausted brain tries to work it into my dream. *It's just a puppy*, it says. *Go back to sleep.* But the second cry is louder, more insistent. My eyes pop open, dry and bleary, and I reach for my phone to check the time.

3:47 a.m.

It's the third time tonight. I crawl out of my comforter cocoon and stagger down the hallway toward her room, the bare-bulb night-light guiding my way. I can't sleep in my room anymore. Her sounds—the rattle of her wet breathing, the soft groans as the pain-killers wear down—keep me awake. Now I sleep on the couch… when she lets me sleep.

"Jamie?" She's been calling me MFM's name all afternoon. She's also been talking to my granddad and I kinda wonder if she can see him. Like, if he's come for her. Sad as it is, the idea gives me some peace.

"I'm here, Granny." I kneel next to her bed and feel in the dark for her hand. "What do you need?"

"It hurts." She tries to swallow, and I can tell her mouth is dry.

I turn on the lamp and check the chart on the nightstand. Thanks to Dr. Lang, morphine has replaced the Vicodin and seems to do a much better job of controlling Granny's pain. It's been about three hours since her last pill. The prescription says she can have one every four hours, but Mrs. Blanchard said, to keep her comfortable, what-ever it takes. So I shake out another pill, open one of the bottles of water on her nightstand, and slide in a straw.

"Sit up now." I lift her shoulders and she winces against the pain. I wedge a pillow behind her and she eases back, wheezing from the effort. "There we go."

"What is it Jamie?" she asks. "You wanna hear about them starfish again?"

I think of that old magazine clipping, still hanging over my bed. "Not right now, Granny. Open up." I slide a pill into her mouth.

She takes a sip of water and hands me the bottle. Her fingers are cold against mine. "Some ol' guy was walking on the beach and he come across a big pile of starfish, washed up and dying." Her chest heaves like she's running a marathon.

"Shh," I say. "Just rest now."

"They's a girl there, and she's chucking them starfish back in the water, one at a time."

I write down the time and the dose of the meds I just gave her, then get another blanket out of the closet and lay it across her as gently as I can. Taking her hand, I sit down on the chair next to the bed.

"Well, that man, he says, 'Honey, why you even bothering with them starfish? They's a million of 'em in that pile. You can't make no difference there.'"

"Hush now." Lying in mine, her hand is tiny, half the size it used to be, and I wonder how that happened. How I became the grown-up and she became the child. I stroke her papery skin, hoping the morphine kicks in soon so she can rest.

"But that lil' girl, she takes up another starfish." Granny's talking to the ceiling, like there's someone up there. I wonder what she can see that I can't. "She throws it way out in the waves. Then she turns to that man and says, 'It made a difference to that one.'"

Her voice is fading, and I sense the pain is too. It dawns on me that one of these times soon, she's going to fall asleep and not wake up. Tears fill my eyes. I don't bother biting my cheek or counting to three—there are too many waiting to take their place. "Get some rest, Granny."

I watch as her eyelids fall once, twice. Another minute and she's breathing softly through her open mouth, pain free for the moment. I coat her lips with Vaseline, then creep back to the couch. Heart aching, I snuggle into my blanket, hoping sleep will take me fast.

* * *

It doesn't.

Around five, I give up and creep out to the kitchen to make some tea. The dogs are whining, so I open the front door to let them out for their morning bathroom break. Then I check on Granny, who's still asleep thanks to the morphine. Hopefully, she'll sleep late and get some good rest.

I empty a bottle of water into a pot and set it on the stove to boil. Looking through the cabinet for a tea bag, I come across a single battered package of hot chocolate mix. Granny used to make it for me on cold mornings, before we milked the goats. It's probably five years old, but powder doesn't go bad, right? I'm willing to risk it.

As the steam fogs up the window, I stare out at the slowly lightening sky. All the things I ever cared about are getting ripped away from me: Iris, Granny, college.

I can't even imagine the future. Georgetown is a distant memory, as hazy as the trees through the steamy kitchen window. For a list-making planner like me, not being able to dream about the future is like having half your senses cut off. I don't know where I am or where I'm going…or why I'm even trying.

I understand why some people give up. You know…on life.

But the water's boiling and the hot chocolate mix has little marshmallows in it. And that's enough, at least for now.

I curl up on the couch under Granny's throw and watch the sky turn violet then periwinkle. I try to come up with names for every color because it's easier than coming up with a plan for the future. About the time I get to tangerine and coral, Granny calls from her room.

She runs her hand through her bed-head hair. "Did I wake you, sugarplum?"

"No. You want some tea?"

She pushes herself to sitting and pulls the edge of the blanket over her legs. "I believe I would, yes."

The dogs are scratching at the door, so I let them in on the way to the kitchen. Silkie and Beethoven rush to Granny's room for pets, but Goldie's not back yet. She's almost fourteen, and it's getting harder and harder for her to get up and down the steps. I wonder what's going to happen to her, to all the dogs, when Granny goes.

I don't think I can take pets to foster care.

After making her tea, I head for the shower and get ready for school. I have homework to finish on the bus, since I didn't get everything done last night. I hate the feeling of last-minute homework. It's so not me. I'm always the one who's overly prepared. I like *that* Liberty—pulled together, in control, charging toward a goal. This new Liberty—stressed out, powerless, drifting, hungry. Her I'm not so fond of.

I pull my still-damp hair into a ponytail and walk into the living room for my backpack, stopping by Granny's room to say good-bye.

I kiss her cheek and pull the fleece up around her. "Love you."

"Love you too. Have a good day."

Down the steps and into the yard, I'm halfway to the top of the drive before I see something strange. Over by the shed, in the old apple tree. It looks like when Granddad used to hang up the stuffed ghost Granny and I made for Halloween. I walk closer, trying to make sense of what I'm seeing, but it's not a ghost. There's no sheet. No round, Magic Marker eyes. I squint through the morning mist, trying to make it out.

And then I'm sucking air, backing away, wishing I hadn't seen. Because there is something hanging in the tree.

It's Goldie. Poor, sweet, patient old Goldie hanging from a noose.

And now I know what a rope dog is.

* * *

I run inside to get something to cut Goldie down with and look twice at the old shotgun Grandaddy used to keep the chicken coop safe. It's hanging on pegs over the doorway, and I'm pretty sure I saw some shells in the junk drawer in the kitchen. Thinking about Goldie, there's a part of me that yearns to take that gun and go after Peabody. Instead, still shaking, I pick up the phone and punch in 911. Then I take the butcher knife outside and cut Goldie down.

Her body's not even cold yet. My hand shakes with rage as I stroke her soft head and rub her ears the way she liked. There are no words for the depth of my hatred for Peabody.

Twenty minutes later, the cops show up, and we have a repeat of the morning the shed burned. Same police officers. Same pathetic attempt at evidence collection. Same faux concern for our well-being.

"Somebody's not happy with you," Officer Hanford says. "You got a pissed-off ex-boyfriend?"

I roll my eyes at him, but as soon as his back is turned, I'm biting my lip, remembering what Cole said yesterday.

Don't say I didn't warn y'all.

Could I be wrong? Is Cole warning me to keep my mouth shut?

I tell the cops to leave Goldie here so we can bury her; then

I head for the house to tell Granny what happened. Just thinking about that sweet, old dog, the way she'd sit next to you for hours, just waiting for a scratch or a pat, I have to stop and count to five three times before I get to Granny's room.

"I'm so sorry."

Tears run like rivers down the wrinkles carved in her cheeks. My heart cracks, right down the middle.

"I know you loved her. I did too." I can't help but feel responsible for everything that's happening. I didn't set the fire or kill Goldie, but whoever did certainly wasn't mad at Granny.

"You didn't do nothing," she says.

"I know but…" I stand at the end of her bed, my splinted finger tapping the footboard.

She's right. I haven't done anything. I haven't done anything to deserve this. *And*, I think grimly, *I haven't done anything about it. Nothing except bitch and moan and fill out a form.*

Granny's fussing with her blankets, barely strong enough to pull them up. She's gotten so weak, but inside, her body is still fighting. That's what I should be doing—fighting Peabody. He's going to start paying for his sins. Somehow. Someway.

"Do I smell bacon?" Granny asks.

I sigh. "No, no bacon." Goddam Peabody.

"Aw well."

"Mrs. Philpott will be here in a few minutes."

"She coming by for a visit?" Granny asks.

"Something like that."

"Aw'right, Jamie," she says. "I'll see you later."

I just head for the car. As much as I hate being called that woman's name, I don't see any sense in correcting Granny. Besides, I have starfish to save.

THIRTY-EIGHT

Thanks to this morning's extracurricular activities, I'm late *again*, which means I can't catch the bus. Which means either I have to stop for gas or hope the two dollars I pumped in yesterday will be enough to get me to school and back. As I hand more of next week's food money to the guy at the gas station, I wonder if I could just slide one of those Milky Ways into my sleeve. He seems to know what I'm thinking, though, and keeps his eyes on my hands the whole time. I guess I'm not the first hungry customer he's had.

Being behind in just about every class, I grab a granola bar from the cafeteria and spend my lunch period making up a math quiz and redoing some homework for Literature that I crapped out on last week. It's not until after school that I catch Dobber, at his locker, and tell him about Goldie.

"Damn! Rope dog?" He glances up the hallway to where Cole's standing with some of the baseball players. "I'm sorry, Liberty."

"Do you think he could have done it?" I ask.

"Shit, I dunno." Dobber slams his locker hard enough to shake the floor. "Me and Cole been buddies long as I can remember. He's a ass when it comes to girls, but I never known him to hurt anybody."

"He hurt me," I remind him.

"Well, that's true."

I watch Cole and his friends walk out into the sunshine toward the baseball field. I wish all I had to worry about this afternoon was running around in the sun, playing games.

Dobber bends down to pick up his cleat bag. "You think it was him?"

I stare through the glass doors a moment longer. "I think he told Peabody about the complaint I filed. But I can't believe he'd kill Goldie."

"Me either," he says. "What happens now? I mean, we was supposed to be safe for a while."

"I know." I take a deep breath. "But we're not. God only knows what he'll try next."

He hooks his bag over his shoulder and leans against the locker next to me. "What're we gonna do?"

"I'm not sure, but sitting around waiting isn't going to work." I look up into his eyes, crinkled around the edges with worry. "I think we have to take the offensive."

"Meaning?"

"I'm not sure yet, but—" I stop and stare at Ashleigh, who's just appeared behind Dobber. "What?"

She looks like whatever she's about to say tastes bitter. "I wanna help."

"What are you talking about?"

Her eyes roll skyward. "Don't play stupid. I know you're going after the mine. The whole town knows."

"Shut up!" I hiss.

Dobber grabs her by the arm and drags her into the empty chemistry lab. "What the hell, Ash. You trying to get us all killed?"

She glances at me. "Tempting as that is, I'd rather go after Peabody."

I try to put together the completely-not-fitting pieces of this puzzle. Ashleigh, who hates me, wants to help us take down the mine, which belongs to her uncle. "Is this a joke?"

Her brown eyes go narrow and evil. "No. You think you're the only person around here who cares?"

"No. But you're related to the mine owner! Or did you forget that?"

"If I could, I would." Her voice drops. "I hate that man. I wish he were dead."

"Is this a new development? Because I asked you for help weeks ago and you slammed a freaking steel door in my face."

"I didn't trust you then," she says.

"And now you do?"

"Don't get excited. It doesn't mean I like you," she says. "I still think you're a self-centered, self-righteous—"

"You know what? We don't need your help."

Dobber steps between us, completely eclipsing Ashleigh's thunderstorm face. "Hang on, Lib. Ashleigh's got a dog in this fight too."

"Why? Because her grandfather's sick?"

"Do you know who my granddad is?" Ashleigh asks from the other side of Mount Dobber.

"Why should I care?"

"Wilson Tanner."

Whoa. "Tanner's Peak Tanner?" I try to step around Dobber but he stays between us.

"Yes."

"What the hell was he thinking?" I ask. "Letting Peabody do that to the mountain?"

"Granddaddy didn't *let* him." Her voice drips acid. "Nobody'd seen a mountaintop removal mine before."

"And the words *mountaintop removal* didn't tip anyone off?"

"Fuck you," she says loudly. "You think you're so—"

"Keep your voice down," Dobber warns.

"Why are you even here?" I ask. "We don't want your—"

Dobber clamps a hand over my mouth and turns to Ashleigh. "If you wanna help, you're gonna have to explain it to her."

She crosses her arms and glares at Dobber. "It's none of her business."

"What's not?" I mumble through Dobber's hand.

Ashleigh chews her lip for a few seconds, clearly mulling her options. "I'm only saying this once, so try to keep up."

Curiosity is the only thing that keeps me from punching her in the face. Dobber drops his hand from my mouth.

"Uncle Robert laid Granddaddy off one year before he was eligible for retirement, so they didn't have to pay his pension. He had no income, no way to live. He scraped by on savings for a while, but that started running out pretty fast. Then, a few years ago, a new geological report came out showing a coal seam near the top of Tanner's Peak."

I see where this is going. "Peabody offered to buy the mountain and your granddad sold it because he needed money to live." The idea leaves me hollow. I know what desperation feels like and how principles can't always be afforded.

"Sold the mountain, yes, but not to Peabody. The deal was with Dragline, a new subsidiary of Peabody Mining. For half a million dollars, to be paid once the coal was removed."

"God, that's a lot of money."

"It would have been," Ashleigh says. "If Dragline hadn't declared bankruptcy the week after Granddaddy signed the papers."

"Wait. Bankrupt? So, he got…nothing?"

Ashleigh sighs. "The bank took control of Dragline's assets before we even heard they were bankrupt. Uncle Robert privately negotiated the purchase of everything Dragline owned from the bank, including Tanner's Peak, which they paid twenty thousand dollars for."

"Twenty thousand?" That's nothing. A person could only live a year or two on that.

"To be paid once all the coal is removed," Ashleigh adds, still standing on the other side of Dobber.

"When's that going to be?" I ask.

Ashleigh shrugs.

"Have they paid him anything?"

"Not a dime."

"Assholes," Dobber says.

"Have you talked to a lawyer?" I ask. "Because that's bullshit."

"We can't," Ashleigh says. "My daddy works for the mine."

"So?"

She gives Dobber an "I told you she wouldn't get it" look. "So who do you think's supporting my granddad now? And paying all his medical bills?"

"Oh," I say, understanding.

"Right. If any of us even look cross-eyed at Uncle Robert, Daddy'll get fired and none of us will eat."

Their situation is a house of cards. A house of cards in a windstorm.

"I'm not asking to be your friend," Ashleigh says. "But...Dobber get out of the way." She punches and pokes him until he steps aside. "I want that man out of our lives."

"And you don't think joining us is going to get your dad fired?" I ask.

"Well, I don't figure you're going to send Uncle Robert a card listing ever'body's names, right?"

"No, but we want to get the mine *shut down*. What's going to happen to your dad's job then?"

"Shut down, he gets unemployment and eventually another job," Ashleigh says. "Fired, he gets nothing but a black mark against him."

"How do we know you're not a spy," I say. "Maybe you're the one who's been watching us. Maybe 'Uncle Robert' put you up to this, to see what our next move is."

"Look," she says. "I don't like you and you don't like me and that's fine. I'm not asking to share your hopes and dreams or borrow your clothes." She gives me a resigned frown. "But you're the only person who's ever even *talked* about taking on the mine. And I'm sick of being a victim."

I know what she's feeling. I know it like I know the taste of salt. It's anger and frustration and pain and loss, and if we could see it, I bet it'd be bright orange. So I get where she's coming from. And I guess, in my gut, I know I can trust her. If Peabody wanted someone to get close to me, he'd find somebody way nicer than Ashleigh.

"It's like any other team, Lib," Dobber says. "You ain't gotta like ever'body on it."

"Fine. Dobber's house. Tonight. Seven o'clock."

She nods at me, but stops short of saying anything. Like *thank you*.

"This'll be interesting," Dobber says.

I watch her walk out the door into the hall. "It'll be fine," I say. "If I have to kill her, we can make it look like Peabody did it."

* * *

Mrs. Philpott's car is gone when I get home. She's supposed to stay and give me a report on Granny's day, so I'm a little irritated as I rush inside. Dropping my stuff at the door, I'm halfway down the hallway before I hear the voices.

One is Granny, laughing softly.

"Liberty?" the other voice calls. "Is that you?"

I freeze in place as my stomach heaves and the dark hallway seems to tilt a little.

She's supposed to be in prison.

I stare toward Granny's door as a shadow moves across the floor.
Why isn't she in prison?

My former mother steps into the hall.

"What are you doing here?" I ask none too kindly.

"Good lawyers," she says. "They compiled enough evidence to prove I wasn't involved in the bombing. Everything was settled out of court, so no trial." Her face is thinner; she's lost some weight. It makes her look younger, even more like my sister than my mom. My former mom. Other than that, she's exactly the same. "I was released yesterday. And just in time too. Looks like you guys could use a little help around here."

"Help? From you?" I snort.

"Liberty…" The smile she gives me is so patronizing, I have to link my hands together to keep from punching her. "The dogs are filthy. There's dust everywhere. For heaven's sake, there's not even any food in the house. It's pretty clear you need some help."

Oh. My. God.

"Get out," I say.

"What?"

"You have no…no fucking idea!"

She reaches forward then drops her arms back to her sides, like she can't decide whether or not to touch me. "Look, sweetie, I know we have some things to patch up."

"No," I say. "We don't. We have nothing to patch up. I don't have a mother. We don't have a relationship. You and I are strangers. And I don't want you here."

"How can you say that?" she says with her annoying, infinite calmness. "You're my everything. All these years, remember? It's just been you and me against the world."

"Is that a joke?"

"Of course not." Her perfectly tweezed eyebrows draw together in confusion and I wonder if she groomed them in prison or if she stopped on the way here to pretty herself up. It pisses me off even more. I'm dealing with cancer and dead dogs. She's fixing her face. "Look, Lib, I'm sorry I wasn't here for this." She tilts her head toward Granny's door. "But I'm here now. And I'm going to make things right."

"You *can't* make this right." I yell. "And I don't need your help. You're not my mom. Not anymore." The last thing I hear before I slam the front door behind me is Granny coughing.

* * *

I spend the rest of the afternoon sitting at the top of the holler, throwing sticks for Silkie and Beethoven, and pulling some early spring ticks out of their fur. From here, I can see the roof of the house and the chimney. MFM must have put extra wood on the fire because the chimney is smoking more than usual. Not so much that I worry it's something else, just enough that I worry we're going to run out of wood. Typical MFM. Instant gratification with no regard for tomorrow.

I wish she were still in prison.

Instead, I'll have to figure out some way to get through these next few weeks or months. It's not like I can tell MFM she can't stay here. First of all, it's Granny's house, and I'm sure she's not going to kick her own daughter out. Second, as much as I loathe the idea of MFM being here, I know she should be. Granny's dying. These are the last days either of us will have with her.

Thinking back to the doctor's office and how much I wanted someone else with us, I try to translate that to MFM. Try to be glad she's here or at least be grateful I don't have to go through this all on my own. But the truth is I've never felt any support from her. Just disappointment. And need. And more disappointment.

It's hard for me to see her as anything other than one of these ticks, trying to suck something out of me when I've got nothing left to give.

THIRTY-NINE

Ashleigh's car is already at Dobber's when I arrive. He's set the table with some stacks of paper and a few pens. His dad is sitting on one side dressed in a clean T-shirt, shaved, and showered. The change is remarkable. For the first time, I see he has Dobber's eyes and nose and is actually kinda good-looking, for an old guy.

"Well, we know why we're here, so we might as well get started," I say. "Getting the mine shut down is our goal. I've filled out the paperwork the EPA sent me to lodge a formal complaint. And I've written to a nonprofit group that helps communities dealing with mountaintop removal mines. Both of those are long shots though. And until we have something we can hold over Peabody's head as a bargaining chip, we're not safe. So…ideas?" I look around the table at blank faces.

Ashleigh levels her round brown eyes at me. "Are you telling me you don't even have a plan?"

"Do you?" I counter.

She screws up her face into something like disgust. "I'm not the one who's been working on this for a solid month."

"Shut up, Ash," Dobber says.

"You shut up," she says, but then settles into silence.

Mr. Dobber watches it all without saying a word.

"We know Peabody bribed the county commissioners to approve the expansion of the mine," I say. "Maybe the commissioners also know the mine is causing these health issues, and Peabody's bribing them to keep quiet."

"So what if he is?" Ashleigh says. "It's not like they're going to tell us."

"There may be documentation of it somewhere," I say, looking around the table. Dobber shakes his head. His dad frowns, toying with the stack of paper.

"*So what?*" Ashleigh says again. "All that's gonna do is maybe get the county commissioners fired. We need to get rid of Peabody."

"Looks like we're back to blowing stuff up, then," Dobber says.

I groan. "To recap ad nauseam: we have no explosives, no know-how, and no viable target."

"That ain't necessarily true," Dobber says. "I came on some new information recently that you might be interested in."

I don't like his smile. "What are you saying?"

Dobber looks at his father. "You wanna tell her?"

"I worked explosives for the mine." His voice is quiet, serious. "Did fifteen years on a blast crew before I got a office job."

"And," Dobber says, a Christmas-morning grin on his face, "you might have forgotten to give back one of the keys to the explosives shed, am I right?"

Dobber's dad nods.

My stomach drops. "Explosives?"

"Just setting there, waiting on us," Dobber says. "Now all we got to do is fix on a target."

I don't like the direction this is going. At all. "Look, I just want to put some pressure on Peabody, to do the right thing: shut down the mine so people stop getting sick. I don't want to hurt anybody. I don't want to destroy property. I don't want to blow anything up."

"What's your plan, then?" Ashleigh asks. "So far, everything you've come up with *doesn't* work." She nods at Dobber. "I like his idea. Make Uncle Robert suffer for the way he's been hurting everybody else."

"Amen to that." Dobber turns to me. "He deserves this, Lib. He brought it on hisself."

"Yes, but there are legal ways to do this," I say.

Mr. Dobber frowns again.

Dobber reaches across the table and covers my fingers with his hand. "Way I see it, he's hurting a whole lotta people. We can stop that by hurting just one." His argument sounds reasonable, but it still feels so wrong. "If we don't do something, more people are gonna get sick. More people are gonna die."

I continue the list in my head—more birth defects, more mutant fish, more poor people starving because they can't eat off the land anymore. I know it's true, but...

"He's basically getting away with murder," Ashleigh says.

Dobber slaps the table. "He's breaking the law, Lib."

"Exactly," I say. "Which means there's a legal way to—"

"Then what is it? Huh?" Ashleigh's in my face, angry and yelling. "Even if he *is* guilty of something, who's gonna arrest him? 'Cause it ain't gonna be Ebbottsville's finest."

"That's the God's honest truth," Mr. Dobber says quietly. "They been on the Peabody payroll since that very first piece a coal come out the ground."

"That's why we need proof—"

"There ain't none!" Dobber's cheeks are turning red. "Don't you see? There ain't no proof. And even if there was, we can't get to it."

"Other people have to know," I say. "Maybe we can get some other people to come forward."

"So their dogs can get killed?" Dobber asks. "Or their sheds burned down. Or their dad fired."

"Well, no. But if enough people come together on this…" I trail off into silence. Even I can see there are too many roadblocks on my route. Getting people united against Peabody…it's an impossibility. Most people aren't like Dobber and me, with families already sick and dying, out of work, ruined by the mine. Most people have things to lose. Things more important than a shed.

"I say we blow up his house," Dobber says.

"What?" My eyes are saucers.

"No!" Ashleigh says. "That'll hurt Aunt Karin."

"Have you all lost your mind?" I say.

Nobody seems to hear me.

"His car, then," says Dobber.

"Perfect," Ashleigh says. "He loves that stupid car."

"Stop. Stop this now," I say, though I have a sick feeling that it's totally out of my control. Is this what happened with MFM? Did the cause she believed in so much just get beyond her control?

My squirming, empty stomach is trying to heave itself out. Ashleigh's going over her uncle's schedule and trying to pinpoint the best time for an attack. Dobber's drawing a crude map and making circles as she talks. But his dad's just sitting in his chair, staring at me, eyes narrowed. I have no idea what he's thinking.

"Daddy, if we're grabbing the explosives tonight, we better go. You ready?"

Mr. Dobber stands up stiffly, wincing, and I am reminded that he's not well. "Reckon so."

"Please," I say to him. "Please don't do this."

Dobber puts his hands on my shoulders. "Lib, we got this. Ever'thing's gonna be fine."

"No." My voice is nearly hysterical. "It won't be fine. This is wrong."

"Trust me, a'ight?" He hugs me fast then grabs his keys and heads outside. His dad follows, limping a little and frowning the whole way.

I'm left alone with Ashleigh—who's looking a little less sure now that things are in motion—and the feeling that something is about to go terribly, terribly wrong.

FORTY

Back at Granny's, I attempt to do homework but end up staring at my calculus book, trying to envision what's happening at the mine right now, and getting a good start on an ulcer.

"Anything I can help with?" MFM asks.

"No."

"Calculus, huh?"

I look up at her, frowning. "What do you want?"

"I just…" She looks around, waves her hands, shrugs. "I don't know what to do with myself."

"Not my problem." I go back to calculus.

"I'm not used to just sitting around the house."

That's because you were never home, I think.

She looks down the hall, to the room where Granny's sleeping fitfully. The morphine's not quite enough to dull the pain for very long, and we can hear her soft groans. "I wish I could do something."

"You could go blow something up." I meant it as a dig, but now that I've said it, I kinda like the idea. I'd much rather see *her* in prison than Dobber or his dad. "That's the kind of stuff you do, right? Only this time, you can help people you care about for a change, instead of complete strangers."

She gives me an exasperated look. "That's not funny."

"I wasn't joking," I mutter as she wanders off to take a bath. Minutes later, opera music from her iPod floats out of the bathroom, accompanied by her horrible singing. Apparently tone-deafness is genetic.

I plug my ears against the sound, debating what to do. My moral pendulum is swinging between (a) praying the Dobbers get safely out of the mine with the explosives, and (b) calling the cops and getting them arrested before they can go through with their plan. I'm wondering if I'll be considered an accomplice when I hear a rattle at the front door.

I look up just in time to see it swing open, and before I can scream, Dobber and his dad rush through.

I'm relieved and pissed all in the same heartbeat. Then I see Dobber's face. His eye is purple and swollen nearly shut. His right hand is bleeding, and he's holding his left on the back of his head. They're both red-faced, and Mr. Dobber's breathing like there's not enough oxygen in the world.

"What happened?"

"They caught us. Leaving the mine." Dobber eases himself gently onto the couch. Mr. Dobber stands by the door. "Two guards."

I tilt Dobber's face toward the light. "They did this?" His black eye makes the one I gave Cole look like a tiny bruise.

"I let 'em catch me so Daddy could get the explosives to the car."

My heart sinks. "You got the explosives?"

Dobber's smile is grotesque, stretched out of place by the swelling in his cheek and his split lip. "Damn straight."

"Where are they?" I ask casually. I'll take them and hide them or cut them up into pieces or—

"Someplace safe."

Damn. Dobber's smarter than I give him credit for. "Please don't do this."

"Lib, I know you want to do this all legal. But Peabody lives outside the law. He buys cops, bribes the county, kills dogs. You seen it. He don't follow nobody's rules."

"That doesn't mean we have to stoop to his level," I argue. The opera music floats on the air like a sound track. "We have to be better than him. Otherwise, we're the same."

He just shakes his head. "You gotta fight fire with fire."

I'm saved the effort of replying by a loud knock on the door. Mr. Dobber jumps a foot before turning to check the peephole. "Looks like trouble," he says.

He opens the door a crack. Cole pushes his way in and slams it shut.

"What are *you* doing here?" Dobber asks.

Cole's hair is drenched with sweat like he ran all the way from town. His black eye is nearly gone, but the dark circles under his eyes are just as bad. It looks like he hasn't slept in days. "They're coming."

"Who's coming?" I ask.

"Peabody's guys," he says. "They know you broke into the mine."

"They're coming *here*?" I think about Granny. And stupid MFM, completely oblivious in her opera-laced bath.

"Not here," Cole says. "They're headed to the Dobber's."

"How do you know?" I ask.

"Are they watching this place?" Dobber interrupts.

"Not sure," Cole says. "But they'll check here eventually, and your car out front's a dead giveaway. Y'all gotta get out of here."

"Leave Liberty and her granny here alone?" Dobber scowls, wincing when his lip opens up again.

I never got a chance to tell Dobber about MFM's arrival. They don't even know she's here.

"They're not after Liberty. They're after you. Dobber…" Cole stares him in the eye. "They have guns."

My mouth drops open. This can't be happening. No. No way.

The ominous chanting of "O Fortuna" floats down the hall.

Mr. Dobber steps forward and presses something into Cole's hand. "Hide it. Wreck it. Whatever. Just get it off this property. I don't want nothing happenin' to Kat 'cause of us."

Cole looks at his palm, where the keys to Dobber's car lay. He closes his fingers around them and nods. Somehow, the sacrifice of Dobber's car makes it all real. People are coming to kill Dobber and his dad. To shoot them, in cold blood. All because of some black rocks that burn nice.

"You better go," Dobber says. "If they find you here, your daddy won't have that job no more."

"I don't care." Cole heads for the door. "I'm sick of this shit."

"Hey, man," Dobber says. Cole stops, his hand on the doorknob. "Thanks."

Cole looks like he's about to tear up, but instead he just says, "Don't let them get you, Dob." Then he heads out into the night.

Dobber looks at his dad. "We better go too."

"Go?" I say. "You can't go. They'll find you."

"More likely to find us if we stay," says Dobber.

"And y'all ain't safe if we're here," Mr. Dobber adds. He takes some papers out of his coat pocket and hands them to me. "These are for you."

"You can't leave!" I understand how them being here puts us in danger, but the idea of not having Dobber around…I don't know. I can't bear it. It's like the last straw. The one thing I refuse to give up.

"Lib, don't be stupid," Dobber says. "Even if my car ain't here, they're gonna be watching the house."

"I know that, but…but…" I'm racking my brain for some way to keep Dobber near. To keep him safe. That's when it hits me. "The springhouse!"

"What about it?"

"You can stay there," I say. "Nobody knows it's there except us."

Mr. Dobber's rubbing his chin. "Might be good to hole up some-wheres. We try to run, we'll be out in the open."

"Exactly," I say. "Hole up. Disappear. Let Peabody think you left town." My brain unhelpfully points out that they can't live in a rock hut forever, but I can't think about that right now. Right now, I just want to have Dobber here. To know he's safe.

I grab some old quilts from the hall closet. After turning off the lights, we head out the back door. Mr. Dobber creeps around the house to make sure no one's lurking before we leave.

I feel like I've fallen into an old Wild West show. Blowing people up. Shooting them. "They wouldn't have actually killed you, right?"

"Why not?" Dobber's crouched next to me beside the back porch. "Daddy's a meth addict and I ain't nothing special. Who's gonna care?"

I feel a little sick when I realize he's right. Nobody in Ebbottsville would be too sad to see them gone. Not Mr. Dobber, anyway.

"Besides, Peabody's killing people all the time," Dobber says. "That mine's like a weapon of mass destruction."

That hits me, hard. It's a perfect analogy. I stare into the dark, listening and thinking how much like a terrorist attack that poisonous water is.

"Only one way to stop a weapon like that," Dobber says.

"What's that?"

"Kill the terrorist."

FORTY-ONE

Midnight. I lie on the couch and stare at the ceiling. Nothing makes sense anymore.

I hate Peabody. Hate him for what he's done to Granny, to the people, and to the land. I can see how him being dead would be a good thing for this valley. But I can't wish that on anybody, not even him.

But Dobber and his dad are sleeping in our springhouse right now because Peabody's trying to kill them. That's just as wrong. Maybe wronger. If I were some kind of God, dealing out death and judgment, I'd say the Dobbers deserve to live a lot more than Robert Peabody.

Granny groans in the other room. The door on MFR (my former room) is closed, so I doubt MFM can hear her. I creep down the hall and peek in. Granny's trying to get the lid off a bottle of water.

I cross the room quietly. "Let me help you."

"Thank you, sugarplum."

I twist off the top and hand it back to her.

She takes a drink and rests the bottle next to her. "You're up awful late. Something wrong?"

Her eyelids are already falling. As much as I'd like to tell her everything, she'd be asleep before I was halfway through. "Nothing," I say.

"She loves you," she says. "Y'all's just too much alike."

She drifts off as I realize she's talking about MFM.

"You're wrong," I say. "On both counts."

I pull the covers up over her arms and watch her face. Because of the cancer, she's aged so fast, but I can see traces of MFM's face in hers still. And I can see what MFM will look like when she's old. Me too, actually. Like Granny says, we're soup from the same pot.

As much as I hate to admit it, there's some truth to that. All three of us are stubborn and outspoken. We're fighters to the death, whether it's a political argument or a Clue game. And if I'm honest with myself, my quest for fairness and justice is just as strong as my mom's. My former mom's, I mean.

The difference is I'd never forget I had a kid to take care of. I'd never ignore my responsibilities just to take up some banner for strangers in China. And I'd never get involved with a political bombing and end up in prison.

Oh no. Never.

And there it is. The sickening, disgusting proof to what Granny keeps saying. We *are* alike, my mother and I. Sure, I'm fighting for Granny and people I know instead of Chinese workers I've never met or seen. And I realize MFM never intended to hurt anyone, just to get those government officials to hear what she was saying. But for whatever reason, we both ended up behind a bomb.

I stare out the window at the blackness beyond. My mother's face stares back in my reflection. I'm so much like her, people think we're sisters. *Too much alike*, Granny said. *She sounds a lot like you*, Dobber said. I know they're right. I can see it, literally, in the mirror. But I don't want to be her. I don't want to make her mistakes. Watching myself in the window, I whisper one quiet question to the night.

"How am I different?"

The reflection offers no answers and Granny's asleep, so I wander back to the living room and sink onto the lounge chair. Something crinkles when I hit the seat. Reaching under me, I pull out the stack of papers Mr. Dobber handed me. In the rush to get to the springhouse, I'd forgotten about them.

Curious, I turn on the lamp and stare at the first page. I know what it is immediately. I've seen it before, or at least one like it. It's a water quality report. This particular one is for a property on Highway 52, near the Dobbers' house, but there must be forty reports in the stack.

I get on the floor and spread them all out, looking for Granny's address. Once I find it, I grab my copy from my backpack and lay them next to each other. They're mostly identical: same sample location, same date and time, same collector. But they differ in one major way:

The levels of chemicals in the water are totally different.

Digging through my backpack again, I find the notes I made about safe limits for drinking water. Looking over the new report, I see the levels in every single category—coliform bacteria, pH, iron, sulfate sulfur, chloride, etc.—are outside the acceptable range.

My hand starts to shake. The paper flutters to the floor and I pick up another. And another. Every report I look at shows unsafe drinking water.

Finally, I have the answers I was looking for.

Granny's well water is poison. The testing report that was paid for by the mine said it was safe. Because of that, she drank it. Now she's dying.

Somebody, somewhere falsified that report. And the proof is sitting right here in front of me. Like a bomb just waiting to go off.

FORTY-TWO

I call Iris at the ungodly hour of 4:00 a.m. As I wait for her to pick up, I look over my plan. Four hours of plotting, and I'm pretty sure I've found a way to take down Peabody without killing anyone or turning into my mother.

"Liberty?"

I can tell from Iris's voice she's already up. Not surprising. Iris sleeps about five hours a night.

"I need your help." I put the last month into a nutshell. Thankfully, Iris is a journalist, with an ear for the story.

"A mine owner falsifying docs? The AP would be all over that. Mountaintop removal is a powder keg on the Hill."

"I'm going to overnight a copy of the reports to you," I say. "You'll have them tomorrow."

"Okay," Iris says. "But what exactly do you want me to do with them?"

"Keep them safe," I say. "I have a few more details to work out, but I'll be in touch."

"Roger that," she says. "Are you okay?"

"You know, I actually think I might be."

* * *

"Wake up, sleepyheads," I call from outside the springhouse. There's some shuffling and groaning inside; then Dobber unfolds his six-and-a-half feet through the tiny wooden door. "Good night?"

His hair is sticking straight up, and he has a zipper mark down one cheek. "I'm alive," he says. "Cold but alive."

"Thank God." Things seem less frightening in the light of day, but I remember they still have a target on their backs. "We have a new plan."

"*New* plan?" Dobber frowns and starts shaking his head.

"We're not bombing anything," I say.

"But—"

"No." My chin juts out in my "don't eff with me" pose. "No bombs."

Mr. Dobber shuffles to the door and leans against the frame. "You look at them papers?"

"I did. You realize what they are?"

He nods. "I was in charge of coordinating them water tests for the mine," he says. "When the results came, Peabody told me to pull out any of 'em that didn't meet the limits and put 'em on his desk. So I did."

"Then what happened?"

"Nothing. I thought he was gonna make it right for them people whose wells was bad." He steps out into the sunlight and rubs his arms.

"But he didn't?"

"Naw." He clears his throat and spits in the dirt. "I knew some of them folks and when their reports come from the county, it said their wells was fine. Even though I seen the report that said clear as day the water weren't no good."

"What did you do?"

"I went to the county. Told 'em the testing company said some people's water wasn't safe to drink." For a moment, the only sounds are squirrels rustling through the leaves. Dobber and I wait silently for him to continue. I can tell he's never heard this story either. "Next thing I know, I got three broken ribs, two less teeth, and no job."

"You've kept those reports all this time?" I ask.

"Naw. I wrote the test company and asked for new copies last week. It occurred to me Mr. Peabody might not'a let them know about my unfortunate job loss." His smile is peppered with black and missing teeth—scars from his meth addiction that'll last a lifetime. Which reminds me…

"Hey." I stare at Mr. Dobber's ankle. "No bracelet?"

"My sentence was up two days ago."

"Good timing, huh?" Dobber slaps him on the back. His dad winces and puts a hand to his chest, and I'm reminded again that he still has cancer. And now, no meth to combat the pain. "Lib, you gonna tell us this plan or not?"

"Listen fast," I say, glancing at my watch. "I need to get to school and fill Ashleigh in on the new plan. We really need her." Those words stick a little in my throat.

I go through everything like I did with Iris this morning, and answer the same questions all over again.

At the end, Dobber's smiling. "I had my heart set on blowing something up, but I reckon this'll work too."

There's a crashing in the bushes near the driveway, and we all freeze. My blood seems to stop in my veins as I watch the shrubs swaying as someone pushes through them. Mr. Dobber stoops down and quietly wraps his hand around a dead branch. Dobber's made fists already. I'm looking around for a weapon when a woman's voice calls, "Liberty? Are you in there?"

MFM.

Dobber heaves an enormous sigh, and his dad drops the branch. I walk around the corner of the springhouse, ready to bitch her out for everything from yelling my name to following me around to her choice in music last night. But she interrupts me, and what she says drives every single one of those thoughts out of my head.

"Liberty." She's out of breath and her eyes are full of tears. "We need to call the hospice nurse. It's time."

FORTY-THREE

I'm sitting in the rocker next to Granny's bed. The windows are open and the faded, flowered curtains are blowing in the breeze. The air smells green—no flower blossom perfume, just leaf buds, wet grass, and damp moss. The notebook with my all-important plan is lying forgotten in the corner.

Granny's dying.

Mrs. Blanchard has been here since this morning. She says Granny's kidneys have shut down, and it won't be long now. There's a morphine drip to keep her comfortable. So now we wait.

MFM is next to me perched on the edge of Granny's bed. Occasionally, she leaves the room, unable to contain her shaking sobs. I guess I've had more time to prepare for this. I've watched it coming for months. Watched Granny sink into herself. Grow smaller. Diminish.

I realize if MFM hadn't gotten arrested, I never would have come here. Granny would have passed away alone. We would have driven down for the funeral, and I wouldn't have had these months with her. These terrible, hard, confusing, agonizing, precious, priceless few months. It scares me to think I almost missed out on them.

I should be working on our plan—there's a meeting to schedule, documents to be sent, people to visit, but none of it matters right now. The whole reason for doing it all is lying in front of me, tiny and thin, a little stick woman with Jolly Rancher hair.

"Liberty?" Granny's mind's been really clear for the last few hours. She and MFM have been talking about old times.

I squeeze her hand. "I'm right here."

"I want you to promise me…" Her blue eyes glare lasers at me. It's the only part of her that hasn't faded. "When I'm gone, this house is goin' to you."

"Granny, stop. Don't talk like that."

"Don't bullshit me. We ain't got the luxury of pretending this ain't happening."

She's right, of course, and I nod.

"You sell the house, you hear? Use that money for your college."

"Okay."

"And I don't mean no community college. I mean Georgetown."

"Sure, Granny. If I get in." She has no idea I'm going to flunk this year, which means the end of my chances at pretty much any major college.

MFM's listening quietly to all this, and I wonder if she even knew about Georgetown. If she ever wondered at all about any of my dreams.

"The second thing," Granny says. "Go back to Worshington, DC, and finish your schooling up there."

I glance at MFM. We haven't talked about what happens next, after Granny's gone, when there's no reason for MFM to stay here and nowhere else for me to go. But I feel like this moment, the *now*, while I have hold of Granny's warm hand, is way more important than the later. Nothing matters except this heartbeat and the next, and as many more as she has.

"We'll worry about that later," I say.

"Lord, girl. Look at yourself. You don't belong here."

"Stop saying that."

"Your dreams got nothing to do with mining or farming or anything else you can find 'round here. You gotta chase down your happy, find where it lives."

"I don't know where my happy lives." My throat tightens at the idea of having to find my happy alone. "I don't even know where to look."

"Look inside." Her voice is softer. Her eyes close, then open, then close.

"Granny!"

"I'm righ'chere."

"Please don't leave me." The inside of my cheek is bleeding as I count to five. To ten. To fifty.

"You'll be awright." Her eyes stay closed. "Y'all got each other. That's what counts."

She sighs. Then nothing. No rise and fall of her chest. No more words. No squeeze of my hand. She's gone.

And so am I. Down the hall, out the front door, with MFM calling after me. I'm not even sure where I'm going until the ground tilts upward and I realize I'm on the ridge trail, climbing up through the rhododendron. The world is sparkly through my tears, like an impressionist painting. At the top of the hill, I collapse onto the ground, the red mud soaking through my jeans.

Then I stop counting and let the tears fall.

FORTY-FOUR

The house feels like an empty shell. An empty shell filled with food. Women started coming at breakfast this morning with casseroles, ham biscuits, and muffins. There's enough on the table to feed an army already, but now the lunches are starting to arrive. Most of the women are from Granny's church, but a few—my Spanish teacher, Mrs. Philpott—are people I know too.

After months of near starvation, we have all this gorgeous food, and I can't eat a thing.

"Hey."

I turn to see Cole standing in the doorway.

"Mind if I come in?"

I shrug. After everything that's happened, being pissed off at Cole just seems like a waste of energy.

"I'm really sorry about your granny."

I nod. I've found it's easier not to cry if I don't open my mouth.

"She was something special."

"Yeah. I know." I walk past him, and he follows me out onto the porch. I stare across the yard, where Myrna Lattimer's getting out of her car with a basket of food. Even from here, I can see her eyes are red. It comforts me a little to know I'm not the only one missing Granny.

"Lib, I wanted to say…I'm really sorry. I was wrong."

Leaning against the railing, I look down at the green splint on my finger. Punching Cole seems to have happened in a different lifetime.

To a different person. It doesn't even matter anymore. "Whatever," I say. "It doesn't hurt much now."

"No, I mean for…" He nods toward the blackened scraps of the shed.

"Wait…" I look from the shed to him, and my blood starts to pound in my ears. "You did that?"

"Peabody's orders." His eyes stay locked on the shed.

"And the spying, the note in my locker?"

He takes a deep breath and nods, blowing it out. "All of it. And I'm sorry. It was—"

My heart stutters. "Goldie? Did you—"

"No!" His eyes close for just a second; then he looks at me. "That wasn't me."

"But you knew it was going to happen!"

"It's not like I coulda stopped it," he says. "If Peabody wants something done, it gets done."

"You could have told me! We could have hidden Goldie. You could have…something. Anything!" I make a fist with my left hand, seriously considering punching him again. But I think for a second instead. "You warned the Dobbers."

"Yeah…" He rubs the back of his neck. "When Peabody called us in and started handing out guns—damn. That was…Well, I realized then you were right. 'Bout him not being a good guy."

It staggers me that Peabody had to resort to murder before Cole could see what a snake he is. And half the town still can't see it. It makes me sick to think about it. Sick and tired. So very, very tired. "Better late than never, I guess."

Cole looks around. "Are they safe?"

I force my eyes to stay on Cole, not to look down the driveway. I still don't trust him. "No idea. They left after you did. I don't know where they went."

He stares at me for a few seconds, then shakes his head. "A'ight. Well, if you see them, tell 'em Dobber's car's in our barn. Keys are in it."

He turns and starts down the steps. It reminds me of the first time he ever came here, picking me up for that party at Dobber's. So much has changed since then. So much poisoned, orange water under the bridge.

"Cole?"

He stops and looks back at me.

"You're a complete shithead."

He's still staring at me when I close the front door.

* * *

People come and go all afternoon. Some bring food; some bring flowers and cards. MFM and I move around each other in our own bubbles of grief. She's still in the denial phase. I've worked my way up to depression and loneliness. I miss Granny so much I feel like a magnet whose partner is held just out of reach. I need and want her with a powerful longing, but she gets no closer. She's gone. Forever.

I sit in the rocking chair in her room, alone. MFM's avoided this room since the funeral people came yesterday. Maybe the image of Granny's body being loaded onto a stretcher is too painful. For me, I feel like what's left of her is strongest here, and I cling to the last cosmic bits of her spirit and soul. I collect a few of her hairs from her pillow, wishing they could bring her back or at least bring me some respite from the loneliness. Instead, MFM appears in the doorway.

"I took the Dobbers some food," she says.

I'd forgotten about them. Forgotten, in fact, that there's a world outside this house. "Good idea."

She sits down on the floor, facing me. From here, I can see strands of gray in her hair. It's comforting in a stupid way. Proof that some part of Granny really does live inside her. "I guess we need to talk."

"We do." I already know what I'm going to say. How could I not honor Granny's last wish? With Granny's hairs clutched in my hand, I mumble the words people have been telling me for months…only with a slight variation. "We don't belong here."

Her shoulders tense, but she nods her agreement. I realize hearing that hurts her as much as it does me. Not to belong in this beautiful place…I wonder if it makes her feel not good enough. A failure. Or worst of all, rootless.

I want to belong here. I want to be a part of the rocks and the crawfish pools, the honeysuckle and the morning mists. But I don't fit. Neither does MFM. We're different species.

"Liberty," she says. "If you don't want to live with me…" Tears drip down her face again. I swear there are grooves in her cheeks now, carved over the past two days. "Mommy told me how I let you down." I've always liked that she still, as an adult, called Granny Mommy. "How I should have been with you more often. Your fancy meals."

I stare at the ceiling, half-glad she's finally realized that and half-irritated she knows I needed her.

"I've talked to Iris's parents and…" She takes a huge breath and holds it for a minute. "They're happy to let you stay there, if you want."

This news hits me like a tidal wave, and once it's passed, I'm surprised to find a little voice in my gut saying no.

"But I'd want to see you," she says. "Whenever and as often as you can stand it." Her smile is stretched across her face, too thin, too tight.

"No, Mom." I stumble a little on the word I thought I'd sworn off. "I want to go back to DC and I want to live with you. Give us another…I dunno, another start or try or chance. Whatever."

"Oh, Liberty." This time the smile is full and genuine, even her eyes crinkle. "Really?"

"Yes, but things have to be different," I warn. The next words stick in my throat like thistle burrs. Admitting weakness is not my strong point. "I need you."

She sputters, her nose running, and I hand her a tissue. I don't know where she got this emotional side, but it sure wasn't from Granny. And I'm glad she didn't pass it on to me. I sit quietly while she pulls herself together.

"There's also the issue of school," I say. Gritting my teeth, I tell her what I've worked out for myself. "Since I'm flunking my junior year here, my scholarship at Westfield will be revoked. I know we can't afford to pay the tuition, so I'll just go to public school and finish up there." Bye-bye, Georgetown. Bye-bye, college scholarship.

"You're failing?" Her brown eyes go round. "You?"

Leave it to MFM to piss me off in the middle of a touching emotional moment. "Do you have any idea how hard it was to take care of Granny all day and night, and try to keep up with school?" I'm yelling. It feels good to yell.

She looks like I might as well have slapped her. "No. I guess not."

"No," I say. "Because as usual, you weren't around to—" I stop myself. This feels too familiar. Our old arguments, our old habits. If we're going to make this work, we have to break them. We might as well start now. "Sorry."

I try to see things from her side. What was it like to be stuck in prison knowing Granny was dying, knowing she might not even see her again.

"I guess it was pretty hellish on your side too."

Mom crawls over and puts her hands on my knees. "You did great."

I bite my cheek, which feels like hamburger after the last twenty-four hours, and count to three. She's never told me that before. She's never told me anything LIKE that before. "I did my best."

She squeezes my legs. "I'll get school figured out," she says. "You leave that to me."

"Really?"

MFM taking on a responsibility, taking care of me, is totally unprecedented.

"Thanks."

"It's my job," she says.

It was always your job, snarky me thinks. But I don't say it. I just smile.

I'm trying too.

FORTY-FIVE

Ashleigh's dressed perfectly—ponytail, jeans, button-down shirt. She's so cute, I want to pinch her cheeks. It doesn't make me like her any more though, especially when Dobber tells her how great she looks.

"Thanks," she says. "I'm nervous. You're sure this is going to work?"

"Yes," I say for the twelve billionth time. I don't blame her for worrying though. If things don't go as planned, it's a sure bet her dad's going to lose his job. And God only knows what'll happen to the Dobbers. And me.

We're waiting in the lobby of Peabody Mining, along with Mr. Dobber, who's wearing a baseball cap and sunglasses. He looks nothing like the man I met two months ago and the receptionist doesn't seem to have recognized him. I'm undercover too, having dyed my hair with red Kool-Aid and put on an absurd amount of makeup. Dobber's just wearing a baseball hat and trying to look small. It's pretty hard to disguise him, but Ashleigh said the mine's reception area is always empty, so hopefully no one will come in while we're waiting.

We're here, supposedly, as a group from the Future Business Leaders of America, led by his darling niece, to interview Mr. Peabody as a successful local businessman. That'll get us into Peabody's office where we'll launch our plan.

Dobber leans close to me and whispers, "You look good too."

"Liar." But I smile a little.

A door opens, and a woman sticks her head out. "Ashleigh?" She leaps to her feet.

"Your uncle's ready for you, hon." The woman watches as we all make for the door.

I try to stay in front of Mr. Dobber, who's wheezing a little from the effort of carrying the camera. He keeps his head down as he maneuvers past her. I pretty much hold my breath until she seats us in a conference room and leaves us alone.

"Okay," I say. "Set up the camera there in the corner. Ashleigh, you sit at the head of the table with Peabody. Dobber, you stand behind them with the mic."

They get set up while I open my laptop and connect Ashleigh's iPhone to it. Next I mute the computer, open Skype, and call Iris. She answers right away.

"I have your sound turned down," I whisper. "You ready?"

She gives me a smile and a thumbs-up. A giant newsroom spreads out behind her. Typical Iris, she picked a perfect spot. It's so good to see her, I'm smiling like a lunatic when Peabody walks in.

"Ho, what's this?" he says, all fake cheery. "I gotta whole team o' Plurd County's finest!" He puts his arm around Ashleigh. "Hey there, darlin'. How's things?"

"Hey, Uncle Robert."

Doing my best not to gag, I hide my face. Ashleigh takes over, and I thank the gods she agreed to do this job. She has her uncle's full attention, talking about Easter plans and Sunday dinner, distracting him completely while Dobber crouches in the corner, pretending to work on the mic stand. Mr. Dobber's doing the same in his corner with the camera. Head down, I plug in a separate webcam, set it next to my computer, and hope like crazy Peabody doesn't notice it.

"I know you're busy," Ashleigh says. "So let's get started."

Peabody winks and says, "Whatever you say, boss."

I'd want to peel my skin off if I were her, but she just smiles, gives me a quick glance, and dives in. "Is there any truth to the rumor that you falsified the water quality tests from people's wells a few years back?"

His smile slips, then goes back up. "What? Who told you that?"

"I did," I say.

His eyebrows go up. "Ms. Briscoe." He leans back in his chair, glancing at the camera. "I'm surprised to see you."

Ignoring him, I spread the pairs of test results I managed to collect from some of the other failing wells on the table. "These reports," I say, gesturing to the left row, "were mailed by the county to the property owners. But these are the ones the testing company has on file as the actual results from the test. As you can see, the ones the county sent out all show the water to be safe." I stare at Peabody. "Which you know is a lie."

"I don't know anything about this." Peabody tries to scoot his chair back to stand, but Dobber is right behind him, pinning him in.

"How do you suppose these reports got changed, Mr. Peabody?" I ask.

His face is a politician's mask—warm smile, fake concern. "Look, this is the first I've heard about any of this. But I assure you, we will absolutely look into it."

I screw up my face. "Why would the mine look into it? Wouldn't that be the county's job?"

His smile just widens. "Well, of course. But as an important member of the community, I will certainly encourage the county commissioners to check into this."

"You know what's odd here?" I say. "It's that the mine had anything to do with the testing in the first place."

"What's odd?" Peabody asks. "We paid for the test at the request of the county. They'd had some complaints about local wells, and we wanted to provide some reasonable assurance that our new mining procedures were safe." He's in full PR mode now. "Obviously, we want to make sure no one is getting hurt or sick. As important as the mine is to the local economy, it's certainly not worth that."

God, I'd love to punch him in the face right now. Watch some of his precious, perfectly healthy red blood drip over his shiny new suit.

"So aside from paying the fees, Peabody mining had nothing else to do with the test?" I ask as innocently as I can.

Peabody narrows his eyes. "None at all, to my knowledge."

He seems to have forgotten about the camera and the microphone entirely. "So this signature here. And here. And..." I gather up the papers and pretend to scrutinize them. "Actually on all these reports. The signature that says Dewey Dobber. You have no idea who that is?"

His smile tightens. "Well, of course I know Dewey. He was an employee of mine some years back." He turns to his niece. "Ashleigh, I'm surprised at you, getting involved in this ridiculousness."

"When Mr. Dobber took the samples for this water test, was he employed by you then?"

"Absolutely not. You can check with human resources." He answers so fast and so confidently, I have no doubt that's exactly what the records would say. "His employment ended several months before the testing even began."

"Bullshit." Mr. Dobber lays the camera against the wall and steps forward.

Peabody's left eyebrow twitches, but that's the only sign of surprise. I read once that true psychopaths can control their reactions completely, no matter what's happening around them. I wonder if Peabody has to list that on his driver's license.

I glance at my computer screen, where Iris is taking this all in like a soap opera.

"You yerself told me to take them samples," Mr. Dobber says. "And when the results come back, you gave me a sheet with safe water levels on it and told me to pull out the ones that was outside the safe range."

"None of that happened," Peabody says, smiling. "I think you're a little confused." He looks at Ashleigh. "And I think we all know why."

"Yeah, I know. I been on meth a long time." Mr. Dobber reaches into his coat pocket, and for a second, I think he has a gun or a knife. But all he pulls out is a piece of paper, which seems to be his weapon of choice. "But the bank don't lie. This here's the record of my last paycheck deposit from the mine. Dated three weeks after the water samples was taken."

Peabody's face doesn't move, but I sense a change. There's no condescending smile. No gentle rebuttal. Just silence. He's getting worried.

"Turn that camera off," he says at last.

Mr. Dobber reaches over and presses a button. The shutter slides closed.

"What do you want?" Peabody asks. "Money? A job? A new house? I'm sure we can come to some agreement. You have my word."

I glance at Mr. Dobber, silently willing him, *Don't believe it. He'll promise you the moon and kill you the second you walk out the door.*

Mr. Dobber busts out a giant belly laugh. I've never heard him laugh before. It's an amazing sound, like rumbly music. "You gotta be kiddin' me. I wouldn't take your word for where to shit in the woods."

I open my notebook and lay it on the table. "We have a list of demands." I launch into it before Peabody has a chance to speak. "One hundred thousand dollars for the Dobbers. One hundred thousand dollars for Ashleigh's grandfather. One hundred thousand dollars for—" I wrote up the demands before Granny passed away. Now I don't know what to say, and even if I did, I couldn't get it past the enormous lump in my throat.

"For the estate of Kathryn Briscoe," Ashleigh says.

I blink a thank-you and get a rare half smile from her.

"Plus, the same restitution for anyone else who was given a falsified water report and develops health issues."

He tries again to stand. This time, Dobber claps his ham-sized hands on his shoulders and forces him down. Peabody makes an effort to collect himself. "Is this a joke? I can't go handing out a hundred thousand dollars to anybody who happens to get sick."

I continue. "In addition, your application for the proposed mine expansion will be canceled. You'll stop the MTR practices at the top of Tanner's Peak. You'll pump out and carry away the contents of the containment pond. And finally…" I pause. This was MFM's idea and I'm a little jealous that I didn't come up with it first. "Finally, you'll extend city water to every house in the valley."

There's not a sound in the room. Then Peabody tilts his head to the ceiling and laughs softly. For a long time. It starts to piss me off. "I'll hand it to you, Ms. Briscoe. You certainly know how to make a Christmas list. But you realize, none of that's going to happen, right?"

"Oh really?"

"No. Because you have no proof Peabody mining had any knowledge of any of this."

"Proof?" I look at the reports still in my hand. "What do you call this? I think the EPA will be very interested in the discrepancies in these reports."

"Again, there's no proof the mine had anything to do with those."

"True," I say. "But do you really think they'll care who's responsible? I think they'll be more concerned that the drinking water at the base of your MTR mine is basically poison. *That* they'll care about."

Peabody goes still, like a fish in a bucket that knows it's caught and is trying to be invisible. Everyone's silent. The seconds drag by. My hopes climb with every heartbeat. Finally, "Fine."

"Fine what?"

"Ten thousand to you, the Dobbers here, and Ashleigh's grandfather."

"That was one hundred thousand each. Plus restitution for anyone else who was given the fake water report."

"Fine." He's too calm. I realize he thinks he'll find a way out of this. Like always. But our sleeves are still packed with aces.

"And," I add, "assurance that Ashleigh's dad won't lose his job."

"Oh, I'm not worried about that." Ashleigh smiles. "I had a nice conversation with Donna Pruitt yesterday."

This is Ashleigh's ace.

"I'm sure Aunt Karin would love to know more about your ex-secretary's new baby." The disgust on Ashleigh's face is about ten times the hatred she's ever shown me.

Peabody's jaw is clenched so tight, I swear I can hear his teeth cracking. "I don't know what you're talking about."

"I think you do."

Peabody turns back to me. "You have no idea what you're asking for. Extending the city water system will cost millions."

"Probably," I say. "But since Peabody Mining is so concerned about the safety of Ebbottsville's residents, I'm sure the cost is the least of your concerns." I smile brightly. "Right?"

He rolls his eyes. "Fine." I can hear the wheels spinning in his head.

He'll get rid of the Dobbers and me—car wrecks, fires, disappearances. And maybe he can bribe Ashleigh. Clothes? A new car? College?

"One more thing." I spin my computer around. He stares at Iris's face and the newsroom behind her. I hold up the webcam. "This is my friend Iris. She works for the *Washington Recorder*."

His face turns white under his fake tan.

"She has our entire conversation recorded, plus copies of these reports. She'll hold on to them for safekeeping. But if anything—I mean *anything*—happens to the Dobbers or Ashleigh or me—"

"Or Daddy or Granddaddy," Ashleigh adds.

"Right. If anything happens to basically anyone we know, Iris takes the tape to her boss and all hell breaks loose," I say. "Forget about the EPA snooping around. You'll have CNN, ABC, MSN, all the letters you can imagine poking their noses in at the mine. With that kind of scrutiny, God only *knows* what they might come across." I cross my arms. That's my ace played.

"Sounds fun, huh, Uncle Robert?" Ashleigh's enjoying this even more than I am.

Peabody glares at her, but he looks different now, like something inside, something that used to be straight and unyielding has been broken.

"I think we're all done here," I say.

"We'll take them checks now though," Mr. Dobber says. "Save you a trip later."

"This is extortion," he says.

"It's a drop in the bucket compared to what you owe Granddaddy," Ashleigh argues.

"That was business," Peabody replies.

"Call it what you want." She takes out a pair of scissors. For the second time this afternoon, I'm pretty sure there's going to be bloodshed. And for the second time, I'm wrong. Ashleigh just snips off a piece of Peabody's hair. "I call this insurance. DNA doesn't lie."

"I suppose you want some money too," Peabody says, eyeing the scissors.

"Nope," Ashleigh replies. "I want that city water extended right away." She holds up the lock of hair. "We'll have DNA results from Donna's baby in two weeks. If construction hasn't started by then, I'm taking them straight to Aunt Karin."

Peabody explodes. "Projects like that can't get started that fast."

"You've got all those diggers and employees sitting up on Tanner's Peak that can't do anything now."

"We need permits and county approvals. It takes time!"

"I'm sure you'll work out something." She smiles. "Checks, please."

There's silence in the room for a minute. Then, to my surprise, Mr. Peabody pulls out his checkbook and writes three identical checks with a freaking astronomical amount of zeros, tears them out, and hands one each to Ashleigh, Mr. Dobber, and me.

"Thanks, Unc. See you at Easter dinner?"

Peabody glares at her. Ashleigh folds the check, shoves it into her pocket, and walks out.

We gather the equipment and head for the door. Dobber stops next to Peabody.

"You can get up now."

The man stands, straightening his coat.

Dobber sets the mic on the table. "Just one more thing," he says.

Peabody's head snaps back before I realize Dobber punched him. Blood pours from the man's nose, dripping on the front of his white button-down shirt. He's gasping in pain, his hands held over his face.

"That's for my daddy," Dobber says.

Outside, we toss our stuff into the trunk of Ashleigh's car and climb in. Dobber's bent nearly double in the backseat with me. Everyone's high-fiving and congratulating each other. Considering our plan worked, I should be celebrating too. But I can't stop thinking about Granny.

"It was a good plan."

I look up to see Ashleigh staring at me in the rearview mirror.

"Thanks," I say. "You did great."

"Ever'body did," Mr. Dobber adds.

We drive under the shadow of the billboard. *Coal Keeps the Lights On.* It's funny that a company that keeps the lights on also keeps so many people in the dark.

Funny but not.

Ashleigh drops us off at Granny's drive. As Mr. Dobber heads for the springhouse to pack up their stuff, Dobber walks up the driveway with me.

"Where will you go?" I ask.

"Straight to the bank," he says, grinning. "Then to the hotel. Cousin Burnett'll put us up for a couple weeks till the check clears."

I think of how much his life has changed in the last thirty minutes. "I'm happy for you."

"Thanks. You okay?" he asks.

"I guess?" I'm not sure how okay is supposed to feel right now. If it's empty and sad and tired, then yes, I'm okay.

He puts his arm around my shoulders. "Your granny was a heck of a lady. I'ma miss her a lot."

The weight of his arm feels nice. Protective, even. But what helps the most is that he knew Granny. He understands what she meant to me. Knowing we'll miss her together makes me feel less alone.

"Thanks." I reach up and hold his hand resting on my shoulder.

"Think Peabody will actually do it?" he asks. "Extend the water?"

"If he doesn't, it'll cost him a lot more than money." My favorite part about today was finally seeing Peabody without a smug look on his face. "Sorry you didn't get to blow anything up."

He gives me that dangerously charming smile. "Maybe next time."

Something tilts—the ground or the sky or something inside me—and I lean into him.

"At least I got to punch him," he says as he joins his hands behind my neck.

In this light, his gray eyes are nearly clear, like a shadow of water. "That was a nice punch."

"Yeah." He's staring at my lips. "Felt good."

I'm conscious of how close we are, hips touching. "Good thing you didn't tuck your thumb," I say.

He smiles again. "Most girls do."

I've completely fallen under his spell. Or maybe it's the other way around. "I'm not most girls."

"Don't I know it."

And then we kiss.

FORTY-SIX

I watch the rocks rolling by as MFM navigates the windy road down the mountain. The tree buds are golden, and the spider webs sparkle with dew in the morning light. I know we'll be back—we have to get the house ready to sell—but this drive has a finality to it. The lingering traces of Granny will all be gone the next time we're here.

But we will be back. MFM agreed that, even after the house is sold, I can come back to visit Dobber and Ashleigh. It's sort of mind-bending to be thinking of Ashleigh as a friend, but I do. A close one. I guess war is like that.

MFM's helping Dobber apply to colleges and said she'd talk to her friend in admissions at the University of Virginia about scholarships. I think she sees him as a new cause. I'm not sure what I see Dobber as. Our kiss was…well…I think about it all the time. But we're both at such big turning points right now. And I keep thinking about Granny's moth-and-flame analogy. Neither of us should singe our wings; who knows how far we might be able to fly? So as much as I'd love a second kiss, we're taking things slow. Still, I'm keeping my fingers crossed for him about UVA. It's just two and a half hours from Georgetown, and wings or not, I know I want to keep him in my life.

MFM also talked to the dean at Westfield, and he agreed I can repeat some classes this summer and go back as a senior in the fall, still on scholarship. I missed early admission to Georgetown, but if I keep my grades up next semester, I should still have a possibility at getting in. And anyway, I promised Granny I'd try.

God, I miss her.

I stare out the window, at the hills Peabody still controls and the creeks I know are still poisoned. Sometimes, it all seems pointless. Everything we did, and the valley is still ruined. It feels like all the grief and anguish of the past months is carved into my bones and the rest of my life will be rooted in grief and anguish.

"How do you do it?" I ask. "All those causes you support. How do you keep going when what you do doesn't make a difference?"

"It does make a difference," she says. "Maybe not the difference I wanted, but it makes a difference nonetheless."

"Pf."

She reaches over and touches my arm. "Hey. What you did here? It mattered. It mattered a lot."

"Doesn't seem like it," I say. "Granny's gone. Mr. Dobber's still sick. Ashleigh's grandpa's dying. The creeks and wells are still ruined."

We drive in silence for a while then Mom says, "Remember the starfish story?"

"Of course." I hear Granny's voice in my mind, as clear as if she's sitting behind me. "It made a difference to that one."

"Exactly. It made a difference. To somebody."

The road flattens out and the rocks and trees turn into fields, fuzzy with corn and soybeans and tobacco. Soon, the honeysuckle will bloom and the scent will fill the creek bottoms. I so wish Granny could have smelled that one last time.

"Is it enough for you?" I ask. "Making a difference to one starfish."

"That depends on the starfish."

I tumble that around in my mind for a while. "The starfish I cared about died."

"We don't always get to pick the ones that make it."

"Well, it sucks."

She takes a deep breath, and I'm sure she's about to launch into a wise ramble about the vagaries of life, but instead, she says, "I'm so proud of you."

"Really?" I can't remember the last time she's said that to me.

"More than I can say."

She's trying to make things up to me. And while telling me she's proud of me doesn't seem like much compared to seventeen years of marginal parenting, at least she's trying.

"Thanks, MFM."

She glances sideways at me. "Still with the 'former mother,' huh?"

"I don't know. *F* stands for a lot of things. Fussy. Frowning." I decide against "felon."

"I see." She smiles. "And how about fetching? Or fascinating?"

I counter with, "Faulty."

She pauses, then asks quietly, "What about forgiven?"

It's a full minute before I answer. "Maybe." I roll the window down so I can smell the moss and the trees and the damp rocks one more time.

ACKNOWLEDGMENTS

To Danielle Chiotti, the hardest-working, best-communicating, sweetest, funniest, most perfect agent in the world. If it weren't for you, this page wouldn't even be. From the bottom of my soul, I thank you…with sprinkles! Here's hoping my next book will have to be sold only once.

To Wendy McClure, my wonderful editor, who was the first person to believe in this book enough to pay real live money for it! Thank you for that and for the wonderful, careful suggestions you provided that made the book so much better. You're awesome!

I've dedicated this book to a group of women who've been with me forever, or so it seems: Hazel Mitchell, Julie Dillard, Kristen Crowley Held, and Sarah McGuire. Thanks for being my crit group, my life coaches, my cheerleaders, and ass-kickers. I love you all. With pants.

A huge thank-you to the Nevada SCBWI Mentor Program, and in particular my incredible mentor, Susan Hart Lindquist. Being a part of that program completely changed my writing life, filled my email box with invisible pink hearts, and made me part of a writing community I'm truly blessed to have.

It's really crazy how many people it takes to create a book. There are so many more people I want to thank… my very first crit group in Boise who didn't ask me to leave, the WAD from Chautauqua, my writer lunch ladies, the Criterati, the Turbo Monkeys, Andrea Cascardi, Steph Blake (someday I'll meet you!), the SCBWI community, The Sweet Sixteens, all the people who read this manuscript along the way, the grocery store folks who sold me the tea and cupcakes that fueled the fifty-eleven drafts of *Dig Too Deep*, my mom and dad, for dragging me all over the Blue Ridge and showing me what a deeply special place it is, whoever invented IPA, and David Schwartz (ILYI.)

Special thanks to my son—an amazing writer in his own right. I know you've eaten more than your fair share of Totino's Frozen Pizza because I was revising this book. Again. Thanks for your patience. I love you immensely and promise in the future—less pizza, more Chiang Mai.

Lastly, and seriously, I want to thank the people living in MTR communities. Thank you for your bravery. Thank you for speaking up when no one listened. Thank you for battling for that beautiful pocket of heaven-on-earth where you live. Keep up the good fight and don't tuck your thumbs. Your efforts matter so very much, to a whole lot of starfish.